TILL JUSTICE

IS SERVED

by

JERRIE ALEXANDER

Till Justice Is Served

ACKNOWLEDGEMENTS

I would be remiss if I didn't acknowledge the following people. Their support, advice, and enthusiasm were invaluable.

To my copy editor, Joyce Lamb, your guidance helped me polish this story until it shone. For that, you have my sincere appreciation.

To Brynna Curry, thank you for your attention to detail. You helped me write a stronger story.

To Alexa Pressley, your creative brain turns brainstorming sessions into bursts of brilliance. I appreciate every minute you spend with me.

Meredith Blair, cover artist extraordinaire, I'm grateful for your patience and talent.

As always, my advisor on all firearms and tactical matters, a retired Navy SEAL. He's a real-life American hero who prefers to remain nameless. Thank you for sharing your knowledge and for your service to our country. Any mistakes are my own!

To Jim, you always said I could do anything I set my mind to. Your love and support mean everything to me.

Last but not least, thanks to my readers. I hope you enjoy reading this story as much as I loved writing it.

CHAPTER 1

Light from the full moon streamed through her window, illuminating her face. Her long hair fanned across the pillow in golden waves. The glow gave her an angelic look.

She didn't fool him for a second. Asleep, her true personality rested, hiding the fact that while awake, she was pure evil.

He lifted the hunting knife high overhead but paused to savor the moment. The time to silence her had come. He plunged the sharp blade into her heart. Her eyes and mouth flew open, but before she could cry out, he slammed the hard steel into her chest again and again. Silence filled the room except for the soft sucking sound of the blade each time it exited.

Adrenaline pumped through his system, flooding every cell and nerve ending in his body. An unexpected thrill raced up his spine. Not from killing the nasty creature, but for the message her death would send to the rest of her vicious girlfriends. They too would pay the ultimate price if they continued their attacks on the woman he loved. The woman he had sworn to protect at all costs.

Rivulets of blood and sweat slid down his face, soaking the front of his jumpsuit. He pulled a handkerchief from his pocket, wiped his eyes, and carefully put it away. There would be no evidence for the cops to find.

He slid his gloved hands under her arms, dragged her limp body to a sitting position, and propped her against the headboard. He dipped his finger into her blood and printed his warning on the wall.

YOU LIE.

YOU DIE.

He checked his watch. The neighborhood would be waking soon. He walked to her bedroom window, stopping long enough to strip off the bloody jumpsuit. Then he stuffed it, the knife, and the gloves into his backpack.

It was only when he reached the back alley and drove away that he sighed a breath of relief. Penny's lies had been silenced forever.

One good thing had come from this incident. Penny's death had afforded him the opportunity to show Erin the depth of his affection for her. In his heart, he knew she cared deeply for him. That she averted her gaze from his when they talked came from her insecurity. Soon, she would shed her inhibitions and be ready to embrace their love.

Erin needed him. Who else would kill to save her? Nobody. And that secret would bind the two of them. Forever.

CHAPTER 2

Rafe Sirilli studied the family portrait in his hand. His mind drifted back to the day his mom and dad had spit-polished him, his twin, Nick, and their little brother, Luke, before insisting they sit still for the photographer. It had been the last time he saw his mother happy. Her depression had only gotten worse, and nothing or no one had been able to help. Rafe shook off the old memory and carefully placed the picture in a box. He'd returned to Westbrook Hills to dispose, donate, and liquidate his dad's belongings, not to analyze the past.

The doorbell rang, surprising him. His first thought was Luke, but it was too soon to be his brother. Luke had been notified of their dad's death, but like Rafe, hadn't made it home in time for the funeral.

Always cautious, Rafe walked to the window and lifted a wooden slat on the blinds with one finger. The tightness between his shoulders relaxed. His dad's old partner, Jeff Paulenski stood on the porch, his hand poised to push the ringer again. Rafe crossed the room and opened the door.

The older man's silver hair and deep-set wrinkles hadn't diminished his presence. Tall and straight-backed, he presented himself with an air of confidence.

"Jeff. It's good to see you." Rafe's words had rushed as Jeff's arms had engulfed him.

The old man's hands pounded Rafe on the back. For a few seconds, he was that kid with the tangled fishing line, and Jeff was helping unravel it. He stepped back, and his gaze scanned Rafe from his hairline to his boots. His fingers caught the hair hanging over Rafe's ears and tugged.

"You're looking a little shopworn, my boy. If the FBI doesn't appreciate your hard work, you can always come home. I'll put in a good word at the Sheriff's Department." The hint of the older man's Scottish brogue brought back memories of camping at the lake, loud laughter, and catching black bass on hot summer days.

"I'm good. Where I've been, poor grooming was expected, even fashionable." Rafe dragged a hand through his shaggy hair. He'd been undercover on an FBI and DEA joint task force for over a year. "We managed to shut down one stream of drugs into the US."

"A pimple," Jeff scoffed.

"Hey, one cartel at a time." Rafe ran his hand over his chin. "An unshaven face and long hair are acceptable in that world." Rafe led his guest farther into the living room, where he'd been packing. "Sit. Want a beer?"

Jeff gave a quick headshake. "Don't have time. I have a question."

"I'm listening."

"You in a hurry to get back to an assignment?"

"No. I'm on a leave of absence. We wrapped up my part of the operation. Unless there's no plea bargain, I won't even have to testify." Rafe's curiosity piqued. He'd expected a lecture for not making it home before his dad died. It was beginning to look like he'd been wrong. Something was troubling the old man. "I understand you were with Dad when he passed. I appreciate it." It was the truth, and Rafe had spoken from his heart.

"Not necessary. He was damn proud of you boys. He understood why you weren't here."

Rafe nodded, trying to ignore the heavy weight sitting on his shoulders. Jeff's comforting words didn't ease his guilt. "If there's something of Dad's you'd like to have, anything, it's yours."

Jeff shook his head, stared at the floor, and then cleared his throat. His gaze scanned the area, seemingly taking in the state of disarray that comes when somebody dies and their belongings are boxed up to be carted off.

The hair on Rafe's arms stood up. "What's wrong?" He'd move mountains to help this man. His dad had considered Jeff the best partner and friend a deputy sheriff could have had.

"You remember Erin Brady, the girl Lotty and I adopted?"

"Tall, skinny, with a mouth?" That hair standing up on Rafe's arms started to vibrate. Damn right, he remembered her.

"Yeah." The old man's eyebrows drew together, resembling a silver caterpillar. "She's in serious trouble. I need your help, she—"

Rafe held up his hands in the universal timeout sign. Helping Jeff was one thing, getting involved with Erin was entirely another. She wouldn't want to see him, and he was fine with that. Sure, their dislike for each other was old news. Way old news. High school news. She'd been a surly brat back then and probably hadn't changed.

"I can't imagine she'd want my help." Rafe returned to his project of clearing the many bookcases lining his father's living room wall. "Dad was my last tie to Westbrook Hills. As soon as I get everything packed or donated, I'll turn the house and property over to a real estate agency. The joint effort between the FBI and DEA worked well in Florida. We're going to try it again in Mexico."

Jeff stared at his shoes again. A wave of guilt hit Rafe. He shoved it from his mind. Erin could handle herself.

"What do you hear from Lucas?"

Rafe had to smile at that. Nobody called his little brother Lucas anymore. "He goes by Luke now," Rafe said, hoping like hell the kid was all right. "Last I heard he was on some secret mission. I'm hoping he'll be home soon."

"Think he knows about your dad?"

"I was assured he'd be told."

"You really don't know where he is?"

Rafe laughed. Luke was the baby of the family. At twenty-six, he was four years younger than Rafe. He and Nick used to sneak off and leave Luke behind. Hell, his accomplishments in the military had eclipsed anything Rafe had ever achieved. He felt great pride in the man the kid had become.

"I have no idea. Ass-deep on some black ops mission."

"From the look on your face, I'm guessing you wish you were still in the military."

"I enjoyed my time, but standing at Nick's grave I made a promise. I had to be stateside to honor it."

"You promised you'd be a fed?"

"Not exactly. I promised I'd join the fight against the cartels. The drug pusher fucked with my family. Now it's my turn."

"Family trumps everything." Jeff's eyes had taken on a sympathetic glow. "And that's why I'm here. My family needs help."

Rafe knew what he had to do. If Jeff needed help badly enough to use the family angle, he couldn't turn his back.

"I get that you want to get back to work," Jeff said, "but this is important."

"I'll do whatever I can." The delay sat on Rafe's shoulders like a heavy boulder. His work was important to him, but this was an obligation he couldn't refuse.

"Thank you." Jeff's words came out with a whoosh. Without further explanation, he moved to the front window. Rafe decided not to push. Jeff had always been one to think before he spoke.

What the hell had Erin had gotten herself into? She'd been the talk of Rafe's senior year when Jeff and Lotty had enrolled her. At the time, Rafe hadn't known or cared whether the rumor that she'd been found living on the street was true or not. His dad had encouraged him and Nick to accept her, assuming the rest of the kids in high school would follow their lead. Erin couldn't have cared less.

Rafe remembered hard edges softened by hair the color of caramel and eyes so green you could almost smell the ocean when you looked into them. She'd had a tough exterior, but behind all that bravado, he'd seen a frightened fawn. His mistake had been asking her to the prom. She'd accepted, and then she'd made a fool of him.

A fool the entire school had laughed about.

Shit, he was a grown man now. Who cared what happened twelve years ago?

Jeff turned to face Rafe. In the span of seconds, the old man had aged. The sadness in his eyes was painful to see. "Did you see the news about the dead high school girl?"

"The teenager who was stabbed multiple times?"

"Yeah."

Rafe's jaw unhinged. He didn't like where this was heading. "Erin killed her?"

"Hell, no." The words fired from Jeff's mouth. "But she's a suspect. The police are interrogating her."

The desperation in Jeff's voice pulled all of Rafe's strings. "Maybe you better back up and tell me what's going on."

"A few years back, Lotty had a stroke," Jeff said, easing down onto the couch. "Erin used the excuse that she was tired of the big-city schools and moved home. She really came back to help us out."

"I remember Dad saying Lotty had been ill. How is she?"

"Doing well. I was lucky and got her to the hospital before permanent damage was done."

"Good to hear. So Erin decided to stay?"

"She's the upper school counselor at Westbrook Hills High School. She worked hard with these kids, giving them someone they could talk to and trust. All of that went to hell the day she reported a student for drug possession. That girl and her friends launched an all-out vendetta to discredit Erin."

"This student she reported has turned up dead?"

"Yeah. The police are looking at Erin for the murder. It's preposterous. Just stupid to waste time grilling Erin when they could be looking for the real killer."

"Shortest distance between two points. Erin's the logical suspect."

"In the spirit of showing her innocence, she drove to the precinct at their request."

"What she needs is a good attorney."

Jeff leaned back on the couch as if exhausted. "I've already called one, but I need you to investigate this mess. Unofficially, of course. Hell, boy, you were a big-shot football hero. Nobody would blink if you turned up for a visit. Whoever sold that student the drugs probably killed her to keep her from rolling over."

Just the reference to drugs and that school lit up Rafe's hot buttons. Nick had started using while attending Westbrook High.

Jeff leaned over and picked up a picture from the coffee table. He ran a finger around the dusty edges of the frame. Rafe's heart grew heavy. The snapshot was of him, Luke, and Nick standing next to Jeff's old pickup. Rafe and his brothers had loved fishing with Jeff and their dad. The five of them would head to the lake every chance they got.

Jeff handed Rafe the picture and stood. His dad's slate-gray eyes seemed to telegraph a message he'd preached to his sons for years. *You get back what you give.* Was his father smiling at Rafe's decision to help?

"I'll see what I can find out," Rafe agreed. Jeff was hurting, and helping was the right thing to do. Erin didn't have to welcome him into her situation. It was enough that Jeff wanted help.

"I owe you." Jeff's sigh of relief made Rafe feel like shit for hesitating to help.

"No. You were always there for me and my family." He stood. "Give me a second to change, then we'll go talk with her."

****

Erin sat in the eight-by-six room and stared at the two-way mirror. She concentrated on keeping her face expressionless. Whoever watched from the other side wasn't going to see how her insides churned. That she'd refused to speak until her lawyer arrived had netted her isolation and total silence.

The door swung open, banging into the wall. She stood, her chair scraping across the floor like fingernails on a blackboard. Retired Judge Harold Penza stepped inside. He wore a black suit, white shirt, and blue tie that matched his eyes. His presence filled the room with an air of authority.

He extended his hand to Erin. He smiled, and the many wrinkles on his face deepened. The warm sparkle in his pale blue eyes gave her confidence her situation was about to get better.

"Judge." She clung to his hand as if she was drowning and he'd just thrown her a lifeline. Quickly, she gathered her wits. "I appreciate you coming."

"It's Harold." He placed his briefcase on the table and sat directly across from her. "I'm no longer on the bench. Jeff Paulenski said you were having a bit of trouble. I'm your attorney, if you'll have me."

"Are you kidding? I'd be thrilled." To have someone on her side with the judge's experience loosened the imaginary band around her chest.

"I understand you haven't been arrested."

"No. I agreed to come to the station."

"You came voluntarily?"

"Yes. Why wouldn't I want to help clear my name?"

His eyebrows furrowed. The look effectively wiped out his curmudgeonly persona. "If I'm going to represent you, I expect you to follow my instructions. Got it?"

"Yes, sir." She'd heard Harold was tough as boot leather on criminals who'd appeared in his court. Jeff respected him, and that was enough for her not to question his direction.

"Then let's get out of here."

Erin grabbed her purse and gym bag, sliding the straps over her shoulders.

Detective Wade Beckett opened the door. She'd met him last year when his niece had played basketball on Erin's team at the

YMCA. Under different circumstances, she'd have thought him handsome. He was tall, had short dark hair, and warm brown eyes. Normally dressed stiff-starch perfect, today he looked a little disheveled with the top button on his shirt undone and his sleeves rolled up, revealing muscular forearms.

He waggled the legal notepad in his hand. "We're not finished."

"Yes, we are." Harold stepped in front of her.

"Judge." The detective nodded. "I heard you were in with Ms. Brady." The detective's eyes narrowed to slits, making Erin think he didn't like going up against the judge. "You're representing her."

"I am." Harold wiggled his fingers, silently telling the detective to move. "I've advised her to speak only through me. If you have questions for my client, call my office."

"Sorry." Erin stepped past the detective, trying to avoid the chill she felt rolling between him and Harold.

"I was under the impression you wanted to clear things up, Ms. Brady," Detective Beckett said to their backs.

Harold paused and looked over his shoulder. "Your time would be better spent looking for the killer."

Detective Beckett caught up with them outside. He handed Erin his card. "Call any time."

Before she could respond, Harold looped his fingers around her bicep and propelled her across the street. "You have something to share with the police, tell me. I'll pass it on."

"I get that I'm a suspect, but pissing off the detective won't help him see my side."

"Beckett is not your friend. He'd be the devil's confidant if it helped him solve this case. We're meeting Jeff at your apartment. I'm parked over here." He gestured to the reserved parking lot. "You can fill in the details on the way."

She opened her mouth to protest that her car was in the

public lot but decided against it. Arguing with Harold didn't seem like a good idea. And hitching a ride with Jeff to the police station to pick up her car wouldn't be a problem. She fell in step with Harold, trying to sort out the events of the past few days. Her career was in ruins. Her freedom in doubt. And her integrity questioned.

"When is this going to stop?" The words fell from her. Pent-up stress had driven her right to the edge of frustration. "I'm ready to rip my hair out."

"You could do that." His tone held no hint of sympathy or humor. "Or you can start at the beginning and fill me in."

"Aren't you going to ask me if I'm guilty?"

"No. I don't want to know."

CHAPTER 3

Erin had yet to return home when Jeff and Rafe arrived. Jeff had unlocked the door and insisted they wait. Rafe used the time to inspect every aspect of her home, starting with the living room. The open floor plan gave him a quick overview. Modest furniture of laminated oak and butter-colored faux leather told him her salary was that of an underpaid educator. Her TV wasn't large, but her DVD collection hinted she enjoyed romantic comedies. A bookcase-lined wall reflected her other interests, running the gamut from books on the psychology of today's teenager to a stack of different sports magazines. A dozen trophies and plaques decorated her counters and tables.

Scattered around the room were pictures of young girls wearing YMCA basketball jerseys. A beautiful woman stood proudly behind them. Erin herself. The tall, lanky girl with the caramel-colored hair had grown into a traffic stopper.

He moved down the hall and found her bedroom. Across the hall, he wandered into her office. Rafe circled the room, walking past the desk and cloth secretary's chair, reading the titles off a stack of training manuals. He found more team pictures and sports memorabilia. Then he crossed to her bedroom. A queen-size bed, dresser, and easy chair took up most of the space. He closed his eyes and breathed in a light floral scent. Yeah, she spent most of her time at home in here. This area was her refuge. For some odd reason, he was reluctant to leave. He shook off the feeling and returned to the living room.

"So? What do you think?" Jeff held out two bottles of flavored water so Rafe could choose one.

"That she lives for others, loves sports, is frugal, and doesn't entertain a lot." He selected the least-disgusting-sounding drink, a lemon-lime something. He left out his surprise at how beautiful she'd become, remembering how disappointed his dad and Jeff had been that Rafe's relationship with Erin had ended before it began.

"How do you know she doesn't entertain a lot?"

"There is one coaster on the coffee table. One cup sitting next to the coffeepot. And the drinks you carried in here? I'm betting there was no beer, and she only keeps flavored water in the fridge. And she shouldn't leave a key hidden under the garden fairy by the door. How am I doing so far?"

"Pretty damn good." The older man smiled, and this time it looked sincere.

The sound of a vehicle pulling into the driveway drew them back into the living room. Rafe moved to the far side of the room and settled in a wing-back chair. He assumed their company was Erin and her attorney, but it was Rafe's nature to be cautious. The only weapon he carried today was the subcompact .45 strapped to his ankle, so he leaned forward with his elbows on his knees. His hands hung loose and at the ready.

The lock on the front door turned, and a second later, Erin stepped inside, followed by a well-dressed man. Jesus. She took his breath away.

"Jeff," Erin said, smiling warmly. "You didn't have to wait here. I would've called."

"I haven't been waiting. I've been getting help," Jeff said.

She stopped halfway across the room. Had she sensed Rafe's presence? Her head snapped to the right, and her gaze settled on him. Her eyes, the color of a sparkling emerald, delivered an icy stare.

"Come now, you remember Rafe Sirilli." Jeff slid his arm around her shoulders.

"Everybody in town remembers Rafe." Her words, coated in sarcasm, pissed him off.

She had no reason to be ticked at him. That she'd

embarrassed the shit out of him was old news. A twelve-year-old scab, but who was counting?

He stood, slapped his brightest smile on his face, then crossed the room. That same fragile scent he'd noticed in her office slammed into his senses.

The urge not to stare was an internal battle. Her skin was flawless, as was her cupid's bow upper lip. Thick hair, pulled off her face and into a low ponytail, put the focus on her eyes. Her body had changed a great deal, too. Nice breasts filled out the YMCA T-shirt she wore. The nylon warm-up bottoms did little to hide the small waist or curve of her hips. She'd matured into a beautiful woman, but apparently, ice water still ran through her veins.

"I doubt that everybody remembers me." He spoke the truth. After graduation, he couldn't wait to get to college. After Nick's funeral, Rafe hadn't come home much. He wasn't proud that he hadn't been back often. It had just worked out that way. "I'm surprised that you do."

She raked her gaze over him, stopping for a minute on his long hair and two-day-old scruff. Would she still dislike the whiskers if he rubbed them along the inside of her thigh?

Shit. He had been undercover far too long.

He extended his hand, half-surprised when her palm met his. Her fingers were warm and soft against his palm. The suit that had walked in with her watched the exchange and then joined them.

"Harold Penza. I knew your daddy. He was mighty proud of his boys." Penza's tone was that of a politician up for reelection. His posture, speech, and mannerisms projected authority. Even his shiny black shoes screamed money. This was a man accustomed to getting his own way.

"Thank you." Rafe towered over him, but the man looked up and held his gaze.

"Hell of a guy, your dad. We need more like him in law enforcement. Are you planning on sticking around?" Harold asked.

"No, sir. I don't plan on being in town for long."

"Then why are you here?" Erin's right eyebrow rose.

"I asked him to help." Jeff's Scottish lilt had thickened.

"Without talking to me?" Her voice jumped up an octave.

"Before you go off half-cocked, let me say this," Rafe said. "You don't have to like that I'm here. Doesn't mean I'm walking away if Jeff needs me." Persuading Rafe to back out now would be easy, but the words had to come from Jeff.

Her gaze met and held his. If she was looking for reassurance, he didn't have it to give. Jeff thought she was innocent, but Rafe remembered the hot-tempered teenage girl whose tongue was sharper than her long fingernails. Was she capable of murder? Given the right circumstances, wasn't everyone?

"Rafe and I are here to help," Jeff insisted to her.

"You understand that if these two sit in on our discussion, I can't guarantee everything you say will remain private." Harold set his briefcase on the coffee table. The snaps opened with a crack, and everybody except Rafe jumped.

Erin dropped to the couch as if surrendering. "For the record, I did not kill Penny. And before you ask, I was home alone last night."

"Keep that information to yourself. If anyone else asks, tell them you've been instructed by council not to comment. All questions are to be directed to me." Harold removed a legal pad from his briefcase and made a couple of notes. "Remember, the burden of proof lies with the police. Exactly what did you tell the detective?"

"Nothing," Erin said. "I called Jeff before I got to the station, and he said for me to wait for my attorney. That's all I said to Wade Beckett. He stuck me in an interrogation room to stare at the two-way mirror until you arrived."

"Good. Let's get started. Penelope Holdstrom was found dead early this morning. Her mother discovered the body when the girl's alarm went off but continued to blare. She'd been stabbed multiple times. Crime scene investigators are analyzing blood spatter and searching for clues. My sources tell me something was printed on the wall of the girl's bedroom." Harold made a note on his pad.

"What did it say?" Erin asked.

"My source either didn't know or couldn't reveal that information."

A look of defeat slid across Erin's face. She dropped her head forward and cradled her face in her hands. Her fingers massaged her temples. If she was faking revulsion to such a heinous crime, Rafe was impressed as hell. When she lifted her head, the pain radiating from her eyes hit him in the gut.

"I can't imagine the horror of walking in to wake your child and finding her murdered." The healthy glow of Erin's creamy complexion had vanished. If anything, she was pasty white. Death, sometimes bloody and gory as hell, had become the norm in Rafe's world, but not hers.

"How could anybody believe I could do something like this?" Erin pulled the rubber thing from her ponytail and dropped it on the coffee table, allowing her hair to fall in waves well past her shoulders.

All those waves tumbling and sliding across her neck sent a bolt of heat blazing through his veins. The image of his hands buried deep in those silky strands flashed through his mind. He started to speak, but his breath caught.

"Everybody in this room is here to support you," Harold assured her.

Rafe didn't comment for fear his voice might crack like a teenager's. Truth be told, he was leaning toward believing in her innocence. Experience had taught him never to assume. This last undercover operation busted a drug ring run by the sweetest-looking grandmother in Dade County. The sixty-five-year-old woman wouldn't have hesitated to slit anyone's throat if they had crossed her or her family. She and her son were currently sitting in a federal prison awaiting trial.

"This murdered girl," Rafe asked. "When did you last have contact with her?"

Erin turned to face him. Her eyes revealed nothing, but her mouth drew to a tight line. "Does that matter?"

"It does to me. I'm going to look into your situation from the perspective that you're innocent."

She turned toward Jeff, who'd folded his arms across his chest. "Erin, girl, Lotty and I love you. I'll call in the devil himself if I have to."

Erin mumbled something that sounded like, "Looks like you already have."

Rafe kept his mouth shut, opting to send her a smile.

"I'm sorry," she added quickly. "I keep waiting to wake up and discover this was all just a nightmare."

"No problem," Rafe said, feeling like a dick for not being a little more understanding. "Let's try this again. When did you last see the girl?"

Erin's shoulders shuddered. "I hadn't seen or spoken to Penny since the day I laid that plastic bag of yellowish powder on Principal Mueller's desk."

"Back up and tell me how the drug came into your possession," Rafe said.

"Penny's grades had fallen drastically over the past semester. I'd called her to my office to talk about them. She became defensive and angrily grabbed her purse to leave. It slipped from her hand and hit the floor. The contents scattered. I knelt down to help her, and there next to my knee was the clear plastic bag. She shoved me, trying to get to it first."

"But you beat her to it."

"Yes. I tried to get her to talk to me. She denied knowing where it came from or how it got into her purse. She refused to say a word, so I escorted her to the principal's office." Erin paused and rubbed her temples again.

Rafe didn't push her to continue. He had to know everything she remembered, but she needed to move at her own pace.

"I left Penny with Principal Mueller's assistant. I went in his office, put the baggie on his desk, and then explained what had happened."

"When did he notify the police?"

"Not until after he'd called Penny into his office and asked where she got the drugs." Erin's color paled. "At first, she claimed to have no idea how they got into her purse. I reminded her that she'd almost knocked me over trying to get it away from me. Her face crumpled, and she began to sob. Principal Mueller waited a few seconds before asking her again where she got the drugs.

"When she lifted her head, there wasn't one sign of a tear. As calmly as anything, she said I'd made sexual advances toward her, that she'd rejected me, and I was trying to get even." Erin's hands covered her stomach. "It was as if she'd flipped a switch in her head. She looked me in the eyes and said I'd warned her that I'd get even. Right in front of us, she'd morphed into a different person."

"Then the principal reported the drug find?" Rafe asked, providing a gentle nudge to keep Erin talking.

"Yes. He notified city law enforcement, the school district police, and Penny's parents." Erin shook her head, keeping her gaze focused on the floor. "The rest of the day only got worse."

"How so?" Rafe asked.

"The police treated me as if they believed her accusation. The district sent an investigator, who at least started out friendly. His attitude changed after he heard Penny's side of the story. By the time they were finished with me, I was embarrassed, hurt, and angry. I was sent home, pending results of the investigation."

"That scenario certainly sounds like a motive for murder, but you're innocent until proven guilty," Harold said. "The police need hard evidence in order to file charges."

Rafe had been so zoned in on Erin, observing every facial and body movement, that he'd almost forgotten Harold was taking notes.

"They may have it." Erin's bottom lip quivered. "Sara Monroe came forward this morning and claimed to have heard me threaten Penny."

Harold dropped his pen on the legal pad and leaned toward Erin. "Why didn't you tell me sooner?"

"I'm sorry." Erin's tone was defensive. "Her statement makes me the logical suspect."

Harold waved his hand as if wiping out Erin's words. "Motive and hearsay do not constitute hard evidence. Finding your DNA or fingerprints at the crime scene would be hard evidence."

Rafe bit back an argument. He'd been involved with more than one trial where a sharp district attorney had spun an airtight case using circumstantial evidence. Harold could soft-pedal the situation all he wanted. Truth was, Erin was in a lot of trouble.

A knock on her front door interrupted the discussion.

Erin sprang to her feet. Rafe caught her arm just before she turned the knob. "Let me take a look first."

"Aren't you being a little paranoid?" Her eyes dropped to his hand on her arm. "My life's not in danger."

"You're sure about that?"

She rolled her eyes. "Wouldn't a plan to discredit me be useless if I'm dead?"

No way was he backing down, but he released her arm. "Humor me."

She huffed out a breath, then peered through the peephole. Yes, sir, she'd grown into a nicely proportioned woman. The evidence was right in front of him. He felt a stirring in his groin that he mentally batted away.

"It's my neighbor."

"Company? That's what you need." He released her arm and

stepped back.

She opened the door and gasped. "What the hell?"

Rafe slid one arm around her waist and pulled her behind him, placing himself between her and the man on her porch. Rafe quickly realized what had shocked her. A handful of local TV station vans were parked in front of her house. Half a dozen reporters ran up the sidewalk, all shouting questions.

Rafe stepped back and allowed the neighbor to come in, then slammed the door closed. "Vultures, every one of them," he mumbled.

"We agree on that." Erin's tone of voice had lost its edge.

Her gaze met his and held for a second. It was long enough for him to see how hard she was working to hide her fear. Erin was scared. He understood. Her entire life was in shambles, and she was about to become nationwide news.

"I found this propped against the door," the neighbor said, handing her a manila envelope.

"What's this?" she asked, ripping the packet open.

Rafe reached to stop her but too late. She'd opened the damn thing and had removed the sheet of paper. She turned toward Rafe, stumbling backward. She held the page away from her body as if it were about to explode. He read the one word aloud.

"Murderer."

Rafe spun toward the neighbor. "Who are you?"

"Linc Hawkins," Erin answered. "He's installing the new computer system for the high school."

Rafe nodded to the neighbor. "Erin," Rafe said, "where would I find a couple of baggies?"

"Check the cabinet by the sink. Middle shelf." Erin still held the note away from her body. He liked her savvy. She knew she was holding something important.

Wearing plastic bags in lieu of gloves, Rafe took the letter from Erin and placed it on her breakfast bar. Then he picked up the envelope, which she'd let flutter to the floor.

Harold studied the note from a few feet away. "You need to give this to the cops."

"Why let them know everybody is passing judgment even before all the facts are in?" Erin's tone was defiant.

"Doesn't matter," Harold insisted. "If you get ten of them, you should call ten times."

"I'll call Detective Beckett." Erin fished a card and her cell from her pocket. She walked to the sliding glass doors overlooking her backyard.

Her hands trembled. She was hiding her shot nerves exceptionally well, and Rafe respected how she hadn't fallen victim to self-pity.

"Erin isn't capable of killing anyone," the neighbor said.

Rafe wanted to know more about the neighbor. "Linc, isn't it?"

"Yes. I live next door."

"How long have you known Erin?"

"Just a few months, but that was enough to learn how much she cares for the kids at the school."

Rafe sized up the neighbor while he talked. Calm and unruffled by the note he'd delivered to Erin, Linc Hawkins looked like he should have been hanging ten off a twenty-foot wave in his board shorts and faded T-shirt. His curly blond hair fell in every direction.

"And you live nearby?" Linc asked, turning the question back on Rafe.

Erin rejoined them. "Rafe's with the FBI. He's a friend of Jeff's."

"I see." Linc nodded while backing away. "I'll get out of the way. If the cops want to talk to me, I'll be home or at the high school." He paused. "Want me to call 911 and complain about these news people?"

"I doubt it would do any good," Harold said. "As long as they stay off private property and don't block traffic flow, they're not breaking any laws." He stood, buttoning his jacket as he rose.

"I couldn't reach Detective Beckett, but a patrol car will be here soon." Erin's voice sounded stronger.

"If I'm outside when they arrive," Harold said to Erin, "give them the note and tell them exactly what your neighbor said. Direct them to him if they have questions. I'll be right out front addressing the media. It's best to meet them head-on."

"When you come back inside, we need to talk about your retainer."

"I'm leaving after I speak with the press. I have a late appointment with another client. You'll be fine, if you do as I said." He smiled, grasped the bottom of his suit coat, and snapped it into perfect alignment. "Your retainer has been covered."

Rafe figured Jeff had already committed to paying whatever it cost to get her the best representation. Exactly like Rafe's dad had done for Nick on a couple of small arrests.

Erin removed her buzzing cell phone from her pocket. She rose and walked toward the kitchen area. Rafe decided to offer his services to Harold.

"You're going to be swarmed. Need an escort?"

"No doubt you could scare them back." Harold waved Rafe off. "But it's not necessary. I'll talk to them. Feed the beast, so to speak. Maybe I can satisfy their hunger."

Rafe watched Harold cross the yard, marveling at the man's forbearance as the press crowded around. He smiled like a rock star, shook hands, and appeared to be completely at ease with questions peppering him from all sides.

Jeff walked up behind Rafe and chuckled. "Harold was a district judge for years before retiring to private practice. That man always loved being in the spotlight."

Erin had stayed back out of sight. Rafe crossed to the

breakfast bar and found her staring at her phone. A swell of sympathy hit him in the chest. He buried that idiotic sentiment. There was no room in an investigation for that emotion. He'd dealt with criminals who could tie a rookie agent in knots with their bullshit. Besides, she wouldn't want him comforting her, even if she was suffering.

Her cell buzzed again. She ignored it.

Jeff wrapped his arm around her shoulders.

"Are you going to answer that?" Rafe asked.

"No." She shoved the cell farther away.

Rafe leaned over and read the display. *Unknown Caller.* "Have you been getting a lot of crank calls?"

"Mostly reporters. If I give them an exclusive on why I murdered Penny, they'll guarantee I get national coverage."

Rafe dragged a hand through his hair. "We'll get this straightened out."

"We?" Again, her eyes filled with doubt. She caught his gaze and held it without blinking.

"Yeah. I'll nose around. See what I can learn about the drug angle. Was she using or selling? The murder doesn't necessarily sound like a minor deal gone wrong, but weirder things have happened. It will be hard to get anyone to talk. Murder tends to shut people up."

"You're calling the shots," Jeff said. "I can nose around. Maybe pick up some intel."

"Good idea. Talk to your friends at the sheriff's office. Call in a few markers. I get why the girl made those accusations against Erin. She was covering her ass. Jeff, you said Penny died from multiple stab wounds. That sounds like a rage killing. We figure out the why, and we'll be that much closer to the who."

Erin reached over, picked up her phone, and turned it off. "I can't stand the buzzing." She shook her head. "Penny was just a kid."

"A kid in possession of heroin. Hell, she might have been

pushing to her classmates." Rafe's hands clenched. He understood that Nick was to blame for his bad decisions, but to hear that after all these years the same crap was still going on at the school made him furious.

Jeff nodded in agreement. "I'll stop by the sheriff's office for coffee in the morning. If anybody opens up to me, I'll give you both a call."

"The message left at the crime scene might give us a hint," Erin said, looking straight at Rafe. "Can you find out what it said?"

Jeff leaned forward. "Rafe can't just step in."

"Because the cops haven't asked the FBI for help?" she asked.

"Right. Even if they invited us to help, I might not be assigned to the case. I'm on leave."

Erin's hand covered her mouth as pink raced up her cheeks. "I'm so sorry. I haven't offered my condolences. Your dad talked about you and Luke all the time."

"You saw him often?" Rafe's curiosity climbed at her words. Did he detect a judgmental tone in her words?

"If we couldn't get enough to round out the table, Erin played poker with us. Most of the time, she held her own around us old folks." Jeff's pride lit up his face.

Rafe stood, went to the window, and looked out. He wasn't comfortable thinking about his dad boring Erin with information about his sons. "A patrol car just pulled up."

Erin walked to the front door. "I'm just glad I didn't find the envelope. They'd just think I planted it."

Rafe intercepted her before she let in the cops. "I'm staying for a few weeks. There's no law against me unofficially poking around. I can also call my partner and get him to help."

"Thank you."

She opened the door and ushered two cops inside. Rafe introduced himself as a friend of the family before Erin had a chance to add the fact he was a federal agent. They jotted down names.

"Where is Detective Beckett?" Erin asked the first police officer.

"On another call. He asked that we bag and deliver the note to the lab. We're to take names and a brief statement. He may contact you later."

The older of the two cops, Sergeant Kelly, peered down at the note. He snapped on his gloves and dropped it and the envelope into a paper bag. After he'd sealed and initialed it, he walked back to Rafe, Jeff, and Erin.

"Ms. Brady, other than yours, whose fingerprints will the lab find on the note?"

"My neighbor handled the envelope, but you'll find mine on both."

"I moved it to the counter, but used baggies in lieu of gloves," Rafe said, knowing the town was too small to keep his identity a secret. He'd been stupid to think he could. "I'm here as a family friend, but I'm also a federal agent."

"I thought I recognized you. You're Rafe Sirilli."

Rafe nodded. "That's correct."

"I hated to hear about your dad." Sergeant Kelly shook Rafe's hand. "He was a good man."

"Yes, he was."

The conversation drifted to football for a few minutes, but Rafe wasn't fooled. Kelly was giving everybody a chance to relax.

"Which neighbor brought the envelope in to you?" Kelly asked.

"That's his house next door. The one with the big oak tree and the tire swing," Erin said. "No kids. Just a swing."

Kelly nodded. "We'll walk over and speak with him. People do crazy things after a murder. There's no telling who left the note. Could have been a reporter baiting you. You know, a 'film at six' kind of news story."

Erin walked the two police officers to the door then pointed out Linc's house. "Tell me, did Detective Beckett really have another appointment or does he think I wrote the note myself?"

"I really don't know what he thinks, ma'am."

Erin sighed. "I'm sorry. Of course, he has other cases." She closed the door and returned to the couch. "Getting bitchy with the cops wasn't a good move."

"They understand." Jeff checked the time. "It might be a good idea if you packed a few things and stayed with me and Lotty until this is over."

She'd started shaking her head before he'd finished the sentence. "I'm not allowing a stupid note and a handful of reporters to send me into hiding." Erin's face softened as she smiled at Jeff. "No way would I add the burden of a houseguest to Lotty."

"You're not a guest," Jeff said.

"You know what I mean. She'd overextend herself. Do me a favor? Hug her and tell her I love her."

"How about staying with Carla?" Jeff glanced at Rafe. "She and Erin are good friends."

"I'm staying here. I'll need a ride to the police parking lot. I rode home with Harold." Her eyes closed for a moment. "But there's no hurry. I have nowhere to go tomorrow."

Rafe knew exactly what she was saying. He understood how a person's work blurred with their personality. Her job as a counselor was her calling. It was as much a part of her as the air she breathed, and she was on the verge of losing everything.

He picked up her cell and programmed in his number, giving himself a special code for speed dial. After all, hadn't she referred to him earlier as the devil?

Then he turned to Jeff. "I'll come by tomorrow and drive Erin to get her car. Give us a chance to talk."

She stood and jammed her fists on her hips. "Don't I have a say in this?"

"Not this time." He paused at the door, battling back a smile. "If you need anything, dial 666. My cell's always on."

CHAPTER 4

Erin closed the door behind Jeff and Rafe. The number of vans in front of her house had thinned out, and she hoped her fifteen minutes of fame had ended. She'd struggled against a poor-poor-pitiful-me frame of mind all day. Finally alone, she allowed the feeling of desperation to overwhelm her. Her knees buckled. She slid down the wall to the floor, brought her knees up, and dropped her forehead forward.

The silence embraced her, almost as if it protected her from outside accusations. She remained huddled in that position on the floor until darkness engulfed the room. Pushing to her feet, she shuffled down the hall, toed off her shoes, lay down on her bed, and then curled into a ball.

Sleep called to her, and she succumbed willingly. Soon, the shrewish voice of Nick Sirilli drifted through the fog. "Rafe knows all about you. Stay away from him. He's planning on telling everybody the truth about you." Tears had streaked the face of the frightened teenager.

Erin woke with a start.

A glance at her clock proved she'd slept only an hour. The last thing she needed was nightmares about her past. Where had that memory come from? Hadn't she put all that behind her? She'd buried that period of her life so deep she'd thought it could never resurface. She gave her pillow a couple of punches and then lay there, staring at the ceiling.

She knew exactly why she'd dreamed of being a kid. Rafe Sirilli standing in her living room as if he belonged there had screwed with her mind. His black T-shirt and black jeans were a testament to his amazing body. Even with long hair and a beard,

Rafe was heart-achingly handsome with his smoldering dark gray eyes.

He'd also reminded her of a time in her life best forgotten. Past humiliation crowded her thoughts. A year ahead of her, he'd left for college before the biggest part of her scandal broke. After the trial, things had died down. The townsfolk had forgotten and moved on. Not Erin. Her memory was vividly intact.

Seeing Rafe had brought back all that old pain. Everybody in town had thought her no more than trash back then. Why was he willing to help her now? Maybe his time with the government had forced him to see that not everything is as it seems.

Her thick comforter was within reach, and she pulled it over her shoulders. This time, she'd dream about warm waters, white sand, and friendly people.

****

The press and onlookers who'd gathered at the front of Erin's house had provided the perfect cover. Hiding in plain sight, he'd been able to check on her a couple of times today. One of the two remaining news vans appeared to be packing up. His ability to blend in was becoming difficult. As much as he hated to leave his vantage point, he had to go.

Erin had been busy all day. Those men in her apartment had troubled him briefly, but he brushed those silly worries aside. Jeff and Harold were pillars of the community. They'd been there to protect her, but the stranger and neighbor had no business sniffing around her.

He'd relaxed a little when all four of the men left. Why had he let it bother him? Erin wouldn't be unfaithful. Hadn't she demonstrated her affection for him repeatedly? What had she called him? Casanova. "Casanova was a great lover," he said aloud, loving the way the name rolled off his tongue.

The lights in Erin's house went off, leaving Casanova to believe she'd gone to straight to bed when the men had finally gone.

He pulled his ball cap low and walked over to a small group of reporters. They paid him no attention, proving to him that hiding in plain sight still worked well.

The word witness stopped him cold. Had someone spotted him crawling out of Penny's window? Blood rushed through his veins, pounding in his ears like huge waves hitting the shore.

"The cops have the counselor cold." A reporter opened the driver's side door of a van.

"How you figure?" asked a tall cameraman.

"Some girl came forward and said she'd overheard the counselor threaten the dead girl." The reporter slammed the van door and started the engine.

"No shit?" Camera Guy said.

"You're out of the loop, man. Small time." The driver smirked. "Everybody has already headed to the witness's house. You're late to the party."

"Well, you follow the crowd. I'm staying right here. One picture of Ms. Brady will net me some quick cash."

The news hadn't mentioned the message he'd written on Penny's wall with the public. Had they done so, maybe her friends might have taken his warning seriously. Damn them and her. Even dead, she was still manipulating people. Which one of her minions had told this lie?

Casanova had no choice but to follow the van to find out which teenager had lied. He'd thought one death would be enough. That his message would get out, prompting the others in Penny's crowd to stop making false allegations against Erin.

He hated to be wrong. Yet, an odd rush of exhilaration rushed through him. He'd kill anyone who came between him and the woman he loved.

There was so much to do before he could take her home. The contractor he'd hired was almost finished with the interior renovations. Soon, the workers would install new thick carpeting.

His next purchase would be bedroom furniture. Erin's style was simple and classic, so he'd select colors and pieces sure to please her. Then he'd have the perfect house for the perfect woman.

Erin would be grateful when she learned everything he'd done for her.

****

Erin woke, swung her feet to the floor, and raked her tangled hair out of her eyes. Sweat had soaked through her clothes, and her empty stomach growled in protest. When had she last eaten?

No way could she go back to sleep, even though it was just four thirty. She showered, washed her hair, and slipped on jeans and a T-shirt. Now what? Taking her morning run was out. Sure as she did, some reporter would catch her away from the house. Sitting around doing nothing was going to drive her crazy.

After she picked up her car, her most important errand today was to visit Lotty. She and Jeff were very close, and by now, he'd told her everything. No doubt, she'd watched the news. She was a worrier and would fret until Erin showed up to talk. Her heart warmed just thinking about the love and affection Lotty and Jeff had given her. They'd taken in a street kid and helped her overcome her past. Because of them, Erin had gone on to college and gotten her master's degree. She literally owed them her life.

Erin flipped off the bathroom light. Today was basketball practice for the girls who played on her YMCA team. She hated the thought of letting them down. Surely, somebody would step up and coach the team in her absence.

She rounded the corner into the living room. Through the sliding glass doors, a series of rapidly flashing bright lights blinded her. White dots blurred her vision. She stumbled and landed hard on the floor.

Where had she left her phone? Rafe had handed it back to her. The coffee table. It was close by. She crawled on her belly, feeling her way along the edge of the table until the cool plastic of her cell cover was under her hand.

She entered the number nine but changed her mind. Instead, she cleared the dial pad and punched in 666.

He answered on the second ring. "What's wrong?"

"Someone's in my backyard."

"Lock yourself in the bathroom and don't come out. And call 911. I'm on my way."

She glanced at the screen. *Call Ended.* He'd disconnected. Knowing he would be there soon sent waves of relief over her. Erin's vision slowly cleared, so she pushed herself to a sitting position and considered a run down the hall to the bathroom. There had been no more flashes, and no one tried to break in, so she decided against calling 911. She stayed right where she was until Rafe arrived.

Fear faded and flashed to anger. The intruder had to be a media type, someone trying for a picture to sell. Images of her half-dressed, looking half-asleep, plastered on every local media Web site sent her blood boiling. For the first time, she regretted not following Jeff's suggestion that she should be certified to carry a gun. Too late now. Texas probably wouldn't give her a license now until she was cleared of Penny's murder.

She stood, ran down the hall, and jerked an old robe off its hanger. Then she walked to the panel of switches on the kitchen wall and flipped on every outside light. Let the bastard come out into the open. She fixed the coffeepot, and while it brewed, she got a rubber band and pulled her still-damp hair into a low ponytail.

The knock on the front door was expected. Nevertheless, she steadied her nerves and checked the peephole before releasing the lock and letting Rafe inside.

"Are you okay?" His voice had a sharp edge. Strong fingers slid up the arms of her robe, stroking and inspecting her for bruises. His eyes scanned her from head to toe and back up. Heat rolled off him. His hard gaze spoke of a man who feared nothing. She wished she were that brave.

"Somebody was in my backyard. A series of flashes blinded me for a minute. I'm guessing they came from a camera."

"Stay put." He pulled a pistol from the holster on his belt and disappeared out the sliding glass door. Chills raced up her arms.

His sharp command hadn't offended her. He was all business and here at her invitation. His touch had been tender and caring when he'd inspected her for injuries. Even with his scruffy appearance, he was compelling. So much so that she'd caught herself leaning toward him.

She filled two mugs and then sat at her small dining room table where she could watch both the front and back doors. A scream sent her scrambling to her feet. Her knees banged into the table and sent hot coffee sloshing over her hand.

Rafe appeared, a dark shadow through the glass, dragging a man by the collar.

He shoved open the door, pulled the man inside, and dropped him on the floor. "Here's your intruder."

"Where'd you find him?" she asked, noticing how the man's forearm hung at an odd angle.

"In a tree." Rafe checked his watch. "You called the cops?"

"No, I waited for you." One corner of his mouth quirked upward, sending electrical charges through her system.

"Call them."

The intruder's face was bright red. His lips were stretched tight over yellowing teeth. He struggled to upright himself, moaning loudly. Erin stepped back.

"Yeah. Call the police. I'm filing charges for assault and suing you for destruction of private property."

"That piece of shit camera was ten years old. You shouldn't have dropped it."

Erin picked up her cell, paused, and looked at Rafe. He gave her a curt nod.

"Tell them to send a car for this garbage. This asshole was on your private property. Tell the operator you're holding a pervert who fell out of a tree while taking your picture."

"He broke my arm," the photographer whined.

"I was helping him down from the tree." Rafe shot her a wink. "He lost his balance."

His playful demeanor sent heat rushing through her veins. Erin turned her back and dialed the phone, keeping her report to the 911 operator short and to the point. When she turned around, Rafe was sitting in her chair and drinking from her mug. The cameraman remained on the floor with his back pressed against the wall.

"This was for me, right?" Rafe sipped the lukewarm coffee.

"Yes and no."

"Come again?"

"I fixed enough for two, but you're drinking out of my cup."

"Too late now." He took another sip and sighed. "I needed that."

The man on the floor leaned forward. "You two want to cut the chitchat and get me to a hospital?"

Rafe's expression hardened. "Shut up, before you fall and break your other arm."

Two police cars stopped in front of her house. Rafe strolled over and opened the door as if he lived there. He introduced himself, passed his ID to the cops, and then turned them over to Erin. Without hesitation, she explained the situation.

One uniformed officer took notes. After a few questions, he closed the pad and said, "You'll have to come down to the station if you want to file charges."

Her sudden burst of laughter drew everyone's attention. "Sorry. The irony of that statement caught me off guard. Just get him out of here. If he comes back, I'll file for sure."

Rafe's hand rested at the small of her back while the intruder was ushered to his car. The possessive move on his part was more than confusing to Erin. Heat sizzled up her spinal cord. She moved away from him.

"You should've pressed charges."

"If I never have to go inside the police station again, I'll be happy. Besides, he didn't really hurt anybody."

"If you don't mind your picture being splashed all over the media, why'd you call me?"

Now this was the Rafe she remembered. "Obviously, I made a mistake. The flashing lights scared the crap out of me, and I fell." Erin rubbed her right wrist. Odd, she hadn't noticed it throbbing until now.

"You're hurt?" Rafe's tone mellowed into something that sounded like concern. "I didn't notice any swelling earlier."

"I'm fine."

He caught her by the elbow, gently lifting her arm. His strong fingers massaging her skin felt intimate and personal. Could he tell she welcomed his touch? It made her feel stronger.

She tugged.

He didn't surrender.

"Wiggle your fingers."

"They worked just fine when I dialed your number."

Standing so near, she became extremely aware of his size. He'd always had broad shoulders, but those had belonged to a boy. The man had matured, his chest had thickened, his muscular biceps rippled with movement. His scent, clean and woodsy, filled her senses. Now was not the time for her knees to get weak, so she concentrated on the bruise forming on her arm.

"I knew you'd remember the 666." He grinned, and his face changed from handsome to heart-stopping.

Erin extracted her arm from his grasp. "I appreciate you coming. I hated to call Jeff. He and Lotty have done so much for me already."

"You should stay with them until this is over."

She shook her head. "I plan on visiting today, but I'm not

bringing my problems to their house. She's doing better, but she's not well enough to deal with reporters and cops. Associating with me right now is like swimming in a sea full of hungry sharks."

"I'm a good swimmer. If you're uncomfortable being alone, I can stay here."

"I'll pass. Why give my neighbors and the reporters more to gossip about?"

"Like I care."

"Easy for you not to give a damn what people think. I'm betting you don't plan on ever coming back once you get your dad's affairs settled."

"That would be a safe bet." He strolled to the door, hesitated, and then turned to face her. "Call me if you need anything."

Again, his smoldering eyes seemed to see into the depths of her soul for a second. Could he see the desire his nearness had created? God, she hoped not. He turned on his heel and sauntered away. The knot of nerves coiled low in her stomach slowly uncurled.

CHAPTER 5

Tagging along behind the news van had proved fruitful. Uniformed cops stationed in front of a large brick home had kept traffic moving. The Monroe name on the mailbox provided the information Casanova needed.

He should have anticipated one of Penny's friends would do something stupid. Sara Monroe was a self-centered, spoiled, malicious brat. Just like the rest of the pack.

She would die for lying.

Casanova dragged his hand across the stubble on his chin. A shower and shave were in order, but he had too much work to do. It was critical he learn which bedroom belonged to Sara, which meant he'd have to get close enough to the house before everyone turned in for the night. Pulling this off would be tricky at best.

With his car parked four blocks from the Monroes' house, he cut down the alley and jogged the distance without breaking a sweat. Being in good physical condition paid off.

He circled to the back of the property, thinking how stupid the family was not to have blinds. Thanks to the sheer panels, he located Sara sitting in the middle of a bed texting on her cell. The purple and green colors splashed throughout her space hinted at school spirit. The pom-poms and cheerleading trophies on the shelves spoke to her physical ability. Nothing in her room reflected her true self, a vicious spreader of lies.

He made his way back to his car and drove home, taking care not to draw attention to himself. Once inside his bedroom, he quickly changed clothes, donning black jeans and a hooded jacket. He knelt down, loosened the screws on the grate covering the air conditioning recirculation vent, and removed the shoebox holding his cache of equipment.

The weight of the hunting knife felt good in his hand. The stainless steel blade bore remnants of Penny's blood. Proof he'd taken action to silence her lies.

He slid the knife into its leather sheath before placing it in his jacket pocket. This method was messy, but it was designed to send a message. His leather gloves were stiff and covered in dried blood, so he eased them on and flexed his fingers until they moved freely.

Tonight, he would make a statement. A louder, clearer declaration than the one he'd made with Penny. People had to understand. If anybody told lies about his Erin, heavy consequences would be levied.

****

Sleep had evaded Rafe last night. He'd returned home from Erin's too stoked to rest. His brain had refused to shut down. Was it the trouble she was in or his ego that had given him insomnia? She'd been so sexy standing there, wrapped in that robe while he rubbed her wrist. One tug of the tie might have opened new doors for them both. She'd smelled of soap, shampoo, and Erin. He'd gotten out of there just in the nick of time.

His X-rated thoughts of Erin, coupled with being home, had been the perfect recipe for no rest. Why would sleeping in his old bed make him feel like an outsider? Who was he kidding? He *was* an outsider. He'd let too many people down to ever belong here again.

He fished his toiletries out of his bag and headed to the bathroom. Normal, everyday tasks such as personal hygiene felt odd. Yeah, he'd been undercover too long. A shower helped wash the funk from his brain. He wrapped a towel around his waist and tackled the job of scraping the excess hair off his face.

Rafe stared at the half-shaved man in the mirror. Nick looked back at him. Or did he? Would they still be the spitting images of each other at thirty years old? They'd hadn't looked like brothers when they'd buried Nick. At twenty-four, his pencil-thin body hadn't remotely resembled Rafe's healthy, robust form. The dark circles under Nick's eyes and the needle tracks on his arms had painted the picture of a life out of control.

Coming home to Westbrook Hills had released a flood of memories for Rafe, some good and some bad. After Nick's overdose, their dad had never looked at Rafe quite the same. There'd never been any overt accusations that he should have been able to stop Nick from using. Behind his dad's eyes, a hint of blame had been noticeable. Rafe's trips home had been limited after that. The military and then the FBI had consumed his life. Once he was squared away here, he had no reason to stay.

He rinsed the razor and continued shaving.

What the fuck had he gotten himself into by agreeing to help Erin? Better yet, what had she gotten herself into? The idea that a handful of teenagers would lie and seek revenge against a teacher didn't surprise him, but the drug aspect worried him. If the girl had been pushing as well as using, the narcotics squad was probably already working on the problem.

Like it or not, some small towns were hotbeds for drug dealers. More than a few states had declared heroin use by the younger generation an epidemic. It had become so widespread because of its easy availability and price. Rafe decided to ask his partner, Colton Weir, to reach out to a few of their contacts. Surely, Westbrook Hills was on the DEA's radar.

Erin's frightened eyes flashed through his memory. Serious, yet defiant, they seemed able to burrow into his thoughts. Her skin, creamy and soft, was flawless. Well, except for a small mole at the upper right corner of her upper lip. Too bad that sensuous mouth held a rapier tongue. He wasn't the smartest guy on the block, but he knew the dangers of touching an open flame.

Rafe slipped on a pair of jeans, a blue pullover, which smelled clean, and his best pair of boots before wandering into the kitchen. For a split second, he expected to find his dad standing at the counter pouring a cup of coffee. He had to give the old man credit. He'd done his best to raise three boys without a wife.

Would Nick have kept his head on straight if he hadn't been the one who found their mother lying on the couch, dead of an overdose of tranquilizers? Hell of a thing for a kid to have seen.

This house seemed to pull mental images and thoughts from deep in Rafe's subconscious. He ignored them and left a message for Colton to dig around quietly and see what he could learn.

Rafe grabbed his keys and walked out of the house. Jeff's SUV pulled into the drive, his window rolled down, and he waved frantically for Rafe to hurry.

"What—"

"Damn the sonofabitch who's doing this," Jeff blurted out. His color rivaled that of a white sheet. Jeff's knuckles gripping the steering wheel, the twitching nerve in his jaw, and the anger pouring off him were all warnings. The man was a ticking time bomb. "Get in."

"I'll drive while you calm down. Then you can talk." Rafe opened the driver's side door, waiting until Jeff moved to the passenger's seat and had buckled up before saying another word. "Where to?"

"Erin's. We may be too late."

"Too late for what?"

"Warning her that another girl was murdered. I called, but she didn't answer."

"I hadn't heard, but then I don't watch much TV." Rafe pressed his boot harder on the accelerator. "You called her attorney?"

"Shit." Jeff fished his cell out of his pocket, stared at it for a second, then pressed a button on the dash. "I forget I have all this newfangled technology available."

Rafe kept his eyes on the road, while listening to the conversation between Harold Penza and Jeff. The judge had already heard about the second murder.

"What can we do?" Jeff asked Harold.

"Remind Erin not to talk to the police. Unless they find hard evidence, they shouldn't be able to convince a judge to issue an arrest warrant. I'm due in court this morning, but if by chance, they take her into custody, call my assistant, she can reach me. I'll meet Erin at the police station as soon as I can."

Jeff disconnected and started calling people, leaving messages for some and speaking with a few of his friends at the sheriff's office. Rafe picked up bits and pieces, while he maneuvered through the small neighborhood. When Jeff ended the last call, he said, "That wasn't much help. All we know is the girls were killed the same way."

Rafe parked Jeff's SUV behind a TV station's van, effectively blocking it in. More than a few vehicles would have to move for the asshole to get out. By the time the engine died, a group of vultures were blocking his and Jeff's path. "You ready for this?"

"Damn right," Jeff spit out the words. His accent thickened when he was upset.

They shouldered their way through the crowd, ignoring questions. The reporters wanted to know who they were and if they thought Erin Brady was a murderess. Rafe whirled at that question. He stood at edge of the porch, daring anyone to come closer while Jeff knocked on Erin's door.

Rafe turned when the door opened and found Linc Hawkins staring at him.

"Come inside," Linc commanded.

New neighbor? Rafe thought not. He was entirely too comfortable with his surroundings to be new.

"Jeff." Erin pushed away from the dining table and hurried into his arms. "Everybody believes I killed again."

"Not everyone." Jeff's tone was soft and soothing. "People who love you know that you're incapable of harming another human."

Rafe didn't look at her. He didn't have to. Her green eyes were burning a hole in his back. She'd accepted that she needed help and was looking to him to provide it. "Depending on the time of death, I may be able to straighten this out."

"Really?" The corner of Linc's mouth lifted, flashing white teeth at Rafe and sending that uneasy feeling to his gut.

"He was here during the wee hours of the morning," Erin said.

"That's true," Rafe confirmed. Why he enjoyed watching Linc's smile disappear was puzzling.

Jeff answered his cell phone. He glanced at Rafe. Maybe this was the call they were waiting for.

"Is the coffee fresh?" Rafe asked, waiting for Jeff's call to end.

"Close enough," Linc answered, walking into the kitchen.

Rafe's curiosity spiked. "Doesn't he work?" he asked Erin.

"Most of the time he works from home. The new system requires him to be at the school some, but not every minute of the day." Erin cocked her head. "Why?"

Rafe shrugged. "No reason," he lied.

Linc set a full carafe on the dining room table. He went back, returning with four mugs, sugar, and a small glass of milk. "Sorry it took me so long. I opened every cabinet before I found the sugar."

Erin filled the cups with coffee while the three of them stood around the table without speaking. Jeff was still on his cell. His tone rose and fell in volume, interspersed between periods of silence.

Jeff's slow footsteps drew Rafe's attention. Nothing could've prepared him for the expression on the older man's face. His eyes were glassy, and he steadied himself by keeping his hand on the wall. His skin matched his silver hair. Erin rushed to his side.

"I'm fine. Don't coddle me, girl."

"News from one of your sources?" Rafe tried to sound

casual.

Jeff walked to the table and eased into a chair. He picked up the spoon and stirred the steaming coffee for a second.

"Sara Monroe is the girl found slaughtered in her bed. Stabbed multiple times, like the first victim."

Erin gasped. "Oh God."

"Too much rage," Rafe spoke, hoping to stem the tide of panic in Erin's eyes. "Anytime a killer stabs the victim over and over, they've lost control."

"Or they're making a point," Linc added.

"He left the same message." Jeff lifted the cup to his mouth, and his hand trembled.

"You know what it said," Erin announced. "Tell us."

"I don't. Apparently, the cops are keeping a tight rein on that information. The rumor is that the detective will ask your permission to search your house and car. If you refuse, they'll ask a judge for a warrant."

"Let them come. I have nothing to hide."

"Call your attorney," Linc said. "I'm betting he'll say the cops can pound sand. They don't have enough to take to a judge." He stood, leaving his coffee untouched. "I've got to get to the school. The upgrade is almost ready to install."

Before anyone could speak, Linc was up and out the door. Ignoring the shouts from the reporters, Rafe followed Linc to the yard, stopping him at the edge of his driveway.

"Who are you really?" Rafe demanded.

Linc's eyebrows rose. "Erin told you. I'm a computer programmer."

"She might believe that crap. I don't."

A smile pulled at Linc's lips. "I believe you're jealous."

Rafe's fingers rolled into a fist. "If you're involved with this mess, I'll find out." He spun on his heel and went back to Erin's house. Damn, he'd wanted to wipe that smirk off Linc's face, but being arrested for assault and battery wouldn't help anybody.

Regardless of what the press or anyone in town thought, Rafe believed in Erin's innocence. He had no doubt the detective on the case knew that female killers weren't normally prone to such violence.

Erin wasn't smiling when he reentered her place. In fact, her jaw was set, and her eyebrows had dipped into a frown. God, she was stunning even when she was mad.

CHAPTER 6

Erin waited just inside the open door until Rafe was back inside. She stepped in front of him. "What was that about?"

"I don't know what you mean." He tried to sidestep her, but she moved, blocking his path.

"Yes, you do. Why were you in Linc's face?"

"He's involved." Rafe stepped closer, crowding into her space. "I don't know how, but I'll find out."

"Involved? Since when is being a caring neighbor a crime?"

Rafe's scent wafted through Erin's senses, almost making her forget the scene she'd watched through the window. She hated to yield and step back, but the heat rolling off his body made it difficult for her to think straight.

Erin reminded herself she'd learned the hard way what kind of person he was, and she hadn't seen anything to convince her that he'd changed. Years ago, he'd been too big of a coward to deliver his message. Instead, he'd sent Nick to do his dirty work. He'd considered her beneath him then and still did.

"He's either with law enforcement or he watches too much *Law & Order*," Rafe insisted.

"If you two can stop arguing long enough," Jeff said, "I'd like to hear more about you being here in the wee hours of the morning. What happened? And why didn't you call me?" He drummed his fingers on the tabletop.

"A photographer hid in the backyard and scared the crap out of me. I called Rafe..." Why had she called him instead of Jeff or the police? "I didn't want to frighten Lotty, and Rafe didn't ask me a bunch of questions like the 911 operator would have."

"So you can alibi her?" Jeff asked.

"It's too soon to say," Rafe said. "We don't know the Monroe girl's time of death."

"How selfish am I?" Erin asked, more of herself than anyone. "I'm sitting here hoping I have an alibi, instead of sympathizing with Sara Monroe's family."

Erin moved to the backside of the kitchen table, pulled out a chair and sat. Rafe followed, dragging his chair close to hers. Their thighs touched, and she squirmed in place. Contact with him sent streaks of lightning to places she didn't want heating up because of him. Sheesh, even in times of crisis he could make her thoughts turn toward sex.

"What's next?" She braced herself for him to tell her nothing.

"I've got some calls to make, but afterward, we'll let Jeff drive us to your car. If one of these news vans pulls out behind us, we'll ditch them."

"I can do that." Jeff smiled.

"Great. You can drop us off. Erin and I will swing by Harold's office. We need to know the time of death."

"Good plan. I'll keep asking around, too." Jeff turned to Erin. "This incident with the camera guy proves my point. You staying here at night alone isn't a good idea. Erin, girl," he said, using his pet name for her, "come home until this is over."

Erin stood, moved behind Jeff, and wrapped her arms around his shoulders. "How lucky was I that you caught me stealing that package of hot dog buns?"

"Depends on your point of view. I'd say it was my good fortune." Jeff patted her hand.

She blinked back the tears floating in her eyes. A look flitted across Rafe's face. Had she seen sympathy? She shook that off, attributing it to his recent loss. He strolled over to a window and lifted the blinds.

"If it gets too crazy here, we can work out of Dad's house," Rafe said.

"I hate to let a few reporters and camera crews run me from my home." She shivered as a chill raced up her spine. "You don't think I'm in danger, do you?"

"It's too soon to tell." Rafe lifted one broad shoulder. "Based on what little I know, it appears that you were the catalyst."

"Then I accept your offer," she said to Rafe. "What can I do?"

"Start thinking about who the girls hung out with. If you ever saw them outside of school, where were they? Stabbings this violent are usually one of two things: rage or to send a message."

"A message?" Erin's stomach rolled into a knot. Did she know the killer?

"Yeah. If the girls were using or reselling, they bought that shit somewhere. Drug dealers don't always look like sleazeballs. They come in all shapes and sizes, but they will eliminate anybody who becomes a threat to their business."

Jeff shook his head. "They used to cut out an informant's tongue."

"Still do, sometimes," Rafe agreed.

"Give me a minute to change." She went to her bedroom, slipped into a nicer pair of jeans, a lemon-yellow blouse, and a pair of multicolored wedges. She redid her hair, pulling it back into a long braid. With a splash of mascara and lip gloss, she was ready. Her insides might be in shreds, but she'd die before showing it.

Halfway down the hall, her bravery slipped. Jesus, they had a killer in their midst. Not some deranged stranger passing through. These murders had been methodical, well planned, and horrifying. Was the killer one of the teachers? One of the students? Where were the girls buying their drugs? The enormity of solving these murders hit her. She stumbled and reached out to brace herself on the wall.

Strong arms gathered her close.

"I've got you." Rafe lifted her as if she were a child and carried her to her bedroom, where he gently placed her on the edge of the bed. "What happened?"

The blood that had rushed from her head found its way to her cheeks. "Killer heels?"

"Nice try." He stroked the back of his hand down her cheek. "It's okay to be scared."

"Good. Because I've never been through anything like this. I feel helpless. It's an emotion I don't like. I'm not sure I can remember everyone."

He knelt in front of her, caught her gaze, and smiled. "Of course you can't. Not unless you possess total recall." His smile widened. "Although, I do think some women have that ability."

Her mind flashed all the way back to high school. "You're right. We remember every slight, every hurtful, embarrassing thing done to us."

"Whoa." Rafe blanched as if she'd slapped him. "What the hell does that mean?"

Jeff entered the room. "Is there a problem back here?"

She tried to stand, but somehow Rafe had wedged himself between her knees.

"She's okay." His gaze never left her face. "Give us a minute?"

Jeff paused, and Erin thought he was going to refuse. Instead, he turned and walked out. "I'm ready to go when you two are."

Rafe hadn't budged. She reached out and grabbed his shoulders. He was too strong for her to push out of the way, and touching him sent vibrations deep into her core. Areas that didn't need to react to him warmed.

"Why do we need a minute?" She met his gaze, trying not to breathe in his clean, snowcapped-mountain scent. He'd always stirred something in her. No way was she setting herself up again.

"You've been pissed since you saw me sitting in your living room. You were a young snot twelve years ago, but it's time to grow up and move on."

"You jerk. My life was miserable back then. You deliberately tried to make it worse. If it hadn't been for Nick..." She clamped her mouth shut.

"My brother?" Rafe's eyes had turned the color of a spinning tornado. "What did he have to do with anything?"

Erin glared back at Rafe, but he didn't seem to be willing to let the subject drop. Maybe he was right. Why not clear the air? "You asked me to the prom, right?"

"And you accepted. Then you changed your mind, announcing it loudly and right in the middle of the hall."

"Because Nick confessed your plan. You thought it would be fun to tell everybody about my past. I should've known you'd never have asked me out for real." After she'd blurted the words out loud, she realized just how childish she sounded. "Look, my feelings were hurt so I lashed out. Why I let something that old flare up is just stupid."

"Then we'll end it. I have no idea why Nick would've said that to you. Not a word of it was true. None. You have my word." He rose to his feet and stepped back. "If we're going to figure out who killed these girls, we can at least be civil. Fair enough?"

"Fair enough," she agreed, glad that was behind them.

His head moved forward slightly in a semi-nod, and he whirled and was out of her room before she could speak. She listened to Rafe's footsteps receding down the hall. She had no reason to think he'd lie. Odd how she'd carried that hurt inside all this time without realizing it.

One good thing had come from clearing the air: She didn't have to regret having hot flashes when he got too close.

****

Damn, Rafe couldn't think why Nick would've pulled that crap, unless he'd been high. Truth be told, more than once, Rafe had suspected his brother of using while at school.

Jeff waited at the end of the hall. The corners of his mouth twitched out a piece of a smile. "You two ready?"

Soft fingers wrapped around Rafe's arm. Erin smiled up at him, and for some stupid-ass reason, his skin heated under her touch. He pulled her hand from his arm and held it in his. She was warm and soft and gripping him tightly.

"Look," Rafe said, "will a belated apology suffice? Because—"

"Don't." She looked up at him, and his chest squeezed. "I should be the one extending an apology. My behavior has been childish. My emotions seem to be controlling me instead of the other way around."

"Dual admissions of guilt." Rafe rolled their hands sideways, effectively turning the hold into a handshake. "I like it."

"Can we go now?" Jeff opened the front door.

"Stay directly behind us." Rafe indicated to her as he moved closer to Jeff until their shoulders touched.

Erin grabbed a handful of his and Jeff's shirts and followed a half step back. They ignored the small group of reporters, got in the SUV, and left the jerks standing in the street.

Erin turned in the seat. "A van is following us."

"We expected as much." Jeff maneuvered the SUV into traffic. "Hang on." He then cut down a side street and circled around through an alley. A few more turns and they were back on track without the tail.

"Nice work," Rafe commented, checking out the area. "It has been a long time since I've been through here. I don't recognize any of these businesses."

Jeff pointed at a barbecue restaurant. "There's one coming up on the right that you'll remember."

Rafe spotted the building before they drove past. It had been a regular hangout of the Sheriff's Department. "You bet I do."

His dad and Jeff had remained partners until they'd retired, but their friendship had changed after Rafe's mother's suicide. The fishing trips had ended. So had the poker games. The laughing, joking Max Sirilli had vanished, too. Thinking back on it, Rafe remembered that he'd never been cruel or mean to him or his brothers. He'd simply withdrawn. His body had been there, but the joy of living had died. Even three robust, noisy boys couldn't pull the shell of a man back into the land of the living. Rafe was glad that his dad had eventually started playing cards again, and that Erin had been accepted into the crew.

Rafe couldn't imagine, not in his wildest dreams, how a person could love as deeply as his dad had loved his mom. Nor could he fathom withdrawing from life because someone died. You kept moving, putting one foot in front of the other.

At first, he'd tried to help his dad snap out of the funk, but had failed miserably. Nick and Rafe were the oldest, and a lot of the responsibility had fallen on Rafe. He'd always wonder if he could've done more.

Jeff drove through the police parking lot and pulled up behind Erin's car. He opened the glove compartment and removed a gun.

"If that's for me—" Erin shook her head.

Rafe adjusted his pistol, making sure he'd pulled his shirt over it. "You need to carry one. Until we figure out who's killing these girls, if you go out of the house, Jeff or I will be with you." He held his hand up to stop her from interrupting, because he knew she was about to let loose. "You can legally keep a gun inside your home. Just be sure you let an intruder step over the threshold before you fire."

She moaned. "That means you babysit me. Lotty isn't well, and Jeff doesn't need the burden of taking care of us both."

"Then we're in agreement on this, right?" Jeff asked. "You'll work with Rafe, and you'll keep your doors at home locked."

"I promise. You also taught me not to be stupid." Erin leaned in and kissed the older man on his cheek. "We're going to find

Harold."

Rafe stopped behind the small car and imagined his six-foot-two body wedged in the seat.

"My car is roomier than it looks." She hit the remote, unlocking the doors. "And eco-friendly."

He chuckled, not because she'd read his mind, but because he didn't believe this sardine tin had room for him. Somehow, he managed to get inside, but his knees were pressed tight against the dashboard.

"Let's go pick up my truck. The quicker I get out of this oversized skateboard the better." This time Erin laughed. The sound came from deep down, hearty and sincere. He liked that. Maybe they'd reached some sort of level ground. At least they could joke and laugh together.

She backed out of the parking spot and hit the gas. His head pinged off the roof, bringing a new round of laughter from her.

Rafe studied her profile. A feminine jawline, perfectly shaped nose, and that mole over the right corner of her mouth made his heart beat faster. Stunning, that's the word he'd use to describe her. Why hadn't some, five-day, forty-hour-week guy swept her off her feet?

"Is there something you want to ask?"

She'd caught him staring. "Sorry, my mind wandered."

"Okay. Then let's focus on this list you want. The teachers who had Penny and Sara in their classes might be able to add a few names."

"Will they help?"

"Some actually believe I'm innocent." Erin cut a glance at him as if surprised at his question. "They're going to the next school board meeting to speak out and ask that I be allowed to return to work."

"If you'll write down their names, I'll drop by the campus. My time is yours, except in the morning, when I'm meeting with the couple who manages the Helping Hands at Dad's church. They're going to take his clothes and some of the household goods."

"Max would like that."

"I thought so." Rafe thought it odd to hear her use his dad's given name. The affection in her tone put a hitch in his heartbeat.

"May I ask a question?" She glanced at him, her cheeks turning pink as she spoke.

"Sure. You might not like the answer, because I tell the truth."

"Why didn't you come home more often? Your dad always hoped you'd marry and settle down."

Rafe tried to scoot farther away, but the car door stopped him. "No marriage."

"Max said you were married to the federal government. He used to joke that was no way to produce a grandchild."

Rafe didn't have to think about his answer. "I witnessed firsthand how a family can fall apart when one of the parents dies. I'm not going to be guilty of putting someone through that kind of pain."

"Your dad didn't die in the line of duty."

"No, but my mother couldn't handle the pressure. After she died, we kids had to learn how to function with one absentee parent."

"I can see how your past might make you feel that way, but you've skewed it to where you think you might die."

"Chances are good. One of these days, I'll be undercover and run into somebody I helped send to prison. It's one of the hazards of living in their world, but it's what I want to do with my life."

"At least you had two parents who loved you."

The touch of bitterness in her tone piqued his interest. He'd never heard the full story about how she'd wound up being adopted by Jeff and Lotty. All he knew was that she'd been living on the street. Today when she'd mentioned that Jeff had caught her stealing food was the first time Rafe had heard how they met.

She parked in his driveway, stopping without killing the engine and blocking his pickup. "I thought we were here to swap vehicles. There's room for your car next to my truck."

"If you think about it, I don't need to physically see Harold. I'll call him on the way home." She put the car in reverse. "And I'll work on the list from my house."

"You don't want to work from here?"

"Even with the press, I'll be more comfortable at home."

Her mood had taken a sharp dive. Dismissed like an unruly student, Rafe had no choice but to peel himself out of her shoebox of a car, grunting as he straightened his spine. Letting her leave alone didn't feel right, but then neither did standing his ground. Not when she was about to back over his feet. He stepped back, leaned down to eye level, and handed her Jeff's gun.

"Remember your promise to Jeff. Take this and lock the doors."

"I will."

He watched as she drove away. There wasn't a valid reason for her not to go home. Nothing truly indicated she was in danger from anybody other than the media. So why had he wanted her to hang out with him? And why had she rushed away? He'd upset her or hurt her feelings.

CHAPTER 7

Erin took a cleansing breath as she sped onto the freeway. Rafe's parents had loved him. Even though his mother had hurt the family by taking her life, he'd known what it was like to feel safe and know somebody cared for him. He'd been one of the lucky ones. Her jealousy of his childhood was ridiculous.

She thumbed the call button on her steering wheel and instructed the computer-voiced woman to get Harold's office on the line. Erin explained the incident with the photographer.

"His pictures will probably have a time stamp," the judge said. "That with the police report will document the time. That's more than one eye witness to your whereabouts."

"I didn't file charges."

"But you called the police?"

"Them and Rafe Sirilli."

"They logged their call to your house. The pictures are probably still good, but his statement and one from a federal agent will carry a lot of sway."

"The photographer may not be agreeable to giving me copies."

"Then have Rafe ask him."

After he reiterated his instructions not to speak to the police without him at her side, Harold hung up. Their timing was perfect, because Erin was only a couple of blocks from her house.

One white media van was parked out front. The local station just wasn't going to give up. She hit the garage remote, hoping she could get inside without a confrontation. A short chubby man came rushing up her driveway. She slid the gun into her purse and got out. He stopped at her back bumper.

"I have no comment." She delivered her words in her chilliest voice.

"Some guy left this on your porch." He held out an envelope, which Erin snatched from his hand.

"Now get off my property."

"It's not from me. It's windy out here today. I figured if I made sure it was safe, you'd appreciate it."

"I said leave." She pulled out her cell. If he didn't do as she asked, she'd call the cops.

The reporter shrugged, backing out of her garage. A question sprang to her mind. "What did this man look like?"

"You don't talk to me, I don't help you."

Erin hurried inside, bolting the door behind her. Her hand trembled when she dropped the envelope on the breakfast counter.

The message light on her home phone blinked frantically, indicating more than one missed call. Dreading the crank calls, she tapped the button, but kept her finger poised to hit delete.

Detective Beckett's baritone voice rumbled through the line, asking that she phone him. Harold's instructions had been clear. She deleted two requests from Beckett and two more from reporters. She called Harold again, leaving a message with his assistant about the latest envelope. Disregarding instructions, she called the detective.

The next number she dialed was 666. Rafe sounded winded. He'd been cleaning out and packing up his dad's garage but would shower and come straight over. Again, he didn't question her. His response meant a lot.

His earlier comment about how death could damage a family troubled her thoughts. Losing his mother must have devastated the family. The pain had apparently destroyed his dad. Rafe had grown up without a woman's guiding touch. In Erin's case, having a stepfather had been the worst thing that happened to her.

She fished out writing material from the kitchen drawer and piled up on the couch to wait for Rafe. Her gaze kept wandering back to the breakfast bar, but she blocked the envelope from her mind.

She hadn't spoken to Jeff or Lotty. No doubt, they were worried, so Erin put everything aside and called them. Jeff answered, putting her on the speaker so she could speak with him and Lotty at the same time. Lotty's progression had been phenomenal, and she was full of questions. Erin did her best to relive any stress she'd caused and closed with a promise to keep them informed.

Erin grabbed the pen and pad, jotting down the names of the kids Penny and Sara had hung out with at school. Erin couldn't remember the names of all the girls' teachers, but knew who would. The school nurse and her best friend, Carla Nye, had a memory like a seasoned game-show winner.

"It's good to hear your voice," Carla said on a sigh. "Just tell me you're okay."

"Thank you for not being mad at me," Erin said, feeling guilty for keeping her friend out of the loop.

"Not mad. Worried. Bring me up to speed."

"So much has happened. After Jeff enlisted help from Harold Penza and Rafe Sirilli, I've had someone with me at all times, except when I was in bed."

"Back up to the Rafe Sirilli part. Isn't he the football player whose picture still hangs in the display case at school? All-America twice, drop-dead handsome as a teenager."

"Arrogant, distant, and now a federal agent? Yeah, that's him."

"Well, tell me. Does he still look good enough to eat, or is he fat with a belly that hangs over his belt?"

Erin laughed. God, it felt good to be frivolous. "You won't believe me."

"You're breaking my heart. He's not only fat, he's bald." The sadness in Carla's voice gave Erin another laugh.

"Okay. I'll tell the truth. He's better-looking now that he's matured. He's definitely grown into that long lanky body."

"Do I hear a hint of interest in your voice?"

"I'm only attracted to his badge. Having an FBI agent willing to help prove I'm innocent makes me feel safer." Carla had moved to town a few years back and knew nothing of Erin and Rafe's history. She had no reason to tell her now.

"Hmm. This good-looking FBI agent just happened to volunteer his services. What are you not telling me?"

"Calm down. Rafe's dad and Jeff were partners. He asked Rafe to help me."

"Shoot. That doesn't sound sexy or romantic." Carla's disappointment flowed through the phone.

"I'm glad I called. You always put me in a good mood," Erin said truthfully. "But I'd better finish this list."

"I'll let you know how it goes at the board meeting. Eight teachers have committed to joining me to protest your suspension."

"Don't get yourself in trouble fighting for a cause you can't win."

Carla's show of solidarity was welcome and gave Erin's attitude a boost. She disconnected and went back to the list. After she finished, she walked to the breakfast bar and stared at the manila monster resting peacefully, daring her to open it. Taunting her.

A knock on the door startled her.

"Erin," Rafe yelled. "Open up."

She fumbled with the lock, opened the door, and pulled him inside.

****

Rafe reached out and caught Erin's hand, fighting the urge to tug her into his arms. "What happened?"

"Come see." She led him toward the kitchen area.

She squeezed his fingers, hanging on as if to keep him from disappearing. Not fucking likely. Erin might be pretending to be brave, but he could tell she was scared out of her wits.

"I called Harold. Left messages at both places. I called Detective Beckett, too."

"Good decision." Rafe nodded, but his attention was on the envelope on the counter. "Son of a bitch."

"A reporter gave it to me. He said a man left it on my porch."

"Which one?" He held on to her hand, allowing her to lead him to the window. She didn't resist when he pulled her back to his chest. He reached around her, lifted a slat on the blinds, and together they scanned the small group. Somebody had brought food, and they had gathered into a cluster. They were laughing and talking like today was just another day.

"Him." She pointed. "The one in the gray pullover. He's looking straight at the house."

She took a step back, pressing tight against Rafe. Under normal circumstances, he'd have allowed his body's natural reaction to surge ahead. Instead, he backed away so as not to tempt fate. Full-body contact with her was a bad idea.

"You think he lied? Maybe brought it himself?"

"Don't know." Rafe studied the man's body language. "But I'm gonna find out."

"I spoke with Harold before I got home about last night. He said between your word, the reporter's picture, and the police report, I have a good alibi."

"He's right. You could have plenty of witnesses, but everything hinges on what time the girl was murdered. He needs to get that information."

Neither had moved from the window. Rafe breathed in her scent again. The warmth and soft curves of her body barely touching his, combined with her soft scent, made his mouth water. It was enough to send blood coursing to his groin. He'd regret it later, but he dropped the blind slat and walked away from her.

She cleared her throat, looking everywhere except at him. She hadn't been quick enough for him to miss the pink in her cheeks.

Maybe she didn't dislike him as much as he thought. The tension in his neck tightened. He'd kept his soft spot for her hidden for years. He couldn't let it surface now...

Her home phone rang, but she ignored it. "You're still getting prank calls?" he asked.

"Yes. Reporters mostly. So far, they haven't called on my cell, but I'm screening all my calls. I'll pick up if it's someone I want to speak with."

"Let's look at the note."

"Shouldn't we wait?"

Rafe's eyebrow lifted. He removed his pocketknife and a pair of purple gloves from his pocket and pulled them on. "Don't say a word about the color. They were the only size-large sterile gloves in the drugstore."

"Wasn't going to say a word," she joked, but her voice held a slight tremble.

He carefully slit the top, shook the envelope, and a small piece of paper slid onto the breakfast bar.

GOD PUNISHES MURDERERS.

"Can my life get any worse?" she said in a whisper.

"You can't let these cranks get to you. As soon as we establish your innocence, these whackjobs will move on to someone else. When Beckett gets here, we'll straighten this out." Rafe wasn't going to allow her to be blamed for these murders. "I'm going to have a chat with that reporter."

"So you don't think 'whackjobs' are dangerous?"

"I wish I knew. Either way, the cops need to see them." He walked to the door. "I'm going to speak with the reporter. Lock the door."

He walked straight to the reporter Erin had indicated, who stepped forward and smiled. Two other men joined them. If they expected to get a story, they were wrong.

"Tom Corman," the man in the gray pullover said.

Rafe studied the ID tag on the man's shirt and the TV station's name on the side of the van. "You have any other identification?"

Corman's eyebrows rose. "Do you?"

Rafe fought the urge to pull his FBI ID. He tried another tactic.

"I'm not the one the cops will be questioning."

"Let them come." Corman dug out his wallet, letting Rafe match the name and picture with the ID tag.

"Describe the man who left the envelope."

"What's in it for me?"

Rafe moved closer. "Your fingerprints are on that envelope. What if its contents are a threat?"

The reporter's eyes flashed wide, filling with a hint of fear. "I saw a guy prop it against the door and run. After he took off, I ran up and snagged it. Thought it might get me a comment from Ms. Brady."

"Description?" Rafe took another step closer. The reporter's face paled.

"Okay. Back off, man. White guy, maybe six-foot, one-ninety. Wearing a dark hoodie and jeans. Really, that's all I saw. Dude kept his head down."

The sound of an engine drew Rafe's attention. A dark blue sedan, the typical county car, turned the corner. "These two guys will have more questions."

Rafe waited on the curb until the two men exited their vehicle. Both wore slacks and shirts, with badges clipped on to their belts. He shook hands with Detectives Wade Beckett and Carl Henry. Rafe handed his ID to Beckett. Last thing he wanted was the press or the police thinking he was interfering. "I'm here strictly as a friend."

"We'll take all the help we can get," Beckett, the younger of the two men, said.

It wasn't an official invitation, but Rafe could work with it. "Thanks. I may be able to clear some of this up. You'll want to go inside to talk."

"This gets more fucked up with each day." The older cop, Carl, pressed his fingers into his temples. "I'll talk to the reporter. You seemed to have better luck with Ms. Brady."

"Erin's expecting you," Rafe said, falling in step with Beckett. No way was either cop questioning her alone. Rafe wasn't an attorney, but he'd do until Harold was at her side.

"How's she holding up?" Beckett asked. Rafe detected a tenderness in the detective's voice.

"Better than most, considering everything she's been through." Rafe stepped up on the porch and lifted his hand to knock.

Erin opened the door, allowing him and the detective inside. "Thanks for coming."

Rafe and Beckett followed her to the breakfast counter.

"You opened it?" Beckett pulled latex gloves from his pocket and slipped them on.

"I wore gloves. My prints aren't on it."

Beckett studied the note a minute before placing it and the envelope in a paper bag. "I doubt if we'll find anybody's prints. Doesn't mean we won't try."

"I'm getting an occasional prank call, but nothing like the notes," Erin said.

"Most of the time they're lonely people wanting attention." Beckett shrugged.

"They're whackjobs. I get it." Erin scowled, clearly disagreeing.

"That doesn't mean you should take them lightly." Beckett jumped on the defensive.

Rafe wanted to clear up any question about Erin's whereabouts last night. "With your help, we can clear Erin as a suspect."

"And that would be how?" Beckett asked.

Rafe glanced at Erin in case she wanted to take the lead. Her head nodded slightly, her silent way of asking him to take over. "I was here last night from ten thirty to around one. 911 has a record of Erin's call and a patrol car was here. If that's not enough, there's a photographer outside who can vouch for most of that time. You know Monroe's TOD. If she was murdered between those times, Erin has an alibi."

"You're sure of the time?"

"Yeah. Check her phone records. She called me after discovering a photographer had climbed up a tree in the backyard. I came straight here, taking maybe twenty minutes. I didn't leave until one."

Beckett looked toward Erin. "Was the trespasser arrested?"

"No." The defiance in her tone was clear. "A federal agent's word isn't good enough?"

"For me? Sure. But you two have a relationship."

"We have no such thing," Erin said, spitting the words as if they tasted bad.

"That's true," Rafe confirmed, only calmer and more pleasant.

Beckett shook his head as if recoiling from her stinging words. "I was referring to your family connection." He looked away from Rafe, directing his comments to Erin. "And there's always the possibility you hired someone to kill the girls."

Her expression iced over. A polar front had taken over her eyes. "There is that possibility."

Apparently unfazed, Beckett turned to Rafe. "I'll need formal statements from both of you."

"Let's get to it," Rafe said, moving closer to Erin.

CHAPTER 8

Beckett placed a small recorder on the coffee table. Erin sat, patting the cushion next to her for Rafe. The couch was a comfortable fit for her, but with Beckett sitting across from them in the recliner, neither he nor Rafe had room to unfold their long legs.

After each of them gave their names, Beckett noted time, date, and subject matter. Then he turned off the recording but left his finger hovering above the on button.

"How about it, Erin? Are you ready to answer questions this time?" Beckett asked her.

Rafe watched different emotions cross her face. She opened her mouth then closed it with a snap. "I called my criminal attorney. He's on his way."

The detective sighed. "I'm not questioning your innocence. I've never believed you murdered anyone, but you may hold the key to stopping the killer. I need your help." Beckett turned to Rafe. "Tell her."

"I can't make that decision for her." Rafe refused to pressure her. "Under the circumstances, I can understand her reluctance. With the exception of a few teachers who've supported her, this whole town has treated her like crap."

Erin's head turned his direction, her eyes misting over. She blinked a couple of times. Again, a desire to protect her slammed into him. He didn't like that feeling a damn bit.

"This is off-topic," Rafe said to Erin. "You used the term criminal attorney. I assume you've asked for help after the school placed you on administrative leave."

"I sure did. I contacted the Professional Educators Organization. Their attorneys have already started the appeal process."

"I figured you had," Beckett said. "The school district police have already been in touch with me. I'll get my information to them as soon as possible. The fact that Sara Monroe was murdered between eleven and one, your alibi should eliminate you as a suspect." He wagged his finger over the recorder on button. "No statement from you?"

"I'll wait for Harold." Erin's expression was grim and determined.

"I'm ready." Rafe defused what he thought was about to be another argument. He succinctly gave his account of last night, finishing off with the intruder's name and media organization. "Check the local hospitals for a patient who broke his arm last night. You'll find him. Get a copy of that picture he took."

Beckett grinned. "How'd he break his arm?"

Rafe shrugged his shoulders. "Clumsy bastard fell out of the tree."

Beckett stopped the recorder. "I'll get this typed up. You'll have to stop by, read, and sign."

Rafe nodded and didn't interrupt. Beckett was aware Rafe knew the procedure, but if his guess was right, the detective was an always-by-the-book kind of man.

Erin escorted Beckett to the door, which gave Rafe the chance to follow up on a call he'd made last night. He pushed open the sliding glass doors and stepped out into the sunlight to call back Colton Weir.

Before Rafe started nosing around the school unofficially, he had to know if he was stepping on someone else's investigation. Nothing made cross-departmental enemies like screwing up another man's undercover operation.

"I'm fast but not that good." Colton, with his East Texas drawl so heavy Rafe wanted to shake the words out of him, always answered before the second ring and without saying hello.

"I'm growing old waiting."

"Take it easy. Getting all wound up won't help. The local narcotics squad is working the case. I'll find out if any other agency is helping out. How's the woman Erin?"

"A second girl was murdered last night, but I was with Erin all the time. The focus will shift off her soon."

"Really?" The word rolled off Colton's tongue like cold molasses. "Want to share info with your partner?"

"I was here. Not in her bed. She's got media crawling like ants, and she's getting notes accusing her of being a murderer. Who knows if it's serious or not, but some of these radicals are crazy as hell and twice as dangerous." Rafe quoted the notes. "Makes me wonder if it's one of the dead girls' mom or dad. Grief does strange things to a person's head."

He whirled in the direction of a loud gasp. Shit, she'd heard. He held out his arm, and she walked right to him, tucking herself close. He gripped her shoulder. Her back went rigid for a second before she relaxed into him. Until the press and townspeople believed her to be innocent, she'd need a shoulder to lean on, and he'd damn well be there for her.

She rested her head against him. Lightning strikes went straight to his groin, which he did his best to ignore. He breathed in deeply, taking that feminine scent that was uniquely Erin into his lungs. Jesus, she smelled good enough to eat.

"Let me know if we or the DEA have somebody on site undercover," he said to Colton.

"Will do," Colton said, ending the call.

"Undercover?" Erin asked.

"Drugs have been a problem at this school for years. Hell, the town made national news once. Yet, kids are still buying, using, and dying. Somebody needs to stop the flow."

They stood in silence for a minute before she moved out of his embrace. She didn't walk away, only broke their contact.

"I think we gave enough information to Detective Beckett to prove I'm not guilty."

"I agree. He's too smart to think otherwise."

"Well..." Her eyes filled with a mischievous glint. "My alibi for last night is pretty reliable." A wide grin lit her face.

If she kept smiling and standing so close, he was going to do something stupid. Yeah, kissing that mole above her lip was a definite possibility. "Beckett knows you didn't kill anybody. We helped him narrow down his suspect pool."

"I hope using your name doesn't get you in trouble."

"I'm on leave, so where I spend my time is my business. Use me any way you want."

Pink rushed up from her neck and disappeared into her hairline. The double entendre had been accidental but oddly enough, he didn't regret a word.

"Rafe, thank—" The doorbell rang, interrupting the moment and sending her rushing to open the door.

Harold stormed into the room. "If you're not going to take my advice, why bother calling?"

****

Erin held back an angry retort. "What are you talking about?"

"You spoke with Detective Beckett?"

"No. Rafe gave a statement. I waited for you." She gave him a short version of last night's events and timeline.

Harold's stance relaxed. "The detective is out front talking with a reporter. If your facts check out, you've probably taken yourself off the suspect list."

She glanced at Rafe. "That's what Rafe said."

Leaning against her breakfast bar, Rafe looked right at home. He winked, and she totally lost track of Harold's words. Rafe holding her close, his arm around her shoulders—none of those actions had frightened her. She'd relaxed and leaned on him, feeling safe so near to him. People touching her often brought back bad memories, but his tenderness and strength had been welcome. Well, not just welcome. His touch, sensuous and seductive, shouldn't have sent heat blasting through her bloodstream, but it had.

She'd become an expert at accepting the things in life she was responsible for and recognizing those she had no control over. It had taken years of love and understanding from Jeff and Lotty, plus a number of therapy sessions, but she'd finally learned to like herself. Sending her stepfather to prison had been cathartic. Patching up childhood misunderstandings seemed to be having the same effect.

Harold's hand waved in front of her eyes. He'd asked her a question. Erin gave him her full attention. "I'm sorry. Say that again."

"Do you believe these notes indicate that you're in danger?" Harold spoke slowly, as if he thought she wouldn't pay attention. "If so, I'll formally request you have police protection. Don't know if we can get it, but I'll ask."

Erin turned to Rafe. "What do you think?"

"It's hard to say. Will you be returning to work soon?"

"I hope so. I need to bring the Professional Educators Organization's attorney up to speed. Schools don't like scandals. I don't know what will happen."

The doorbell rang again. This time, Erin ushered Beckett and his partner, Carl Henry, inside.

Detective Henry's scowl drifted past Erin and settled on Rafe. "Was breaking the photographer's arm necessary? As far as we know, he wasn't a threat to Ms. Brady."

"He fell." She inserted herself into the conversation. Of course, Rafe had jerked the guy out of the tree and let him fall. The jerk deserved a broken arm. "I take that to mean you located the photographer?"

"It does," Henry answered.

"Did you get a copy of one of the pictures?" Rafe asked calmly.

Again, Henry answered, "That may take a warrant."

Erin's tempered flared. She opened her mouth to ask why Carl Henry had such a crappy attitude, but Beckett stepped between her and his partner.

"We got his statement. The picture would be nice to have, but he gave us a timeline. We'll get his statement on paper."

She wasn't finished with Carl. "So you're sure the phone calls and notes are just pranks."

"Good." Harold spoke up. "Are we done here?"

"Looks like it." Beckett and his partner said their good-byes and left.

"Jackass," she muttered as she closed the door behind the detectives.

Harold cleared his throat. "I think Wade Beckett is a good man."

"He probably is. Hell, they're both probably wonderful people. It felt like Carl Henry cared more about the broken arm than my innocence."

"I'm going, too," Harold said, "but I'll stop for a chat with the media. They'll be disappointed to hear you have an alibi for last night. But they'll gobble up a front-page story in which an FBI agent helped clear a schoolteacher of murder charges."

"The police didn't file charges," Erin protested.

"You obviously haven't been keeping up with the news. If you had, you'd know the media had already found you guilty." Harold picked up his briefcase and left.

All of a sudden, her house was empty except for her and Rafe. The quiet took her breath away. She lowered herself to a barstool in front of the counter. "I can't believe it's over."

Rafe scrubbed a hand across the stubble on his chin. His dark eyes briefly studied her from across the room, sending chills up her arms. "I hope you're right."

"After Harold gets finished spinning his tale, the media will have me nominated for mayor."

"There's still the drugs. And who did kill those girls?"

"I'm glad you're going to keep working the drug angle. You'll want the list I made of Penny and Sara's friends." Erin ripped off the page and hurried back to her office. She made a copy and carried it to Rafe. "The first two names complete Penny and Sara's circle. I heard they were all backing their friend."

"Thanks. The detectives may have already spoken with them, but these two girls should be trembling in their shoes today. Maybe they'll open up to me."

"I can see how they might. What red-blooded teenage girl wouldn't be thrilled to talk with a hunk like you?"

"I'm no such..." He took a menacing step toward her. "Are you being funny?"

"Please." She waved him off. "It's not like you haven't heard that all your life."

He pulled his keys out of his jeans pocket, twirled them around his index finger, and walked to the door. "Call if you need me."

"I will." She followed him to the door.

He covered her hand with his. Heat from his body washed across hers. God, how she wanted to bury her face in his neck and just breathe. He didn't move closer, nor did he touch her anywhere except her hand, so she didn't.

"So you think I'm a hunk? I'm flattered." One corner of his mouth quirked into a smile. "Lock the door."

Erin watched as he strode across the lawn to his car. His wide shoulders swayed with each stride. His jeans strained to contain muscular thighs. He moved with power and authority, a man to be reckoned with, yet each movement was graceful, almost as if choreographed.

He glanced back and caught her looking. She slammed the door and flipped the deadbolt. She'd been running on fear and adrenaline for days. Suddenly, all the energy leaked out of her.

The quiet in her house felt odd. After all the talking and male voices in the house, she missed having them around. She wandered through each room, looking for something to keep her mind occupied.

First thing in the morning, she was going to the Y. Just as the school had sent her home, Domingo Ramirez, the administrator at the YMCA, had removed Erin as coach of the girls basketball team. She believed his sincerity when he'd said the staff and the young women would miss having Erin as a volunteer. She counted on him allowing her to return a lot quicker than the school.

She called the attorney handling the school board and then her friend Carla. Who, after she stopped squealing, decided she wasn't canceling tonight's trip to the school board meeting. Maybe if the group pressed for Erin's reinstatement, the board's resolution would come faster. Then Erin settled down on the couch and dialed Jeff and Lotty's number.

By the time Erin had hung up, she was happily exhausted. She made herself a peanut butter and jelly sandwich, selected a book from her unread pile, and then stretched out on the couch. Trying hard to concentrate was a failure. Nothing held her attention.

The silence was making her jumpy. The wind was gusty, or as the weatherman liked to describe it, breezy, this time of year. Still, every brush of a tree branch across the roof spooked her. She fished out Jeff's nine-millimeter pistol from her purse and put it on the coffee table. If anyone tried to break in, she'd be ready.

She turned on the TV and settled back. One of her favorite shows filled the screen, giving her the perfect temporary escape.

****

Using the reporters who'd grouped around Erin's attorney, Casanova had blended in with the crowd and listened. He'd formulated a believable story, just in case somebody recognized him, but as usual, people had been too caught up with their own wants and needs to notice him.

He'd breathed a sigh of relief to hear that Erin's alibi had removed her from the suspect pool. At the same time, anger at himself had bubbled up to the back of his throat. He should've planned better. If he'd killed those little bitches while Erin was with someone who could vouch for her, she'd have been spared the trauma, and he could've professed his love sooner. Damn it. His oversight had allowed the FBI man to come to her rescue.

Waiting to approach her got harder every day. However, proving his love and gaining Erin's gratitude were critical to his plan. She wasn't the type of woman to rush, not his Erin. She was level-headed and cautious, which behooved him to rein in his desires and proceed slowly. The reward would be wedded bliss.

Now that there were only two of Penny's venomous friends left, were they through causing Erin trouble? It was troublesome that the police had kept his messages from the press. Why would the authorities not alert the public? The other girls needed to know that lying about Erin wouldn't be tolerated.

Casanova had been mingling with the media over the past couple of days, biting his tongue when they made comments about the killer teacher. The idiots had believed him when he'd said he was on assignment, sent to do a personality profile on Erin.

He'd overheard one of the photographers talking about what happened to his arm. The man had admitted to sneaking into Erin's backyard last night. He'd taken a series of pictures of her. Her boyfriend had shown up and jerked him from his hiding place.

Hearing that she'd been spied on, startled, and had fallen, sent flashes of heat in front of Casanova's eyes. Rage had the blood rushing through his veins. Anyone who'd hurt her would suffer his wrath, but this photographer had lied when he said Erin's boyfriend had saved her. The bastard had sealed his own fate.

Casanova had to get away from the media crowd before he blew his cover. As calmly as he could, he walked down the street, then circled back to the vacant house on the corner.

This place provided him with the ideal vantage point. Once he was safely inside, he lashed out with his foot and kicked a hole in the sheetrock. God, the release felt great, but the act of losing his temper wasn't a good sign. Besides, venting wouldn't save the photographer's life, but for now, the rage had to be relieved.

He went to the window facing Erin's house, picked up his binoculars, and watched through the small window in the kitchen.

Relief had settled on his heart when all those men left her house. Had she been treated with respect and dignity? She needed him with her to protect her. Waiting was hard on her, too.

His legs and back grew tired, but he refused to budge. Comfort played no part in this exercise. Keeping an eye on the woman he loved was worth any sacrifice. After all, soon they'd be together. He hardened just thinking about it.

"Damn it," he yelled, the sound reverberating off the walls. That Hollywood-looking neighbor had just jogged across the lawns carrying a sack from the local fried chicken hut. He knocked on her door. Erin would turn that guy away. There was no logical reason for her to allow him inside.

She opened the door. A big smile spread across her face as the bastard entered her house. Casanova's stomach knotted. No. She wasn't that kind of woman. He'd kill anyone who said differently. No one would question her virtue.

The cameraman walked into Casanova's line of vision. It appeared the media were closing up shop as camera equipment was being stowed in the back of a van. Between his job and keeping up with construction on his house, it was difficult to keep an eye on her. But he had to know where to find the camera guy later tonight. He stuffed the binoculars in his bag and ran for his car.

****

"For me?" The aroma rising from the sack in Linc's hands sent Erin's salivary glands into overdrive.

"I know it's late," he said, flashing a grin. "I brought enough chicken for two people."

"Oh." Erin stepped back, feeling stupid for not recognizing he'd brought enough for them both. "Sorry. I didn't realize—"

"It's okay." Again, he hit her with his sparkling smile. "I'm not hitting on you. Just looking for a dinner companion. And I figured you could use a friend."

"Now, I really am sorry." She waved him inside. "Come sit down. I'll get a couple of plates and something for us to drink, and then I'll join you." Erin bolted to the kitchen, fighting the heat in her cheeks.

Oddly enough, she wasn't disappointed he hadn't used food to make a pass. Not that he wasn't model perfect with his square jaw and sea-blue eyes. She guessed him to be at least six-two. She liked Linc, but her blood didn't heat up like it did when... God, why had Rafe's name popped into her thoughts?

Linc had emptied the sack and was dividing the packages of ketchup when she joined him at the table. "Thanks." He took his bottle of water from her and pushed a bucket of fried chicken toward her. "Ladies first."

Erin selected a chicken breast and piled french fries on her plate. "How's the job going?"

"I ran into a few glitches, but isn't that always what happens with a new installation?" He closed his eyes and bit into a piece of chicken. "Nothing like greasy food to soothe the nerves after a day at that school."

"I wish I had that problem." Erin longed for the everyday problems. Most of all, she missed the kids streaming in and out of her office. "I'm hoping my appeal will be heard by the school board soon."

"I'm sorry. That was insensitive of me." Linc wiped his hands on a paper towel.

"Not at all. The school may take awhile, but in the morning,

I'm marching into the YMCA and asking for my volunteer spot as coach back."

"Good for you."

"I miss the team," she said, taking another bite of fries.

"How are you?"

"You saw the news?"

"Yeah. At this point, the police can't think you killed either girl."

They ate in silence, polishing off every bite of food on the table. Erin gathered all the paper and stuffed it in the bag. "Thank you for supper. I was starving. And you make a great friend."

Linc carried the plates to the kitchen. He followed her to the living room and made himself comfortable on the couch. "That girl you turned in for narcotics possession, she bought them from somebody. Had you heard rumors about drug use prior to that day?"

"The subject comes up regularly. The police hold awareness classes, but no one's ever been arrested. Not that I know of. Why?"

"Curiosity, I guess. I thought as a counselor, you might have heard rumblings from some of the students."

"They confided a lot of things to me. Drug use never came up."

Linc's gaze drifted to her pistol on the coffee table. He picked up her notebook and wrote something down. "Here's my number. You get scared, I'm right next door."

Erin watched from her porch until he crossed her yard into his. His walk said confidence and strength. He could handle himself if she needed help.

The absence of people shouting her name was refreshing. The media had apparently decided she was no longer of interest. Even the newshound Rafe had pulled out of her tree had left.

Or had he?

She moved the gun to the end table, turned the TV back on, and curled up on the couch where she could keep an eye on both doors. Maybe Harold's interview had made it to television. For the first time in days, she was looking forward to the news.

A reporter's voice drew her attention. Her breath caught when Rafe's face filled the screen. His conversation with a reporter had been caught on film. Even angry with a storm brewing behind his eyes, he made her heart skip a beat and heat settle low in her stomach. His walk, heck, his stance, every move he made screamed power, authority, and courage. She couldn't imagine him being scared of anything.

He dragged his fingers through his long hair, glanced over his shoulder, and pinned the person filming with a deadly stare. Goodness, the camera loved him. Nobody should be that handsome without being airbrushed.

Erin couldn't help but wonder how those fingers would feel caressing her skin. Running through her hair. Stroking her... She shook her foolish ideas out of her head. Having romantic daydreams about him was ludicrous.

Mr. I Can't Wait To Get Out Of This Town was a heartbreak waiting to happen. His brother's addiction had turned Rafe into a machine. She remembered him devoting himself to football. His prowess on the field and dedication to sports had resulted in a ticket out of Westbrook Hills.

He hadn't changed in that regard. He was still driven. Only this time, his passion was his job.

CHAPTER 9

Casanova had followed the cameraman from a safe distance, made a mental note of which apartment his target had entered, and then he'd gone home to change clothes and gather his equipment. The man's apartment complex had cameras scattered around the parking lot. While that complicated matters, nothing would deter him from killing the bastard who'd scared Erin.

He threw his gear in the trunk, drove back to the apartment, and parked in front of a movie theater a block away. Time passed slowly, but Casanova was known for his patience, and from this location, he could watch the front door. Having lived through enough stress in his childhood, he'd learned to compartmentalize his emotions. Rage built to a destructive level if he allowed it, as evidenced by him kicking the walls out earlier. That couldn't happen again.

That the man had hidden in Erin's yard, frightened her, caused her to fall, was enough to warrant his death. But the fact he'd thought his behavior was funny had sealed his fate.

The cameraman exited his apartment, jogged down the stairs, but walked past the van. He crossed the street and headed straight for the bar on the corner. Fate had dealt Casanova a winning hand. Intercepting the bastard on the way home would work.

He moved his car a block behind Hunney's Hang Out, walked to the bar, and hid in the shadows. The night air was warm, but he didn't remove the hooded sweatshirt. It wasn't long before sweat broke out and ran down his sides.

Time passed. People came and went. Nobody noticed him lurking in the dark. His knees grew weary from standing in one position. Still, he refused to move. His mission was clear.

The bar door opened and out walked the man with a cast. He made it to the curb before Casanova slid the knife blade up through a kidney and into the liver, puncturing his diaphragm. The beauty of this method was the target couldn't breathe. Therefore, he couldn't scream as he crumbled to the pavement.

A lingering coppery stench followed Casanova almost all the way back to the car.

Too bad there hadn't been a way to leave a message.

****

Rafe woke half-surprised at his surroundings. He'd been home three days, and waking up in his old bedroom still felt out of place. Coming home had him picking at old sores. Open wounds, because he kept digging up bad memories to dissect his teenage years to see what he should have done differently. He'd been so caught up in his own life that his brother's drug habit had been completely out of hand before he'd realized it.

Twins read each other's thoughts and minds, right? Then why hadn't he "seen" inside Nick's troubled mind?

Twenty minutes from Dallas, Westbrook Hills was a millionaire suburb where manicured lawns and long circular driveways fronted elaborate homes. Many parents commuted or traveled, leaving the kids to their own devices. Hell, the teenagers from this area drove cars that cost more than Rafe's father's annual salary had been.

One thing hadn't changed since he'd been gone: Rafe's deep-seated belief that the town was a hotbed of drugs was even stronger. Two additional high schools had been built in the past twelve years. No doubt, they shared the same problem.

The Sirillis had lived comfortably. It meant his dad pulled lots of overtime, but Rafe and his brothers had survived just fine without the lavish swimming pools, maids, and nannies. He snorted. Just fine was a stretch. Things stopped being "just fine" with their mother's death and had completely fallen apart when Nick started hanging with the high-dollar crowd. From his sophomore year on, their family life had been one constant fight.

Rafe pulled on a pair of sweats and wandered to the kitchen. Damn, would the odd expectation he'd round the corner and find his dad waiting ever go away?

He checked his messages, relieved to hear Luke's voice. Word had finally reached him that their dad had died. Rafe was pleased to know his baby brother was on his way. Maybe with Luke in the house, the place would feel more like a home.

Rafe headed for the shower. Fifteen minutes later, he bought a cup of coffee on the way to the school. That Westbrook High had doubled in size didn't surprise Rafe. The shock came at seeing the new sports complex, which spread out over more than a couple of acres.

Rafe paused at the flagpole and considered the opulence of the buildings. Odd that he'd never paid much attention back in his youth. Now all he could do was compare it to some of the poverty-stricken neighborhoods he'd seen since signing on with the feds.

"Rafe," a male voice called out.

Across the campus, his briefcase slung over his shoulder, Linc Hawkins was headed directly toward him. Rafe made a mental note to call Colton. Information on Hawkins should be easy to gather.

"How's it going?" he asked, walking up the steps to the entryway. "You about got the new system up and running?"

"Almost. Ran into a few bugs."

"Where to after this job's finished?" For some reason, Rafe was hoping the move would be soon.

"I have no idea." Linc stopped and studied the trophy case. "Your mug is in more than a few of these pictures." He nodded his approval. "State champions twice. Old memories bring you to the school?"

"You could say that," Rafe answered, glancing down at the

picture. "We had a good coach and team."

"Too bad the school has neither now." Linc moved down the case, looking at pictures.

"That bad, huh?"

"I played for a tough coach, but wouldn't get on the field with this one." Linc leaned closer to the display case. "You have a twin? The guy on the back row looks just like you."

"Had," Rafe corrected. "He died of an overdose. We were identical. My dad had trouble telling us apart when we were little."

Linc's smile vanished. "Tough break. Sorry to hear that."

"Yeah, thanks." Rafe turned toward the principal's office, but hesitated. "Your company must be flush to rent you a house instead of sticking you in a motel."

"Unlimited funds. Since this was a long-term assignment, they ponied up the money for a rental." Linc shifted his bag to the other shoulder and went back to staring at the pictures. "I'm thinking of buying a place here. Be nice to have a home base."

"Really?" The hair on the back of Rafe's neck rose. He didn't dislike Linc, but the man was hiding something. "And you think Westbrook Hills is the right place?"

"I have no family, so here is as good as any." He shrugged one shoulder. "I'd better get back to work."

Rafe nodded once. He watched until Linc was out of sight, then hustled to the main office where he'd request to speak with the principal. He gave the older woman behind the counter his best shot of charm to no avail. Without an appointment, he figured he'd have to wait.

He studied her familiar face. Her silver hair had been pulled back in a knot. Tall and slim, she wore navy slacks and a soft, cream-colored blouse. She was a cross between regal and scary with her straight back and furrowed brows. She lifted glasses that hung on a long, gold chain around her neck and perched them on the tip of her nose. Her gaze narrowed as she scrutinized him. Years vanished.

No way could he forget the Iron Maiden. Mrs. Henley used to be the librarian.

"Mr. Sirilli, you haven't been around for a long time."

"Yes, ma'am. I wondered if you'd remember me."

"Of course I remember you. The only boy harder to keep quiet in the library was your younger brother, Lucas."

"Luke," he corrected, immediately wishing he'd left the subject alone. It had taken years to get people to call him Rafe instead of Rafael.

"Whatever." Her tone had Rafe sitting up straighter. "What brings you to the school?"

Was this small talk or was she grilling him? She had always been full of questions. "My father passed. I'm home to handle the legal matters and get the house ready to sell."

Her face softened. "I'm sorry for your loss. How can we help?"

"Thank you. I appreciate your offer. I just needed a break and decided I'd stop by to take a look at all the changes, maybe meet the new coach. Figured protocol demanded I check in here first."

She rested her hand on his arm. He remembered her even more clearly now. She'd always been tough on the outside but a marshmallow at heart.

"You go on out to the field house. I'll clear things with Principal Mueller as soon as he gets here."

She used to be a bit of a gossip, so Rafe decided to gamble. He leaned his elbows on the counter separating them. "What's this I hear about drugs and girls getting killed? Morale must be at an all-time low."

"It's worse than that," she said, lowering her voice. "Some of these kids are out of hand. Not all, mind you, but there's a handful who have no respect for anyone, including themselves."

"How so?" he prodded.

"All the trouble they caused for Ms. Brady. And for what?

Everybody knows the accusations are false." She shook her head. "And now two of them are dead. Somebody needs to figure out what the heck's going on."

"I heard the trouble started when Ms. Brady turned one of the girls in for drugs."

"Darn right she did. See what it got her? No job. No career. It's not right." Her eyes narrowed. "Now that she's been cleared, I hope she puts a full-court press on the school board."

His heart warmed with Mrs. Henley's passion and support for Erin. "If there's a drug problem here at school, surely the cops are investigating."

"These kids are too smart to get caught. Principal Mueller had every locker searched but came up with nothing. The parents showed up at the next board meeting. You'd have thought he'd had their kids frisked. It's hard to get through to teenagers, especially without their mothers and fathers backing us up." Her grip on his arm tightened. "I'm retiring soon. I gave up the library and moved into the office for my last few years. My husband and I are moving to Florida." She frowned, then glanced over her shoulder.

Rafe got the message. She was afraid she'd talked too much. "Nothing you said will be repeated." He gave her his card. "You can tell me anything."

She smiled again as she studied the card. "I always knew you'd make something of yourself." The card went into her pocket. "Now go. Principal Mueller won't care that you stopped by. If the coach asks, you cleared your visit with the front office."

Rafe left, feeling even more sure that drugs were rampant at his alma mater. They'd been in the shadows when he and Nick were in high school. Back then, the use and sales had mostly happened off-campus. Today, it sounded as if they were commonplace. He hoped Mrs. Henley thought of something helpful and called. Having a friend inside the school would be invaluable.

Rafe walked toward the side exit, the quickest route to the

field house. The deeper into the bowels of the building he went, the more out of place he felt. Suddenly, teenagers poured out of classrooms into the hall. Seeing him, they reacted as if he were Moses parting the water. Their curiosity entertained them for a minute, and then they hustled off to their next classes.

He jogged down the stairs, stepped outside, breathed in the spring air, and headed down the path to the field house. Rapid footsteps on the concrete drew his attention. A pretty brunette with an armful of books was locked on him, and she was gaining ground. He moved off the path and waited.

The student slid to a stop, looking him up and down. He remained silent, allowing her to catch her breath and start the conversation on her terms.

"One of the guys said you were on TV." She shuffled her feet as if standing barefoot on hot pavement, which she wasn't. "Were they lying? Are you really an FBI agent?"

This young girl's face screamed fear. "Guilty as charged, but I'm not here on business. I graduated from Westbrook."

"Really?" Her eyebrows lifted.

"For real. Go look at the pictures in the trophy case. I'm the football player wearing the number fourteen on my jersey." He smiled, and her bunched shoulders relaxed. "I'm Rafe Sirilli. And you are?"

"Grace...just Grace." She bit down on her bottom lip.

Rafe decided to approach her carefully. She was scared shitless and would bolt like a frightened rabbit if he pressed. "Why did you ask if I'm FBI?"

"I heard you were Ms. Brady's friend." She shifted again, this time looking over her shoulder.

"That's true. We went to school together." Rafe slowly maneuvered Grace to the bleachers. He sat down and patted the bench next to him. "I can't help if I don't know what's frightening you."

She hesitated and then moved to his other side. It was obvious she was uncomfortable being seen with him, so he shifted his body to shield her from prying eyes.

"I'm the new girl at school. We moved from Houston a couple of months ago." A thin sheen of sweat highlighted her forehead. "I didn't know anybody, and people weren't falling all over themselves to be my friend. Penny and her girls were the first who let me hang out with them."

"Are you somehow caught up in the lie about Ms. Brady?" He paused, waiting until she nodded. "Have you told the principal Ms. Brady didn't make inappropriate advances or threats?"

"I can't. I'm not opening my mouth." She jumped up. Her movements were so jerky the books she carried fell to the ground.

"Grace." He scooped up her books and handed them to her. "Telling the truth is the right thing to do."

"If you tell, I'll deny it." Books clutched to her chest, she stared at him for a long heartbeat. "There are two of us still alive. We just want to stay that way."

"Take my card. Call when you're ready to talk." He reached for his pocket. She waved him off. "Just take a look at it."

Her fingers trembled as she accepted the card. Her gaze dropped and then flashed back to his face. "I just wanted Ms. Brady to know I'm glad she was cleared."

"I'll pass that on for you. But I need to know more about the drugs that were in Penny's purse."

"I have to go."

"Stay safe, Grace. Call me if you change your mind."

"You should be careful, too. First Penny, then Sara, and last night some photographer who was covering the story. Looks to me like anybody close to this mess could be next." She rushed back inside the building.

What was this about a photographer? Fuck. Was he going to have to watch every news show that aired to keep up with this killer?

He grabbed his cell and pulled up the news. Son of a bitch. The guy Rafe had pulled out of Erin's tree had been killed outside a bar. Stabbed in the back. Did the fact a knife was the murder weapon worry Rafe? Hell, yes.

Minutes later, he had Colton on the line.

"You're sitting on a bed of hot coals." As always, Colton had skipped the pleasantries. "You can't even go home without getting shit stirred up."

"What does that mean?"

"According to the boss, there's already a joint effort in Westbrook Hills, and you're not to get involved."

"How'd he know you were looking into the drug angle for me?" Rafe wasn't questioning if Colton had leaked information. He knew better. Yet here was a message to back off.

Colton chuckled. "While you had me discreetly poking around, somebody inquired about you. I was told to remind you that you're taking some time off."

Rafe's neck muscles tensed. "I knew it. I fucking knew it. Systems programmer, my dying ass. He's a federal agent."

"If you're referring to Linc Hawkins, you're right. While you and I were undercover in Mexico, he made quite a name for himself. Got a brother with the DEA. I suspect they're working the drug angle together. You'd better keep an eye on your lady friend. I hear Hawkins is almost as good with women as I am."

Rafe heard Colton laugh, but nothing he'd said really registered. Nothing past the fact that Linc was a fed. That should have made him happy. It didn't. Should have eased his concern about an ongoing investigation into drugs. It didn't. Should have assured him that Erin was well protected with Linc next door. It didn't.

However, it did make him curious. Was Hawkins really thinking about settling down in Westbrook Hills? Or had he been yanking Rafe's chain to piss him off?

What the hell? He didn't give a damn where Hawkins lived.

Rafe asked Colton to get the inside scoop on the murdered photographer and then ended the call. He arrived at the field house just as the door opened. Young men poured out onto the football field. There'd be no talking to the coach for a while.

He climbed the bleachers and found a good spot to watch practice. The first time the wide receiver ran downfield for a pass, Rafe visualized Nick doing the same, arms in the air, ready to catch the football. Once upon a time, Rafael and Nicholas Sirilli had made one hell of a team.

The young players had broad shoulders and thighs the size of tree stumps. Within minutes of practice starting, things turned ugly. Rafe remembered workouts so brutal that half the team puked. Aggression was expected, but the young men on the field today were vicious. Words were exchanged, and more than one confrontation turned into a shoving match.

Rafe's coach had been tough, preached teamwork and ethics. This man was encouraging the violent behavior. Hell, he was setting an example with his own taunts, shoves, and kicks.

Rafe had seen enough. He jumped to the ground and jogged to the sidelines.

"Coach," he called, interrupting a tirade directed at one particular kid.

The coach whirled. His lips were drawn back over his teeth. He released the kid's jersey. "Practice isn't open to the public. You'll have to leave."

Rafe flashed his badge, exposing enough to identify himself as a federal agent. This had to remain informal, but he had to interrupt.

"Rafe Sirilli," he said. Without hesitation, he walked to the young player and clapped him on the shoulder pads. "You okay?"

The kid's lower jaw moved, but no words came out. He swallowed, glanced at the coach, and then nodded. He jogged back to the action on the field.

"What can I do for you?" The coach moved to stand on Rafe's right side.

"I noticed things were getting out of hand. Thought a timeout might be welcome." Sometimes staying casual and keeping things light worked better than the tactic he wanted to use. He held back the urge to give the asshole a taste of his own medicine.

"If you're not here on official business, I'll get back to the team."

"You go ahead. There's no law against me watching from the stands." No way was he getting anything out of the man or his players.

Rafe climbed to the top of the bleachers where he could stretch his legs out in front of him. The coach called a huddle, and the players grouped around him. Rafe could only guess what was being said. He leaned forward, paying close attention to the big kid who'd most recently been on the wrong end of the coach's wrath.

Movement to the left of the end zone caught Rafe's attention. The girl he'd talked to earlier, Grace, was running across the parking lot toward the street. He stood, keeping her in his line of vision. She paused at the passenger door of a waiting car, caught his gaze, and held it for a minute. She disappeared inside.

Rafe couldn't see the license number, but he knew that particular yellow sports car cost eighty and a hundred grand and was recognizable from any angle. Why was she leaving school early?

Enough of this unofficial crap. It was time he was assigned to this case. Rafe pulled out his cell to call his supervisor. Maybe he could get Rafe assigned to the task force. His cell vibrated before he'd dialed the number. The name on the screen wasn't the boss. Now why'd his heart speed up at seeing Erin's phone number?

"What's up?"

CHAPTER 10

Why had it gotten difficult to talk with Rafe? And why did she allow his looks to sidetrack her thoughts? Erin had been acutely aware of his rock-hard chest and muscular arms the day she'd stumbled in her hallway. He'd swept her up as if she weighed nothing. The tenderness he'd displayed had been endearing. In the span of a little more than ten years, he'd hardened, forged a rough exterior while nature had polished his physical attributes to a razor-sharp edge.

His Italian ancestry oozed from his pores. His strong jaw blanketed in dark stubble, smoldering gray eyes that looked right through her, and those tempting lips made it hard to concentrate. But damn, he wasn't in the room. He wasn't even in the house.

"Erin. Talk to me." His tone of voice held a hint of worry and a demand for a response.

"Sorry. I got distracted." She decided against telling him she'd been wondering if his lips were soft. "Detective Beckett is coming by. He's asking about a couple of people on the list I gave him. You..." Her mouth had gone bone dry. Erin swallowed and prepared for a rejection. "Do you want to join us?"

"Yeah. I'll head your way right now."

"I make a mean chicken-fried steak. I'll share with you if you want to stay for supper."

"Is Beckett joining us?"

His chilly tone surprised her. Was Rafe jealous? Heat rolled through her system and settled, snuggly and low, in her stomach. "I didn't invite him."

"What wine goes with chicken-fried steak?"

"Any kind you like." The heat in her belly slid lower with his soft chuckle.

"I'll think of something."

Erin disconnected and flopped down on the couch. Had Rafe's low sexy tone hinted he'd assumed this was more than dinner between friends? Was it? He wouldn't be in town much longer. Could she let her guard down and fulfill a few fantasies? A smile pulled at her lips. Why not? He'd be gone soon, and she'd never see him again.

Sex without emotional attachment. Could she do it? Why not? She couldn't remember the last time she'd had sex. A reminder might be just the thing she needed.

She raced through a shower, took particular care with her makeup and hair, and finished minutes before the doorbell rang. Her heart pounded against her ribs, until she looked through the peephole. Hiding her disappointment that it wasn't Rafe, she opened the door.

"Detective Beckett, come in." Erin peeked around his wide body, scanning the porch and yard for his partner. "Where's Detective Henry?"

"Busy. Can we dispense with formality? My name is Wade." He waved a hand toward the empty street. "I see you've lost your audience."

"I heard about the photographer. I guess they're following his story." Erin caught movement from the corner of her eye.

She held the door while Rafe parked in her driveway and came inside. He shook the detective's hand. She took the bottle of wine and cake box from Rafe, leaving the two men to talk. She turned to find them at her breakfast counter. Both were over six feet tall, broad-shouldered, and they filled the room.

"Iced tea?" At their nods, she poured three glasses and set them on the counter. "You found somebody on the list interesting?"

"A couple of them warrant talking about." Wade flipped open a small notebook. "What's your opinion of Coach Terry Evans and YMCA Administrator Domingo Ramirez?"

"I wouldn't think it unusual for the girls to be seen talking with either one. Terry is always talking with students. A lot of the kids use the Y, so Dom would logically be in contact with them."

"How about the principal?"

"The same. Professional. He spends more time on administrative duties. Vice Principal Bushnell handles the staff and students."

Rafe frowned. "There's no Bushnell on my list."

"Her name is Rachael Bushnell."

"Oh." He nodded. "Give me your personal take on the men I mentioned," Wade continued.

"I think Coach is a sleazeball, and Dom is friendly but always professional." Deciding she might have been too hasty, Erin took a second to collect her thoughts. "Terry's a jerk. He bullies the boys and flirts with every female, from teachers to students. Principal Mueller is a politician. He's a little awkward around women. Dom loves everybody. He enjoys working with the girls at the Y. He's always giving pointers to any player who wants to improve her game." Erin shook her head.

Rafe held up a finger. "What are you not telling us?" he asked Wade.

Wade hesitated. "Two of them have had run-ins with the law. A few complaints, but nothing that resulted in arrests."

Rafe placed his empty glass on the breakfast bar. Erin moved to give him a refill. His hand covered hers. His strong fingers wrapped around hers as she gripped the handle of the pitcher.

"I'll pour." Rafe refilled his own glass. "Not good enough," he said to Wade. "Define complaints."

Wade hesitated. "You know I can't share that with you."

Erin had to ask, "Do you think one of them sold the drugs to Penny?"

"I'm just working your list against our records," Wade said. "Until I have proof, I'm not commenting. Right now, I'm looking for loose ends."

"Here's one. Erin initiated the whole investigation by reporting the drugs. If she's in danger, I want to know." Rafe's words chilled the air. Harsh and flat, his tone was menacing.

"I can see you're itching to get involved." Wade's back straightened. "I can't allow you to interfere."

"Me?" Rafe's eyes flashed wide. Erin guessed this was his innocent look. "I won't get in anybody's way." He casually brought his glass to his lips and drank a sip of tea.

"Anyone else interesting?" Erin decided to route the conversation back to the list.

"No one stood out." Wade shifted on the stool, turning so he faced only Erin. "Your response to Terry Evans makes me want to chat with him."

Rafe stood, moving to stand behind her. She resisted the urge to lean back and seek out his support. How easily she'd shifted from blaming him for the misunderstanding they'd had as teenagers to trusting him to look out for her best interests.

"I met Evans today," Rafe said. "He has no business working with kids."

"I heard he was pushing too hard. That doesn't mean he's selling drugs on the side." Wade stood. "Thanks for the tea. I'd better run."

Erin walked Wade to the door. He paused and nodded toward Rafe. "He'll make sure you're safe."

"Yeah. He will do that."

She closed the door, half-expecting Rafe to be standing right behind her. The sudden banging noises coming from her kitchen indicated otherwise.

"What are you doing?" A smile pulled at her lips. The tall, muscular, gorgeous man stood in her kitchen with a frying pan in one hand and the flour canister in the other.

"I'm starving. How about you?"

"I could eat." Erin removed the tenderized steaks from the fridge. She let a chuckle escape. "You cook?"

"I'm a confirmed bachelor. Learning to cook was a matter of self-preservation."

Her chest tightened. Rafe's statement had been a direct hit. A reality check. Not that he'd directed it at her as a warning, nor was it a surprise. He was probably available to borrow, but he had no intentions of sticking around.

Erin took charge of the meat, assigning him to biscuit duty. His eyebrows went up when she removed the bag from the freezer. "Use one of these." She handed him a pan from under the counter.

He opened the bag and removed a frozen biscuit. He held it between two fingers for inspection. "I'm supposed to believe this is edible?"

"In twenty-five minutes."

He pursed his lips and tilted his head to the right as he studied the frozen dough. Erin turned on the oven then grabbed her phone and snapped a picture of him. The camera loved the slope of his jawline, his tempting lips, and the mischievous glint in his eyes. She laughed, turning the shot of him around so he could see.

"Now that's a keeper." She slid the cell into her pocket. "Follow the instructions. You can do that, right?"

"Depends on the situation and who's giving them."

Her thoughts went triple-X-rated and weren't the kind she could share. She turned her attention to the steak and worked in silence. If he noticed, he spared her any embarrassment by putting the pan of biscuits in the oven and starting a salad. Erin finished the last dish, a thick white gravy, while Rafe set the table.

He reached around her, and his strong hands covered hers, dwarfing the bowl. "I'll take it."

"Deal. I'll grab the biscuits."

"Not without me. I want to see this miracle."

"Go. You can look all you want after they're on the table."

"I like this side of you," he said, standing close behind her. His deep, sexy voice warmed and unnerved her, while his breath brushed a caress across her ear.

Her insides melted. No way could she look at him, not with heat rushing up her cheeks. She dumped the biscuits into a warming basket and brushed past him. He held her chair at the table, sliding it forward before taking a seat.

"What side of me?" Now that she'd forced out a couple of words, the tension in her shoulders relaxed.

"The side that's not mad at me anymore. It may be old news, but it bothers me that I was too stupid to realize you lashed out because you'd been hurt."

"It's not important." She spooned gravy over her steak. "To hang on to a hurt this long was childish."

"Sure it's important. I would never intentionally hurt you."

The sincerity in his tone and the serious set of his mouth made her wonder. Did he really not know? She handed him the breadbasket in hopes he'd drop the subject.

He peeled back the kitchen towel and stared at the biscuits. "As my Southern granddaddy would've said, 'Well, I'll be damned.'" He picked one up and took a tentative bite. "Good. With gravy, they'll be even better."

"They'll do in a pinch," she said. Pleasure washed over her as he piled his plate high.

Except for an occasional moan from Rafe, they ate in peace for a few minutes. She loved how he enjoyed her cooking.

His hand paused inches from his mouth. "As great as this food tastes, it's not going to get you out of answering my question." He rested his fork on his plate, reached over, and ran the backs of his fingers down her cheek. "A man would be a fool to hurt you."

"You weren't a man, you were a teenage boy."

"That's no excuse. Nick acted out a lot back then, but to deliberately lie and hurt other people. That was wrong. We had probably argued about him using drugs. I can only guess that by hurting you, he must have felt like he was getting even with me."

"I'm sure I said equally horrible things to you."

"You said you'd rather die than be seen in public with me." Rafe's eyebrows lifted.

"You remember my words verbatim?"

"Hey. I'm a guy. Our egos are fragile, especially when we're teenagers." Rafe caught her hand in his. "Nick must've overheard a conversation I had with Dad and Jeff. They wanted me to ask you on a date. Not Nick."

"They what?" Erin's supper rolled into a knot in her stomach. "A boyfriend was the last thing I needed back then."

"Don't you think Jeff was just trying to help?"

"Maybe so, but I realize now that I wasn't ready for a social life. I'd have flipped out if you'd put your arms around me."

"I heard you mention that he'd caught you stealing hot dog buns. You weren't joking."

She'd never been comfortable talking about her childhood. She met Rafe's gaze, prepared to end the conversation. His expression stopped her cold. A softness and compassion radiated from him, pulling her to a level of comfort.

"Yes. I'd been sleeping under a bridge with a small group of runaways. He caught me stealing a package of hot dog buns because I hadn't eaten in days. Instead of arresting me, he hauled me to the youth center and turned me over to Lotty. They saved my life."

"Thank you for telling me." Rafe squeezed Erin's hand. "Jeff's a good man."

She appreciated that Rafe didn't push or ask for more information. "Maybe someday I'll share the rest of the story. But for now, let's eat the dessert you brought."

Time flew by as they ate their slices of coconut cake. After Rafe's second piece, she had to ask if he worked out to stay in shape.

"Genetics and a long run every morning."

"I love to run. I haven't felt safe enough to strike out by myself."

"I'm come get you in the morning."

"Oh," she said as heat shot up her cheeks. "That wasn't a hint."

"I didn't think it was. Six o'clock okay?" The gleam in his eyes said the time was a challenge. No way could she ignore the gauntlet he'd thrown at her feet.

"I usually run earlier, but if you need to sleep in, six is fine."

Erin cleared the table, filling the dishwasher as she went. He brought her his plate and glass, rinsing them before handing them to her.

"We'll drive out to the fairgrounds. The trails out there used to be quiet and safe."

For a moment, images and sounds flew through her mind. The carousel music, the smells wafting off fried turkey drumsticks and cotton candy dragged her close to the abyss. Wrists pinned tightly over her head by a huge hand. Body odor mingled with the stench of stale liquor filled her nostrils. Pain arrowed through her body. Hate crawled up from deep in her subconscious, slithering its way to the here and now.

"My stepfather worked out there. Safe or not, I don't care for that area." She blinked back old memories, refusing to allow the past to control her today.

"Then we won't. But you know I'd never let anyone hurt you, right?"

CHAPTER 11

Rafe took the carafe from Erin and placed it back on the warmer. Despite her apparent resolve not to allow tears to fall, one broke free and slid down her cheek. Before he could react, she wiped it away as if it had offended her. What had happened to her as a child to trigger such a visceral reaction? His blood pressure soared along with his anger. Careful not to frighten her, he moved closer.

"Come here." He spoke softly and pulled her into his arms. "It's okay to cry."

Her body, tight and rigid, relaxed into him briefly. Then she stepped away, and he immediately dropped his arms to his sides. Pink rushed up her neck, running all the way to her hairline. Wide green eyes briefly met his. Then she turned away and walked to the glass doors leading to her backyard. Embarrassment had colored her cheeks, yet she'd held back her tears.

"I'm sorry. I haven't had a meltdown in years."

Rafe followed. Standing behind her, he ached to comfort her. "There's nothing wrong with having an occasional meltdown." He gave in to the urge to touch her and put his hands on her arms. "I need you to believe that as long as I'm around, nothing bad will happen to you."

"I do. Thanks." She leaned into him, the top of her head resting under his chin. "But you won't be around forever."

Her words landed like a kick to the gut. She was right. She wasn't a murder suspect any longer, but the drug situation at the school still had to be resolved. "I'll stay until we bust the narcotics supplier."

She turned in his arms to face him. The movement of her hair sent a lemony aroma wafting across his face. Warning bells went off.

Getting involved with Erin would be a mistake. Hurting her would be inevitable and unforgivable.

"You can do that?"

"If I have to, I'll tack on vacation to the end of my leave." His brain was firing warning shots, but his desire to hold her grew. He'd never wanted to touch a woman as badly as he did this second. To feel her warm body yield to his. "My boss suggested I reconnect with real people." His hands slid around her small waist. "And you feel very real to me."

He had to taste her. Had to know if her lips were as soft as he thought they'd be. The kiss would be only a light touch, an exploratory meeting.

She lifted onto her toes to meet him. Erin's eyelids fluttered closed, and her mouth opened slightly. She molded against him on contact. Her hands dived into his hair. Damn, he was never getting the stuff cut, not if she liked tunneling her fingers through a long mane.

He increased the pressure, coaxed her to open wider, and then he swept his tongue inside when she did. Sweet heaven, blood rushed to his groin. She rose higher on her toes, placing his growing erection against her stomach.

Erin pulled back. Her eyes glazed with desire. Rafe cupped her cheeks, rubbing his thumb over her swollen lips. "That was much better than I expected."

"Too much too soon, don't you think?" She rested the weight of her head in his hand.

"Do you?" The way his body had reacted to her, he couldn't see it.

"I'm not answering that." She lifted her head, leading Rafe to believe she was about to walk away. Instead, she combed his hair in place with her fingers. "That was quite a leap from not wanting to be in the same room to almost tearing off each other's clothes."

"Naked would be good." Sounded like a good plan to his

body, but his brain said otherwise. He didn't have room in his life for attachments. "Okay, I'll buy that we've come a long way in the past few days."

"It's late." Taking him by the hand, she led him to the door and stepped onto the porch with him.

God, he wanted to kiss her until she lost her mind. Instead, he leaned down and covered her lips with his, breaking away after a second. "Where's the gun?"

"On my nightstand."

"Good. I'll see you in the morning. We'll find a nice peaceful path to run."

"I know just the place." She lifted onto her toes for another kiss.

"Lock the door." He didn't dare pull her into his arms. The desire to carry her to her bed was still powering his thoughts. He gently brushed her lips with his, moved back, then waited until the bolt on her door slid home. He got in his car and drove away, acutely aware of her scent on his shirt and her taste on his tongue.

Between thoughts of Erin, two dead teenagers, Nick, and a drug dealer who needed to meet his maker, there'd be little rest for Rafe tonight.

At dinner, he'd paid close attention to Beckett's facial expressions. If the detective was aware of the joint undercover operation, he'd shown no signs of it. Maybe narcotics had kept it a secret. Not smart when Beckett was trying to solve two homicides.

****

The binoculars hit the floor at his feet. The sound reverberated off the hardwood floor, amplified by the fact the house was devoid of furniture.

He tried so hard not to be angry with Erin. Casanova clamped his hands over his ears and pressed. He feared his head would explode when his heartbeat rose to such levels.

He stormed away from the window, unable to watch any

longer. Surely, his eyes had been playing tricks on him. She would never betray him with another. Not after all he'd done for her.

Erin belonged to him. Why did she flaunt another man under his nose? Was there no end to the hoops she'd force him to jump through? No doubt, the bastard had kissed her against her wishes.

The sound of a car's engine drew his attention. He returned to his vantage point and watched as her friend got into his car and drove away.

He paced, running different scenarios though his mind, until he knew what he had to do. She had to be taught a lesson.

****

Erin opened her eyes and stared at the ceiling, wondering why she'd woken from such a lovely dream about Rafe and regretting not taking him to bed last night. Now, getting him out of her head was going to be difficult. Admittedly, having him around for a few weeks was going to be nice.

Who would've guessed his lips were so soft when everything about him was so hard? That monster erection of his had burned through layers of clothing and demanded her attention. She snuggled deeper under her comforter, hoping she could pick up the dream where she'd left off.

A noise from outside grabbed her attention before she could close her eyes. She'd bought an older home and the porch had a few loose boards. Footsteps made an undeniable creaking sound. Was someone trying to break into her house? She slipped out of bed, grabbed the phone, and quickly dialed 911. In a loud voice, she announced to the operator that an intruder was on her front porch and the gun in her hand was pointed at the door. She ignored instructions to stay on the line, opting to dial 666 instead.

"You all right?" His voice was thick with sleep.

"Somebody is on my porch. I heard footsteps."

"I'm on my way."

Again, she'd needed him, and without hesitation, he'd reacted as if she were his priority.

Erin ran to the living room and flipped on the outside lights. She paused in the dark and listened. Had the intruder gone?

When she heard the sirens, she hurriedly pulled on a pair of sweat pants and shirt. Someone knocked on her front door.

"Erin," Linc called out. Her next-door neighbor's voice calling her name gave her courage. She hurried to open the door.

On the porch at his feet was another envelope. "Not again," she said.

"I didn't touch it." Linc held up his hands. He was barefoot, his hair mussed, and he wore nothing but jogging shorts. Erin thought he looked more like a college running back than a technology geek. Behind him, two police cars rolled to a stop.

Her knees weakened. Tears brimmed in her eyes. She refused to give in to either. Damn it, she refused to allow the feeling of being powerless and vulnerable to take over.

****

Rafe parked, sprang from his car, and was greeted by two uniformed cops. He handed over his identification, biting back expletives at being kept from Erin. A few seconds passed before they allowed him to enter the house. Erin stood next to Linc while a patrolman spoke with her.

Rafe's gaze stopped on the manila envelope on the counter. An officer wearing gloves was staring at the hand-printed note.

YOU TEST MY LOVE.

The meaning slammed into Rafe. Had someone witnessed their kisses on the porch and lashed out at her?

"Erin?" he said. Her head turned in his direction, and the fear in her eyes chilled his soul.

"Thank God." She crossed the room into his arms. Her hands clutched his shirt, and the fear he'd seen shifted to anger. Her body trembled. "I thought someone was breaking in, but apparently, he was just leaving the note."

"You're okay. That's all that matters," Rafe whispered into her hair.

Linc joined them. "It's a good thing she didn't try to confront him."

"He's right," Rafe added, reluctantly releasing her. "This message is different. The first two were accusations. This was a warning. It's also personal. Does it spark any new ideas about who it might be from?"

"None." Erin shook her head. "But it is different from the others. This one is typed."

Linc frowned. "The delivery was the same, but I think we're looking at different people."

"I haven't seen the other notes," a uniformed officer said. "Did you notice anything else different, Ms. Brady?"

"The envelope is larger." Erin thought a second.

"Maybe the lab will find DNA. I'll drop the note off, but first I have a few more questions," the officer said.

"I'm ready." Erin followed the officer to the breakfast bar.

"Looks like she's in good hands," Linc said. "Let me know if you need me."

"Thanks for getting over here so fast. I appreciate it," Erin said.

Rafe wasn't going to get too far away from Erin, but he walked to the yard with Linc.

"You had me pegged all along," Linc said with a grin.

"Not completely. Your cover's a good one." Getting the truth out into the open was a good thing. "I promised Erin I'd stick around until things were resolved."

"Hell, I'm glad. The city's narcotics department's resources are limited because of budget cuts. You ask me, they don't have enough manpower." Linc jerked his head toward the house. "You staying because of Erin?"

"I guess." The question caught Rafe off guard. "My brother

died of an overdose. I'd like to know the stream of drugs here has dried up. At least for a while."

Linc nodded his understanding but asked nothing more. "What do you make of tonight's message? Saying 'you test my love' is a lot more personal than calling someone a murderer."

"All roads lead to Erin." Rafe glanced back toward the open front door. She'd moved out of his line of sight. "Hey, if you need some extra help, you can call on my partner. Colton Weir. He's probably bored out of his mind, doing grunt work. Ask for him."

"I just may do that. Thanks." Linc jogged across to his yard.

Rafe laughed on his way back to Erin's house. Linc and Colton on the same operation was going to be interesting. A California surfer and a die-hard country boy from south Texas would be interesting.

Rafe joined Erin. She and the officers were just finishing their Q&A. The corners of Erin's mouth lifted slightly, making Rafe feel as if she drew comfort from his presence. "You're still pale." He tucked a strand of her hair behind her ear. "You can't stay here. My place is your best choice."

"I know. Lotty is doing well, but she's also still doing physical therapy. She needs to concentrate on herself. If I'm there, she'll try to take care of me."

She constantly amazed Rafe. "Selfless and smart. You're one hell of a combination."

"Don't you believe it. It's purely selfish. I'm a counselor and a coach because it makes me feel good. I learn something from those kids every day."

"Pack a bag. I'll walk the cops out. Make sure you lock up tight. If this gets out, you'll have another yard full of reporters and curiosity seekers."

"Yes, dear," she said with a tilt of her head.

"Sorry. You don't need me to tell you that." Rafe was proud of the way she'd taken tonight in stride. She'd slow down soon. The adrenaline pumping through her veins would keep her going just so long.

After she'd disappeared down the hallway, he walked outside to talk with the CSI in charge, Tyler Hurst. They'd exchanged IDs earlier, but Rafe had stayed out of the way, yielding to the experts.

"Not much information to go on," Rafe said. "I appreciate anything you can come up with."

"If there's something to find, we'll find it," Tyler said. He glanced around the yard. "What do you know about the neighbor?"

"You won't have to worry about him. He's clear." Rafe paused on the porch and watched the orange blaze ascend as the sun broke over the horizon.

Erin was in her bedroom packing, and Rafe took a couple of steps down the hallway. The fact that it was her *bedroom* caused him to pause. If he went back there tonight, he'd cross a line that maybe shouldn't be crossed. The desire to pull her into his arms and kiss her until she begged him to join her on the bed was too strong.

He'd hurt her once, inadvertently, but the pain had been real. No way did he want to do it again.

CHAPTER 12

"Erin?" Rafe's tone had a strange effect on Erin. Like a favorite song she wanted to hear again and again.

"Coming." She shook off the stupor she'd slipped into. How long had she sat on the side of the bed and stared at the tennis shoes at her feet? All the air seemed to have left her lungs, draining every ounce of energy she had left.

Dragging her suitcase and carrying her shoes, she hurried down the hall. Rafe took her bag while never taking his eyes off of her. "Let's get you out of here."

She nodded. Too tired to speak, she opened the door and stepped out into the morning air. The sun washed across her face, and a light breeze warned that summer was right around the corner. "I love this kind of day. Everything is new and fresh, ready to begin anew."

Rafe's hand slid around her waist. "You're getting maudlin, which tells me it's time you got some sleep."

"You owe me a run. And I dressed for it." She held her shoes up for his inspection. "See?" She sat on the porch steps and slipped on a pair of socks and the tennis shoes.

"We'll stop for breakfast and coffee. Then we'll see if you're together enough to run. If you fell and got hurt on my watch, Jeff would have my hide."

She tied her shoestrings then accepted his hand, allowing him to help her stand. Neither spoke as they got into his car. Rafe backed out of her driveway and headed toward the highway. Erin took one quick glance at her house as they turned the corner. She'd held back her anger since the first police officer walked through her front door.

"You've been very quiet," Rafe said. "If somebody sent me a

threatening note, it would piss me off."

"You really should stop reading my mind."

"Afraid I might learn your secrets?"

"We all have secrets," she snapped, but immediately wished she hadn't.

"Hey." His large hand covered her knee. "I was joking."

"Sorry. I'm a little touchy." She forged ahead without waiting for a response. "This last note convinced me. The messages, the drugs, and the murders all tie back to me."

"You're pretty smart. I'm not sure it registered with the cops today. Beckett gets that somehow it connects to you." He glanced at her. If she'd read him correctly, a hint of pride backlit his dark eyes.

"This last note was very different. Scared me just a little."

"A little. Scares me a lot. It was delivered using the same method as the others. Whoever left it knew you'd received the other envelopes."

"You think tonight's note isn't related to the murders?"

"We need to look at all the angles. Hell, it could be one of those reporters who staked out your house. We have to figure that out." Rafe took the ramp onto the freeway, took his sunglasses from the console, then slid them on. "Did the cops who interviewed you ask about old boyfriends?"

"Yes. And I told them the truth."

"Are you going to tell me about him?"

"I don't see why not. He taught history at the high school. Our relationship lasted a couple of years. It ended when he moved to Minnesota to take the headmaster's position at a private school. There's been nobody since."

"He was in love with you." Rafe's words were a statement, not a question.

"If you mean did he ask me to go with him, yes. I said no, and he understood."

"Well, somebody thinks he's in love with you now. If I'm

right, he saw me kiss you good night, and that set him off."

"So the first time I kiss a man in a year, somebody cares? Why hasn't this person come forward? Nobody has asked me out in a long time." Erin's brain sorted through any possible suspects.

"Then you're surrounded by fools."

Erin blinked as he glanced at her, sending that trademark wink of his.

"Thank you."

"Just calling it like I see it."

"You really think somebody could be jealous?"

"There are a couple of possibilities. We have a reporter trying to goad you into a story. Or some guy who's trying to prove his love."

"You think this guy who fancies himself in love with me killed two young women to prove his love? How sick would that be?"

"Damn sick and damn dangerous."

She realized Rafe had led her to answer her own questions. She punched him in the arm. "You'd already figured it out. Why didn't you just tell me?"

"Because I'm not a hundred percent sure, and sometimes talking it out helps." Rafe glanced at her. A sexy smile tugged at the corners of his lips. "I was the first guy you'd kissed in how long?"

She thought about her answer. "Maybe a year."

"Sweet. Now I feel special."

"Stop or we won't have room in the car for all three of us."

"Three?"

"Yeah. You, me, and your ego."

He laughed, and she joined him. "You did it again. This time you calmed my nerves. I'll bet you're very good at your job."

"I try."

Erin's thoughts went back to the idea of having a stalker, one who thought they had a relationship. "There's a name for this behavior." She dug deep into her memory. "Erotomania." A band tightened around her chest.

"Yeah." Rafe nodded. "That's the technical name for it. Some celebrities have to deal with people who've really gone off the deep end. You're sure nobody has made a pass—"

"Nobody."

"Don't be too quick to answer. Sometimes all it takes is a few kind words to set off this type of personality. A pat on the back, a smile, maybe you thanked him for something. Any or all of those can be seen as a declaration of love."

"Then the killer could be anyone in town. I try to get along with everybody."

"This bastard apparently believes you initiated the imagined affair with him. He felt that you disrespected him or your relationship, and he lashed out."

"Like leaving me a warning not to do it again."

"Exactly. He's saying you aren't allowed to betray him."

"I remember reading that egomaniacs don't normally kill."

"If this is the correct scenario, this bastard in not like most." Rafe drove into the parking lot of Mom's Kitchen, a café known for its home-style breakfasts. He wove through the jumble of cars and eighteen-wheelers and parked. He killed the engine and turned in his seat. "I'll talk to Beckett today. He'll see the report, and I'll wager he agrees with me."

"After we eat, I'll pass on the run. I should tell Jeff and Lotty what's happened. They need to hear this from me."

"You're right. We'll drive over after breakfast. We can exercise later," he said with a wink.

Erin walked in front of him, feeling his eyes on her and thinking about a different kind of exercise.

****

Rafe hadn't been inside Jeff and Lotty's home in many years. Erin had cautioned against expecting the Lotty of old, but the friendly, warm-hearted woman who opened her arms and ushered guests inside pulled him in for a hug. She moved slower, her steps were cautious and more deliberate. Her smile and the sincerity in her welcome hadn't faded.

"Shame on you for not coming sooner," Lotty chastised, but with a sparkle in her eyes.

Rafe chuckled. "No excuses." He kissed her forehead. "I'm sorry."

"No fun if you're not going to argue." She slipped her hand into the crook of his arm and leaned against him as he walked her to an easy chair.

"You're looking good. I'm guessing this old grouch has been taking good care of you," Rafe said, sitting on the couch close to Lotty.

"Between Jeff and Erin, I can't move without them hovering." Lotty settled back in her chair. Her gaze shifted between Rafe and Erin. "Whatever it is, best you just spit it out."

Erin scooted next to Rafe, allowing Jeff to sit next to her. "I'll let Rafe explain."

Hitting the high spots, Rafe explained the latest note left at Erin's. No one spoke or interrupted. He finished with the news that he would stay until the case was resolved. An uneasy crawl of foreboding nagged at him for making such a promise. What if this dragged on for years?

"So while you're packing up the house and working on the case, Erin should stay here, so I can protect her," Jeff said.

"We talked about this." Erin joined the conversation. "The last thing I want you worrying about is my safety. I knew you'd want to stay in the loop on what's happening, which is why we're here."

"My partner, Colton Weir, may be assigned to the narcotics case. One of us will be around to provide security. Erin will be fine."

Jeff rose and started pacing. The nerve in his jaw jerked. His agitation was obvious, but he remained silent.

"Are you staying at Rafe's?" Lotty asked.

"Yes," Erin said. "Everybody in town knows you and Jeff raised me. If I stayed here and anything newsworthy happened, the media would be crawling all over your place. Rafe's house is farther out and more secluded."

"It's a good plan." Lotty looked directly at her husband.

"It will work," Jeff agreed. He stopped behind his wife's chair and patted her on the shoulder.

An unspoken message had passed between Lotty and Jeff. Damned if Rafe knew how she'd calmed Jeff down. That kind of communication had to be something that came from being married to each other for many years.

Rafe stood, offering Erin his hand. "I'll take good care of her."

"You'd better," Jeff said.

"I'm right here. Stop talking about me as if I'm invisible."

"Erin, girl." Jeff's accent thickened.

"You two go on. Just check in every now and then." Lotty stood, issuing hugs and then walking Rafe and Erin to the door. "He worries." Lotty nodded in Jeff's direction.

"I understand." Rafe leaned down for a hug. "Luke will be home soon. He'll make the perfect bodyguard."

"If I need one," Erin muttered under her breath.

Rafe escorted her to the car, slid behind the wheel, then drove toward the freeway. "There is no 'if I need one,'" he said. "I'm not a profiler. In fact, my career has been focused on slowing the flood of drugs coming into the country. I'm not an expert on erotomania or any other kind of mania. I do know that those two young women were stabbed repeatedly, violently, and that indicates rage. The killer was furious. Maybe he was angry that you suffered because they'd fabricated a story about you. That's a big maybe, but if I'm right, when he realizes you're not in love with him, he'll come after you."

Erin simply nodded. Was she thinking over what he'd said? She was a smart woman, and Rafe had no doubt that he'd gotten her attention. Now he felt like crap for coming on so strong. "I wasn't trying to scare you. Just trying to impress the need to be cautious."

"I'm not going to do anything stupid."

Rafe pulled into his driveway and killed the engine. "Home sweet home."

"Refresh my memory," she said. "How many bedrooms do you have?"

"Three. Why?"

"I was just counting heads. That's you, me, Luke, and your partner, right?"

"Colton. Right." Rafe laughed. "I see where you're headed. You're outnumbered."

"That doesn't bother me. I was just wondering how you were going to divvy up three bedrooms between four of us. Because one of them is mine."

"You're assuming Colton will be assigned to work with Linc." Rafe grabbed her bag from the trunk, unlocked the front door, and stepped back. "You'll have to excuse the packing boxes. As far as rooms, you take the master bedroom. The twin beds in my room will work for me and Luke."

"But isn't the master the largest of the three?"

"Yeah. But that's not why you get it. It's the only one with its own bathroom."

"Oh." She smiled, and her green eyes twinkled. "Good call."

Rafe carried her bag down the hall and placed it next to the bed. He turned to find Erin standing in the doorway. He tracked her gaze as she took in the room. "Come in. You're safe with me."

"A lie if I ever heard one." She joined him next to the bed. "It's lovely."

"I don't think Dad changed it much after Mom died. The comforter is new, but the rest looks just like it did when I left."

"He loved her very much." Erin's lips curved slightly, making her even more beautiful.

"Best I can remember, the feeling was mutual. I don't remember a time where either raised their voice at the other. Now, when it came to getting the attention of three rowdy boys, they did. But never at each other."

The wistful expression on Erin's face dropped a boulder on his chest. What kind of life had she lived before Jeff found her? "I'll let you get unpacked."

Rafe went to the back porch, slid his cell out, and called Colton. Linc had taken the initiative, and Colton would be joining them soon.

"So you're okay with this?"

Colton's low, slow laugh rumbled through the line. "Little late to ask. Hell, I just finished filling out my last expense report. I need to get out of here before it gets to the boss."

"I'll text you my address."

He disconnected just as the back door opened. "I need to go to the YMCA in the morning," Erin said. "Now that I'm not a murder suspect, I'm hoping Dom will allow me to return to my volunteer position."

"That's an easy fix." Rafe joined her inside. "I'll drive you. You get unpacked?"

"I hung a few things."

"I have an idea." Rafe left then returned with a cardboard box. "Come on, let's make you some more space." He led her back to the master and emptied two of the dresser drawers, trying to ignore the pinch in his chest at handling his dad's things. Instead, he concentrated on making space for Erin's clothes. "Now you have room."

A warm hand caught his wrist. Her green eyes glistened with honesty as she looked up at him. "Thank you. For everything. I think I'll be able to sleep tonight."

"I don't need a lot of sleep. You find yourself awake and want to talk, knock on my door."

She lifted up on her toes and kissed his cheek. He nodded, turned, and walked away, leaving her to finish. Funny how the simple gesture of a kiss had almost knocked him to his knees.

He rounded up more cartons and bags, escalating his efforts to clean out closets and drawers. More items went into the boxes he'd set aside for Luke. A couple of things caught Rafe's attention, but his brother deserved first shot at choosing what he wanted to keep.

With Erin in the master, Rafe was never going to get any sleep. If he did, his dreams would be X-rated for sure. Colton could take the room across from her. Luke and Rafe could bunk together. Their feet would hang off the ends of the twin beds, but they had both slept in worse places.

Rafe wrapped their dad's badge in a frayed handkerchief and carefully placed it in the keepsake box. Seeing Luke would be a good thing. The reason they'd both had to come home, not so much.

****

Agitated didn't fully describe Casanova's mood. Between work, remodeling the house, and keeping an eye on Erin, his body was rebelling, demanding sleep. But he simply had too much to do. Everything seemed to conspire to pull him away from her.

Women were funny creatures. If they didn't receive the proper amount of love and affection, they'd run off with someone who would give them what they wanted. Hadn't his mother proved that fact? Hadn't his father hammered it home, repeatedly telling Casanova how women expected too much? He'd grown up believing that, until he'd met Erin. She wasn't like that. She was a caring, giving person. And soon, she'd belong to him. She'd appreciate everything he'd done and was doing. If she didn't, well, he'd prepared for that, too. Eventually, she'd grow to love him as he did her.

The sound of hammers had given him a splitting headache.

The workers had ripped up the hardwood flooring, making way for the installation of the new thick, sound-dulling carpet. Nobody had questioned his request for an underground safe room, not with the number of tornadoes this area experienced. The sales representative had explained that Casanova could survive any storm that might blow through.

 He had a few personal final additions, but those final touches would have to wait until the update on the house was complete. He hoped with all his heart not to have to use the room for long, but it would be there. Just in case.

He tossed back two painkillers and carried his lunch to the backyard. Eating and listening to the radio, his mood improved when the news broadcast announced Erin had been eliminated as a suspect in the homicide of at least one of the two female students. The police no longer considered her a person of interest.

He hung out and watched the men work on the renovation of his house for a few minutes. All of them were lazy bastards. No sense of urgency from them. Too bad they didn't report to him. He went back inside and informed the construction supervisor that slow work would not be tolerated.

Casanova understood the danger of being seen around Erin's house too often, but on the way back to work, he had to swing by to check on her. The absence of reporters and media vans helped his mood. That the only car in her driveway was hers perked him up, too. He should've known that she would chase those other men away.

After work, he'd drive to Dallas. The wedding dress he'd purchased had been delivered to the PO box he'd rented. He hoped he'd guessed correctly when selecting her style and size.

CHAPTER 13

The rumble from a vehicle's engine drew Rafe's attention. By the time he reached the window, Linc had stepped onto the porch.

Rafe opened the door and waved Linc into the living room. "Erin is here, so before we talk about work, you might want to bring her into the loop."

"What loop?" Erin's voice came from behind Rafe. He turned and found her frowning as her gaze settled on Linc.

"Linc has something to tell you." Rafe pointed to the couch. "Let's get comfortable."

Rafe shut up and left the conversation to Linc. After he and Erin had taken spots on the couch, Rafe sat in his dad's easy chair. Sadness tried to creep in but he shoved it aside to listen.

"I'm not a programmer, although I am good enough to use my knowledge as a cover." Linc launched into an explanation. "I'm an FBI agent. Here at the request of your city's narcotics squad and the school district police department."

Erin waved off his comment as if shooing away a fly. "I was close. I figured DEA." With the same hand, she motioned stop. "Stay calm. Nobody else knows." She glanced at Rafe. "Okay, I think Rafe had you figured out. I'm just glad somebody is in the school investigating."

"I guess my cover wasn't all that good. Maybe I'll get a haircut." Linc frowned as he dragged a hand through his mop of hair.

"Colton will be here officially to work with you and the narcotics squad. I'll help on the side when I can," Rafe said.

"The police department will be pleased you're willing to lend a hand. They'll see that you get whatever you need." Linc turned to Erin. "What are your plans?"

"I'm staying here at Rafe's for a few days. My teacher's union attorney is working to get me reinstated, and I'm hoping the YMCA will allow me to resume coaching."

"Good for you."

Rafe listened, observing body language as Linc and Erin chatted about the school and sports. He didn't detect any romantic interest toward Erin from Linc, which made Rafe wonder about the man's eyesight.

Linc stood. "One more piece of information. One of the senior boys was rushed to the hospital last night. He almost died of an overdose of heroin. The paramedics saved him with a dose of Narcan."

"Who was it?" Erin moved to the edge of her chair.

"James Mayboy. He was lucky."

"I read an article that some towns hold training classes for families that teach them how to use the Narcan nasal spray," Erin said. "Maybe I'll suggest that to the school board. If it saves one life, it will be worth it."

Rafe handed Linc his card. "My cell's always on. After Colton checks in at the precinct, we'll do some interviews."

Rafe closed the door and turned to Erin. "When you're ready, I'll drive you to the YMCA."

"How's it going to look with you following me around? People will think you're tailing me."

"People will think we're friends. There's only been the one overt action from your stalker, but I consider it a threat. Driving you will give me a chance to look around the Y. Anywhere a bunch of kids hang out is a prime piece of real estate to a drug dealer."

"I'll change." Erin took off toward the bedroom but stopped and looked back. "You know, there's a great barbershop next door to the Y."

"I get paid to look like this." He laughed as she disappeared down the hallway. Maybe he should hit the barbershop. Better to get rid of the long hair before Luke got home. If he didn't, the scruffy appearance would be open season with Luke.

Rafe texted Colton to let him know they were headed to the YMCA on South Porter Street. Depending on where he was on his journey, they'd either meet up there or back at the house. Then Rafe headed to the extra bathroom to shave. Truth was, he'd be better received after a little polishing.

Emerging without the face stubble, he walked toward the smell of food. "You're cooking? We just ate."

"Check your watch. It's lunch time." Erin looked right at home standing in front of the kitchen stove. "I figured this way would be quicker. Lucky for you, I make a mean fried bologna and cheese sandwich, because your fridge is a barren wasteland." She slid his grilled lunch onto a plate and handed it to him. "I'm fixing two for you."

Rafe dumped a handful of chips on his plate and ate while leaning against the counter. "If you're going to assume the responsibility of feeding me, we're going to need groceries."

"Fair warning, if this house fills up with men, you're all going to pitch in or go hungry." She slid a second sandwich onto his plate.

"Thanks," he mumbled around a mouthful of food.

She stared at him. Her smile softened her gaze and heated his skin. "What?" he asked.

"I'd forgotten how gorgeous you are. No wonder you let your hair grow out and stop shaving. Otherwise, you'd never convince anyone that you're a thug."

Her announcement had been so matter-of-fact and unexpected that Rafe was stumped for a response. Silence was the best way to end a one-sided conversation, so he kept his mouth shut. He took another big bite and chewed slowly. The idea that she was a little prejudiced in his favor made him happy.

Rafe finished eating first. He rinsed the dishes then loaded them in the dishwasher. He felt Erin's presence behind him. He turned and took the plate from her hand. Her tongue slid across her bottom lip as if searching for any errant pieces of food. Or was she thinking about kissing him? Before she could decide, he made up her mind by cupping her cheek with his hand. He started with her sexy mole, placing little pecks there, before covering her mouth with his.

She moaned softly, leaned into him, and swiped her tongue across his. A small earthquake ripped through Rafe. Nothing had ever felt so right. His free hand slid around her waist, and he crushed her tight against his chest, pressing her breasts against him.

Her hands slid under his shirt. Supple fingers kneaded his back, stroked across his skin, and made it difficult to think. He left her soft lips to work his way to her neck and behind her ear.

She shivered.

He whispered, "You have no idea how often I've threatened to do that."

A sexy smile lifted the corners of her mouth. "What took you so long?"

Rafe dropped his hands to her waist. "I'm here now." He dragged her even closer, molding her body into his. Desire had blinded him to anything except her nearness. He forced himself to take a deep breath. "Still too much too soon?"

She glanced down. While she couldn't see how he strained against his zipper, she'd definitely felt his erection pressing against her. "It's not enough."

He lifted her away from the counter, and her legs locked around him. He turned and sat her on the edge. He grabbed the edge of her T-shirt and pulled it over her head. Leaning back, he let his eyes devour her. Her chest rose and fell rapidly. Jesus, her creamy, soft skin begged to be stroked.

"You are incredible." He lowered his head and ran his tongue along the flesh at the top of her lacy bra.

"Rafe?" Her tone was breathy.

"Little busy here," he joked, sucking her nipple into his mouth through the material.

"I'm a big girl."

That got his attention. "Huh?"

"I want your word that I'm not going to get the 'I'm not ready for a permanent relationship' speech. You're leaving as soon as you can. I get it."

Her gaze was steady, and the smile on her face appeared to be sincere. She was right. He should make sure she understood this was sex and not permanent. At that thought, his erection deflated faster than if he'd jumped naked into the lake in winter. "You get it?"

She nodded. "It's no big deal."

"Excuse me?" Now why had that sent a ping of hurt to his pride? "You said earlier you hadn't been kissed in a year. Now you want me to believe you have two- or three-week flings. Can't have it both ways. Which is it?"

Her eyes broke contact with his. "All right. No flings but I'm okay with this being temporary."

"Listen, tough guy." He decided to get everything on the table. "I've never wanted anybody as much as I do you. You've always hit my hot buttons. Even when we were too young to know where all those buttons were or exactly what they meant, you stirred my blood." Her gaze returned and met his. "An assignment will be waiting on me when I get back to work. Where to? Who knows? There isn't room in my life for a perm—"

"You're not telling me anything I don't already know." She slid off the counter into the narrow space between them. "We'd better go."

Rafe placed a hand on either side of her hips. Grasping the counter top, he effectively trapped her. "I remember a young, innocent girl. One who's grown into a beautiful, desirable woman. Don't get pissed because I don't want to hurt you."

"I wasn't innocent." Again, she averted her gaze, but not

before he saw the suffering in her eyes. "I'd been through more at that age than you can imagine."

"I didn't know. I swear." The pain in her eyes and the fire in her tone slammed into Rafe. She'd been through a lot more than being homeless. That somebody had hurt her sent anger rushing through his system. He cupped her cheek. "I hope you'll trust me enough to tell me." Her eyebrows dipped. "Someday."

"Thank you."

"Whatever happened, it won't change my desire to make love to you."

The tension around her eyes relaxed. The corners of her mouth twitched. "Good to know."

He kissed the mole above her lip, caught her by the hand, and then walked her to the car. Damn, he'd wanted to carry her to bed. Wanted to see, touch, and taste every part of her soft skin. But she'd stopped them twice. Hell, maybe she was just too smart to hook up with someone like him. Either way, the next move had to be hers.

The drive to the YMCA took them past areas of town Rafe hadn't seen in years. The elementary school playground was full of kids. "See those monkey bars? Nick and I used to race to see who could get there first. Even then we were competitive."

"And you always won?"

"Hardly ever," Rafe said. "Nick was a good athlete and student. He pushed me to try harder, get stronger, and be smarter. I tried, but he was usually a step faster and a little brainier. All that changed when he started experimenting with drugs. After he became addicted, he lost interest in sports and school."

"I've read that losing your twin is like having a part of yourself missing." Erin's tone was sincere, without sounding like pity, and Rafe appreciated that. "I can't imagine how much his death hurt you."

"I took it hard. At first, I was filled with anger at him. It took a long time for me to forgive him, but I'll never forgive the drugs."

"Which is why you're dedicated to your job."

"If you're trying to make up for telling me my hair needs to be cut, it's not working," he joked, figuring he'd already spilled too much personal shit to her. Nick wasn't a subject Rafe liked to discuss. Why he'd brought him up to Erin was a mystery, except she was so damn easy to talk to.

He parked his car in the lot across from the YMCA and walked across the street with her, stopping at the entrance. "I'll catch up with you in a few."

The sunlight bounced off her face as she graced him with a big grin. "You're going to the barbershop."

"Don't start thinking it's because of you," he teased, and her eyes sparkled in the light. "I'd been planning on getting a haircut. I just hadn't had time."

She'd never know how close he'd come to kissing her again.

****

Erin couldn't wipe the smile off her face as she entered the Y and walked to the office. The sound of squeaking tennis shoes and a whistle blowing filled her with joy. It was like waking up from a nightmare. Her step was lively as she walked around the corner to the basketball court. The girls were in a huddle, listening to the school principal. One of the players spotted her and called out her name. The entire group looked up, squealed, and ran to her, all talking at once.

Erin's heart was so full she was sure it would explode. Smiling teenage faces crowded around her, everyone patting and hugging her. Tears filled Erin's eyes. She swallowed and tried to sound serious. "Why aren't you ladies in school?"

"Teacher in-service day," Gayle, one of the seniors, said.

"I seem to have lost track of time," Erin said.

"You're back, right?" one of the girls asked. The rest of the team echoed the question.

"We'll see. I'm here to speak with the director about it."

Movement caught Erin's attention, and she glanced up to see Principal Mueller waiting to speak with her. "When did the principal take over?"

"Just for today," Gayle whispered. "Principal Mueller said he could sneak off easier than Coach Evans, which was fine with us. We were glad he couldn't make it today."

"I wasn't aware he coached basketball." Erin had a bad feeling considering every girl standing around her was frowning.

"He doesn't," Gayle answered. "We're all ready to quit rather than have him yell and trash-talk us..."

Sensing Gayle had stopped talking for a reason, Erin turned to find the principal had walked closer.

"Ms. Brady," he said. "It's good to see you."

"You, too. This is my lucky day," she said. "After I spoke with Dom, you were going to be my next stop."

"You girls divide up and scrimmage for a minute." Principal Mueller shooed the team back to the court. "Last time I saw Dom, he was in his office. I'll walk with you."

The principal seemed overly pleased to see her, which she tried to ignore since he tended to be a flirt. No matter, Erin edged away from him. She took a deep breath and thought through what she wanted to say before speaking. "I appreciate you and Coach Evans filling in. The girls are important to me, and I look forward to getting back to coaching here and my counseling work at school."

"It's a matter of formality. The district police contacted me this morning. They've already filed their report. Your reinstatement should come soon."

"Great news. I'm ready. My normally quiet life was perfect without all the notoriety." Erin knocked on the office door, expecting the principal to move on. Instead, he stood a little too close. His fingers wrapped around her arm, causing her to jump. Could he be the one who'd left the last message at her house? Had he killed Penny and Sara?

"You're an asset to the school, and I'm glad the trouble is over. I'd better get back to the girls."

Before she could speak, he released her arm and jogged back to the basketball court. Erin felt like a fool. Was she going to view every male she knew as if he were a suspect?

"Looking for me?"

"Dom?" She whirled to find him strolling down the hall. "As a matter of fact, I was."

"I hate sitting in an office. Walk with me. We can talk while I check on the water aerobics class."

"Perfect." Erin fell in step with him. "I'm hoping you've heard that I'm no longer a suspect in the murders."

"It was on the news, and Principal Mueller stopped by my office this morning. I hated to ask you not to come back until this mess was cleared up, but my primary concern will always be the kids."

"I expected nothing less. But I'd like to come back. The girls need me."

"Excuse me just a second." He walked to the edge of the pool and spoke with the instructor.

Erin didn't recognize the new woman. She wore her dark hair pulled up in a knot, and her flashing brown eyes brightened as Dom dropped to one knee and chatted with her. From where Erin stood, it appeared to be a rather friendly conversation. Dom was all smiles as the young woman spoke.

Erin gave herself a mental shake. She'd done it again. Overanalyzing was going to get her nowhere. Besides, Dom's private life was none of her business.

Dom returned, smiling from ear to ear. Had he been flirting? Here at work?

"She's lovely." Erin hoped that would open a line of dialogue.

"Indeed. She's new." He restarted their walk. "As to your job as coach, based on what I've heard, I support you coming back. The girls have complained that Terry Evans pushes too hard."

Erin stopped in her tracks. Shocked to think her life might be getting back to normal, she felt lightheaded. "How's today sound?"

"Go for it. The girls will be thrilled." With a nod, Dom strode around the corner.

She breathed a sigh of relief on the way back to the basketball court. She interrupted practice again to extract a promise from the principal to call off Coach Evans. Her heart soared when the players cheered at her return.

"Why are you ladies standing around?" Erin dug out her whistle, which she'd tucked away in her bag just in case she was reinstated, and joined the team, hanging the lanyard around her neck. It was like being hugged by an old friend. "I need ten free throws from each of you. Run a lap for each one you miss."

Every player grinned from ear to ear. The chorus of "Yes, Coach" was a welcome sound. The girls ran drills and sprints and worked on defense without one complaint.

Grace McCain, one of the newer players on the team, jogged over to Erin. "I'm glad you're back."

"Thank you," Erin said, knowing how hard it must have been for the teenager to initiate contact. "It feels good to be back."

The girl shifted from one foot to the other. Her gaze seemed locked on her shoelaces. "I...I..."

Erin's heart melted. "I'm okay, Grace. If you need to talk, I'll make time for you."

The teenager lifted her head and smiled. "Thanks, Coach."

"You better get back to the drills."

"Oh," Grace said, her gaze shifting to something behind Erin. "Don't look now, but there's a stranger watching you."

Icy fingers crawled up Erin's spine. "Where is he?"

"Sitting in the stands."

"Maybe he's a college scout." Erin tried to sound convincing, hoping she was right.

"If he is, I'll play on his team." Grace's eyes sparkled. "He's hot."

Feeling a little foolish for being paranoid, Erin knew without looking who was in the stands. "He's a friend."

"Guys who look like that aren't 'friends.'"

Erin gave in to curiosity and glanced over her shoulder. The man smiled, nodded, and then removed his Western hat. Without breaking eye contact, he walked toward them.

"Who is he?" Grace asked.

"I was wrong. I have no idea." Erin had expected to see Rafe, but this man was a stranger. "Now go back to the team and let me find out what he wants." Erin didn't wait for a response. She joined the stranger where he'd stopped at the edge of the court.

Grace had been right about his looks. His sandy-colored hair was neatly trimmed, a white shirt covered his broad shoulders, and black jeans fit snugly across his trim hips. With a face structured like Matthew McConaughey's, he could've been a stand-in for the star. By the time her gaze got to his Western boots, she'd solved the riddle.

"You must be Colton Weir." Erin extended her hand.

His grip was strong and his smile wide. "Yes, ma'am. Rafe texted me where you two were going, but I haven't located him. Figured he wouldn't be too far away. Is it okay if I wait?"

"Of course, although I'm not sure my girls will pay me any attention with you in the stands."

"It appears to me that Rafe left out a lot of information about you. He failed to tell me that you're beautiful and charming."

Erin held back a laugh. Rafe had also failed to mention his partner's heavy Southern drawl. "Rafe is two doors down at the barbershop, if you'd like to join him."

Colton looked behind her. A grin spread, flashing his straight white teeth. Erin hadn't heard a ball hit the floor since they started talking. No doubt, the entire team was staring.

"Thanks for the intel. Maybe I'd better go check in with him." He put on his hat, tipped the brim with his finger, then swaggered out of sight.

Erin whirled and caught the team standing perfectly still. She clamped her hand over her mouth to keep from busting out laughing. "Okay, ladies, wipe your chins. You act as if you've never seen a handsome man." She blew her whistle and tried to get the girls' minds back on basketball.

Rafe's partner was eye candy for sure. But his looks paled in comparison to Rafe's. His olive skin, stormy gray eyes, and perfectly shaped lips won in Erin's opinion poll.

CHAPTER 14

Rafe heard the bell over the door to the barbershop jingle. He paid little attention as he paid for his haircut. The familiar voice turned him around. He and Colton had both grown up in Texas, though in different parts, and Colton spoke with a much heavier accent. Colton had grown up in Midland, where oil wells, heat, and dust were the norm. Rafe, on the other hand, had lived here, just thirty miles west of Dallas, until he'd left for college.

"Aww. He got prettied up to impress the coach next door," Colton said to no one in particular. He could mask his heavy drawl with a Jersey accent faster than you could blink.

"You made good time," Rafe said, choosing to ignore the comment about getting prettied up.

Colton nodded. "I missed the heavy traffic coming out of Dallas. Must've been luck."

"Erin told you where to find me." They walked out onto the sidewalk and headed back to the gym.

"Yeah. I watched her and the basketball team for a few minutes."

"She was coaching the girls?"

"Yeah. Why?"

"That means she's been allowed to resume her volunteer work." Rafe brought Colton up to speed on her situation with the Y.

"You could've warned me that she's the hottest thing within a three-state radius."

"I hadn't noticed," Rafe said.

"You lie."

Rafe didn't dispute it. "Let's get back to the gym. I'll leave my keys with Erin just in case something happens, which it shouldn't.

We need to be back in time for me to drive her home. You need to check in with the narcs and Linc."

"I spoke at length with Linc while I was on the road."

"Good. You already know most of what's happening. The guys at the precinct can tell you the rest."

They entered the YMCA and walked back to the basketball court. The silence unsettled Rafe's nerves. He'd expected squeaking tennis shoes and female voices.

"Hell of a lot quieter than ten minutes ago," Colton said, reading Rafe's thoughts.

Rafe increased his pace, stopping as they turned the corner. Sitting on the floor in the middle of the court, surrounded by teenage girls, Erin had never been so beautiful. The team was focused on her every word, and she was lost in the moment.

"That's the first time since I got home that I've seen her looking relaxed."

"Partner," Colton said, drawing out the word and pronouncing it as *pardner*. "Do you have history with this woman?"

"Not the kind you're thinking. We went to the same school." Rafe sat on one of the metal bench seats that sufficed for bleachers. "These damn things were built for people the size of a first-grader."

Erin's gaze lifted in his direction. She nodded then returned her attention to the team. They stood, circled her, each girl stuck one hand out, and then cheered. The girls changed shoes, grabbed their backpacks, and took the long way to the front door.

"Afternoon," Colton said as each girl passed the bleachers. His slow drawl caused pink hues to race up all but one of the girls' cheeks.

Rafe watched as she swung wide and left quickly. He'd recognized Grace. He'd spoken with her at the high school. He turned his attention back to Colton. "You made their day. Just keep in mind the average age of this team is sixteen."

"What?" Colton made an exaggerated show of folding his

arms across his chest and burying his hands in his armpits. "These girls remind me of my baby sister, which is why I was interested in helping you bust this drug supplier."

Erin stopped at the bottom of the stands. She planted both hands on her hips and scowled up at Rafe and Colton. "I may have to ban you two from practice."

"It was his fault." Rafe pointed at Colton.

Erin raised an eyebrow. "Right."

"Why are they out of school?" Colton asked.

"Teacher in-service day," Erin said. "So what's the game plan?"

"We were going to drop by and let Colton make nice with the local narcs, but if you're finished, those plans just changed."

"I'm easy. Just tell me what to do." Colton stepped down off the bleachers and waited.

"First," Rafe said to Erin, "tell me about Grace."

Erin's eyebrows rose. "How do you know her?"

"She stopped me the day I went by the school. I could tell she wanted to tell the truth, but she was just too scared."

"Her family moved from Houston at the beginning of this semester. I believe she's a good kid who got swept up by the wrong crowd."

"Is her family wealthy?"

"That's what I've heard, yes."

"That's probably why that particular group befriended her so quickly," Colton said.

"Could be." Rafe and Erin followed Colton out of the gym.

"You think Grace's money made her attractive to the other girls?" Erin asked.

"It's a good guess." Rafe stopped next to his car. "If she ponied up a little cash for drugs, it would've lifted the burden off the rest of them."

Erin shook her head. "Grace is smart and a great athlete. I'd hate to see her ruin her chances to get into a good college because of drugs."

"Maybe that's why she wanted to speak with me. We were interrupted when another girl kept calling her name, which noticeably spooked her. A few minutes later, she ran out the front door and got into a yellow sports car."

"That would be her brother's car."

"Interesting." Rafe turned to Colton. "Follow us out to the house. Then we can make a run downtown." Rafe opened Erin's door for her. "Does that work for you?"

"It does if you'll swing by my house and pick up my mail." Erin slid into the car.

Rafe drove out of the parking lot and drove toward the highway. "You'll like Colton. I wouldn't take anybody else with me to a gunfight."

"Look, I'm going back to work soon and will have to be at the Y two or three times a week. My moving to your house might not have been a good idea. We're not even sure my admirer is dangerous to me."

"Give us at least a few days to figure it out. It's safer if one of us drives you wherever you need to go."

"Won't I be the talk of the school? My own entourage of good-looking men taking turns dropping me off and picking me up. That should give the gossips something to talk about." Erin laughed.

"I'm afraid your entourage will consist of one man. Me."

"In that case, how can I refuse?"

Rafe parked in his driveway and killed the engine. "Truth be told, I'm not comfortable leaving you alone out here."

"Are you kidding?" she said on a laugh. "My whereabouts are safer than most state secrets. I have Jeff's gun, and I'll lock the door."

****

Rafe was pleased with the reception he and Colton had received during their meeting with the narcotics squad. They'd allowed Rafe to sit in unofficially and listen. The empty desks in the bullpen were indicative of the cutbacks the city had made. Rafe understood budget cuts, but he'd didn't get reducing the size of the police department. Westbrook Hills had three high schools. If drugs were a problem at one, he'd bet the other two were experiencing issues, too.

Colton had met with two detectives and their sergeant for two hours, going over interviews, drug busts, and recent arrests. The flow of narcotics had been slowed, but the main supplier was still at large. The meeting ended with the sergeant emailing the case files to Colton.

"Let's check in with Wade Beckett," Rafe said. "See if he's looked at the note left at Erin's last night." They turned right and walked down the hall to the homicide division.

"What's your take on Beckett?" Colton asked.

"He's okay. Serious. All business." Rafe walked through the open door and scanned the open space. "That's him coming out of the side office."

Wade waved, dropped a manila folder on a desk, and walked to meet them.

"Granite-faced. He must be a shitload of fun," Colton observed.

"Can't say. I haven't socialized with him."

Rafe made introductions then followed Wade back inside a small office. One chair sat across from a weathered gray metal desk, but the detective dragged one from an empty desk outside the office and let Rafe position it to suit himself. Colton remained standing, moving around the room.

"Colton. I heard you'd been temporarily assigned to the narcotics squad." Wade smiled. "I'm guessing you're going to back up Rafe, too."

"I lend a hand when it's needed." Colton's gaze was on the diploma hanging on the wall. "University of Texas at Austin," he read aloud.

"You an alumni?" Wade asked.

Colton responded by flashing the famous Hook 'em Horns sign, which consisted of a closed fist except for the index and little finger, which he waved in the air.

"Anything we learn," Rafe said, choosing not to remind them Texas A&M was, in his opinion, the better college, "we'll pass on to you. Have you studied the latest note sent to Erin?"

"I had a copy waiting for me this morning. Damn near missed it." Wade slapped a stack of paperwork. "If it had gotten buried here, it might've been days before I got to it. The lab tech left it on my chair."

"What did you make of it?" Rafe asked.

Wade stood, walked over, and closed the door. "I assume you know the killer left a message on the wall of each murdered girl." He held his hands out in the stop-don't-talk position. "Don't deny it, and don't tell me how you know. I'm fairly sure how you learned about it, so please, don't confirm it." He returned to his chair.

"We have no idea what the message said," Rafe answered honestly. "I'd like to know if it was anything like the note Erin received."

Wade shuffled around pieces of paper on his desk as if looking for something. Rafe could see the struggle behind the detective's eyes. "I intentionally kept this information away from the press. I expect you to do the same."

"You have my word," Rafe said.

"And mine," Colton said.

"The messages were written using each girl's blood. Big and bold, in all capital letters. Each read, 'You lie, you die.'"

"Shit," Colton said. "What a warning."

"And so was Erin's note," Rafe said. "Think about it. The killer and Erin's stalker are one and the same. Her note wasn't written in blood, but he made it clear that she had tested his patience. You have the proof you need. The cases are connected."

"I agree," Wade said. "The girls' lies hurt Erin. Maybe their actions were the impetus this bastard needed to crawl out of the woodwork."

"Maybe he already had Erin on the radar, and the girls interfered," Rafe said, pleased not to have to argue his idea. "Now we just have to figure out who he is."

****

Casanova emptied his shopping bag. He wrapped the nylon rope around his palms and pulled hard. This would be easy to handle and wouldn't harm Erin's skin. A camping toilet and refrigerator were the best he could do without raising suspicions. She'd just have to make do. He hoped putting her in the safe room long term wouldn't be necessary. This was just until she realized she was safe and with him. She'd quickly come around when she realized how much he'd done for her.

He hoped those men hanging around her hadn't confused her. Mixed up her thinking. Made her doubt her love for him.

Concentrating on anything except Erin was getting more difficult by the day. His heart ached to be with her, and he knew she felt the same way.

He went upstairs and showered before carrying the white wedding gown to the safe room. He wrapped his arms around the lace bodice, closed his eyes, and then swayed to the music drifting down from upstairs. His body ached for the real woman rather than this empty dress, so he carefully spread the gown across the foot of the small cot he'd installed. Then he went upstairs and closed and locked the storm shelter door. He pressed the new carpet and molding back in place. To the unsuspecting eye, the carpet would appear to be properly installed.

Soon, he'd bring his bride home. She'd prove to him that the room had been a waste of time. Then it would become a shelter to protect them during bad weather.

He had to see her. A quick look to ensure she was okay would suffice. He hopped into his SUV and drove by her house. The man who'd been hanging around Erin was getting her mail out of her mailbox. And who was the new guy driving the pickup? A stranger. His lunch rebelled, forcing its way up the back of his throat.

A horn sounded, snapping Casanova out of his rage. He jerked his steering wheel to the right, swerving and barely missing an oncoming car.

Keeping her under surveillance presented problems, but he had no choice. He'd take her home with him as soon as the situation presented itself. In the meantime, he wouldn't tolerate any more men hanging around.

Good thing the house on the corner was still empty.

****

"Crazy bastard," Colton muttered as two cars barely missed having a head-on collision.

"Lucky bastard. He was inches from meeting his maker." Rafe dropped Erin's mail on the front seat of Colton's pickup. "We don't have to wait until school is in session to talk with these kids. In fact, they might be quicker to open up away from their friends."

"Pick one. My new GPS system will guide us."

Rafe studied the list for a minute before he programmed an address into the truck's computer.

"There you go," Rafe said while the vehicle's brain calculated directions. "You saw Grace McCain at the YMCA. I loaded her address."

"Ah, the girl who avoided us," Colton said.

"She ran with the two dead girls. Probably scared shitless. I didn't get the sense she was using. That's not saying she doesn't. She just wasn't high the day I met her."

Colton slowed for the upcoming turn, taking a right into a new neighborhood on the outskirts of town.

Rafe scanned the area. "All this is new. Wasn't here when I

left."

Colton let out a low whistle. "The gardeners probably make more money than we do. Bet there's a riding mower in every shed."

Rafe chuckled. "Big houses. Big lots. We're talking serious money here."

A horseshoe driveway led to a two-story house set toward the back of the property. All dark brick and glass, with thick green shrubs and no flowers, the house came across as cold and distant to Rafe. The outside projected an image of wealth. Wealth without welcome or warmth.

Colton parked in front of the house. "Let's go see if the natives are friendly."

Rafe waited while Colton put on his hat and clipped his badge to his belt. They walked up the few steps, but before they could ring the bell, the door opened. Grace, still wearing her gym warm-ups, stood wide-eyed.

"What are you doing here?" she asked.

"I thought it might be easier if we talked today instead of tomorrow on school grounds." Rafe could almost smell the fear rolling off her. "If you'd rather have one of your parents with you, we'll wait here."

"My mom and dad are out of the country. They both travel a lot. Why do you need to talk to me anyway?" The defiant tone in her voice indicated she'd calmed down a little.

"Look, Grace, we don't want to get you in trouble, but you were friends with two girls who were brutally murdered. The FBI is helping sort this out, and you need to tell us what you know." Rafe was being very formal for a reason. She'd clammed up on him once. He didn't want her to think she could get away with that again. He decided to soften his approach. "Grace, Erin Brady says you're a good kid, and we trust her judgment. It would help if you extended us the same courtesy."

"Drive your truck around back. I'll meet you by the pool."

Grace closed the door.

"Okay," Colton said, spinning on his boot heel and heading to the truck.

Rafe got in, closed the door, and turned to his partner. "Let's see what the young lady has to say."

CHAPTER 15

Grace was perched on the edge of a lounge chair, waiting. Based on her body language, she looked like a bird about to take flight. Her face showed a layer of panic even an unseasoned agent would've seen. Rafe cut a glance at Colton as they sat in chairs across from her. Yeah. He'd noticed it, too.

"Grace, I'm Colton Weir," Colton said, getting straight to business. "Rafe here? He's one of the good guys. He cares enough about you kids to want the drugs and the dealers off the street."

Rafe watched as her shoulders relaxed. He knew what was coming. She didn't. Colton's smile disappeared.

"Me, on the other hand? Not so much." The warmth in Colton's voice had turned cold. "My job is to send that drug dealer to prison. I don't want the jerk who sells a small bag on the corner. I want the supplier. So together, Rafe and I make a good team. Understand?"

Grace nodded, her gaze locked on her feet.

Rafe leaned closer. "Tell us about Penny. Who her friends were."

"I don't know much about her. She wasn't friendly toward me until my brother dropped me off at school. She was standing next to my car door before he got stopped. Acted as if we were old friends. That was the day I became part of her group."

"He drives a fancy sports car," Rafe said, drawing her attention from her feet to his face.

"Yes. How did you know?" she asked.

"Where is your brother?" Rafe turned in his chair and glanced toward the house. "Is he here?"

"Bradley went back to college. He only comes home on

weekends. He's the smart kid in the family." The resentment lacing her words chilled the air.

"We get it. You've never measured up," Colton said. "Lots of us take a backseat to a sibling. We don't sit around and shoot that shit into our system. Tell us where you got the drugs."

"I don't use drugs and don't know what you're talking—"

"Don't lie to us," Rafe said. "We know the truth. We need to know who sold them to you." Damn, they needed a break on this case. Grace could give it to them. Her chest rose and air whooshed from her lungs. A sign of surrender? Rafe hoped so. "Back up and start with who you and Penny hung out with."

"Penny didn't include me in everything. After we'd hung out a few weeks, she asked me if I could get to any of my parents' drugs. She said all the popular kids were doing some sort of junk."

"What did you give her?" Rafe prompted when she fell silent.

"A few hydrocodone pills. When Mom and Dad travel, they take their meds with them. Penny was okay with me not bringing her drugs as long as I had cash when she needed it."

"After you gave her money, who did she contact?" Rafe asked.

"I don't know. Every now and then, she'd collect names and cash. The next day she'd meet everybody behind the field house and pass out the drugs. I only went with her a couple of times."

"Why'd you stop?" Colton asked.

"My mom and dad keep a tight control on my spending. The minute Penny found out I wasn't flush with cash, she started leaving me out." Grace stood. "Are we done?"

"Soon as you tell me a little about Melanie Summers," Rafe said. "Is she going to be helpful?"

"No. She's too smart. She warned me not to talk to the cops or we might wind up like Penny and Sara." Her hand went to her chest, covering her heart. She was frightened. A little girl trying to be tough.

"Then you do know something." Colton took that aggressive tone again.

"Only what I told you." Grace walked to the edge of the swimming pool.

Rafe and Colton joined her. "Then they're still buying? The deaths didn't slow the deliveries down?"

"Not from what I've heard."

"Who is collecting money now that Penny is gone?" Rafe asked.

"I don't know. I swear."

Colton stepped closer to her. He leaned down and got next to her ear. "I don't completely buy your innocence. You're lying and withholding information. When I can prove it, I'll be back."

"Now's not the time to hold back." Rafe gave her one more chance to talk but was met with silence. "You still have my card?" She nodded. "Call if you need to talk."

He and Colton walked around the house past the immaculately groomed landscape and got into the truck. Rafe and Nick had shared the responsibility for keeping the shrubs trimmed and lawn mowed when they were kids. Voicing an objection had resulted in extra duties being piled on. So they'd bitched and moaned amongst themselves. Didn't seem like such a big job now.

"Where to now?" Colton asked, driving out of the neighborhood.

"Hang on." Rafe looked up an address. "Turn right at the next street. Melanie Summers lives directly behind Grace. Let's pay her a visit."

Colton jockeyed the truck into a U-turn, and within a couple of minutes, he'd parked in front of a Southern plantation-looking house. "Wish I'd been the construction contractor on a few of these houses."

They stepped onto the brick sidewalk and made their way to the expansive porch, where Rafe rang the doorbell. The door opened, and a fortyish Latina woman filled the space with her short, sturdy body. Her hair had been pulled back into a knot, and she wore a simple blue dress with dark shoes. Her thick soles indicated she spent a lot of time on her feet.

"We don't want what you're selling," she said behind tightly drawn lips.

Rafe held out his identification for her inspection. "We're here to speak with Melanie."

She studied the ID then raised her gaze to meet his. "I don't think her parents would approve."

"Would you rather we call for a patrol car?" Rafe looked around the neighborhood. "I'll have them pick up Melanie and drive her to the station where she can wait until her parents arrive or arrange for an attorney for her."

The woman hesitated but then stepped back, waving them inside. "Stay here." She turned and hurried up the staircase.

Colton picked up a vase and studied it. Light reflected off the glass, giving it a slight glow. He carefully returned it to its place. "Shit," he whispered. "The furniture here in the foyer cost more than everything in my house put together.

A girl strolled down the staircase. She wore skin-hugging blue jeans shorts and a form-fitting tank top. Jet-black hair had been shaved to the scalp over her left ear, but the rest hung past her right shoulder and covered her eye. The blank expression on her face told Rafe that she wasn't happy with their presence.

"What do you want?" she said.

"We'd like to ask you a few questions about Penny and Sara," Rafe said.

"Talking got them killed. I have nothing to say."

"That's harsh." Colton stepped closer to her. "They were your friends."

"He's right," Rafe said. "Don't make this any harder than it has to be." Something moved to Rafe's left. He looked but saw nothing. He'd have bet money someone had been listening. Maybe the housekeeper was keeping tabs on Melanie. "Would you rather speak with us at the police station? You choose."

She turned and walked away, stopping after a few steps to turn to motion them to join her. "We can talk in the living room."

Melanie sat on the oversized couch with her bare feet pulled under her. She tucked her hair behind her ear and leveled her gaze at Rafe. "If the killer knows I talked to you, he'll come here. I don't want to die."

"Nobody else knows that Agent Weir or I are here. So I think you're safe answering our questions. First, you need to understand that if you're addicted to heroin, we can get you help, but there's no way to keep your parents out of it."

"I'm not an addict."

"That's good," Colton said with a doubtful shrug. "Tell us who sells you drugs."

"And be dead by morning? Even if I knew, I wouldn't tell you. We never cared enough to find out his name."

Again, Rafe caught movement off to his left. "Who is we? Is it Grace?"

Melanie met his gaze with a blank stare. Rafe walked to one of the chairs and sat.

"Yes." Grace entered the room, walked straight to her friend, and curled up next to her on the couch.

Colton slid to the edge of his chair and locked gazes with Grace. "I gotta give it to you. You're good. I bought your innocent act. Once. Don't try it again." He rose and paced a couple of steps. His jaw was set tight when he turned to face the girls. "You answer our questions, or I'll have your asses hauled to juvenile detention. You can stay there until we contact your parents and have them join us."

Damn, Rafe liked to watch his partner in action. And for once, Rafe was getting to be the good guy. He smiled what he thought would be a comforting expression. "Let's begin again. I'll start by promising that no one has to know what you tell us." He paused to let that sink in. "That's if we can gather proof that will stand up in a court of law without your testimony."

Melanie said, "There's a back road into the city baseball fields. Be there Friday right after dark. You'll see who passes out the drugs and who buys them." She glanced at Grace and then folded her arms across her chest. "We're done talking."

Rafe held her gaze for a minute before he stood. "Good enough."

He and Colton walked to the door. As they exited, Rafe glanced back and both girls were watching. Neither had moved.

Colton drove away from the property, got Linc on the phone and filled him in on the visit with Grace and Melanie. "I'll keep an eye on the girls tonight," Colton said. "If they leave, it might be interesting to see where they go."

"That's not a bad idea. They could lead you to somebody important."

Colton pulled onto the freeway. The quick acceleration of the pickup shifted Erin's mail, sliding it next to Rafe's leg. He dropped his hand on an envelope. He'd grown too fond of her too quick.

"Where to?" Colton asked. "Back to your place?"

Rafe nodded. "Yeah. Take I-22 west. We should check on Erin."

"Any idea where to start looking for her stalker?"

"Hell, no. Wait until you see the list of men she's friendly with—not dated—just those she knows." Rafe's stomach growled. "Let's grab a sack of burgers. I'll ask Linc to join us. Maybe you can talk him into sharing surveillance duties with you."

"Shouldn't you call your girl and ask what she wants to eat?" A grin spread across Colton's face.

"What are you?" The top of Rafe's ears burned, which pissed him off. "Still in high school? Erin is not my girl."

"Easy," Colton said. "I'm finding that hard to believe. I know you. Careful, or I'll think you've mellowed."

Rafe's head almost spun around backward. Mellowed? That was the worst thing an agent could do. Even worse, he'd felt a shift in his emotions this morning. Holding Erin in his arms had opened a part of him he'd intentionally kept buried. Affection. He actually cared about her.

"What's really bugging you?" Colton asked.

"I wish the hell I knew." The answer had been the best Rafe could do. That Erin had awakened emotions inside him, emotions he didn't know how to explain, wasn't up for discussion. He had to keep his focus. Keep his wheels on the ground. If he and Erin had sex, and he hoped they did, he had to keep his perspective.

"You know I was joking about getting mellow. I was trying to get a rise out of you."

"You succeeded." Rafe texted Linc, who agreed to come to the house. "Take the next exit. There used to be a mom-and-pop burger place at the bottom of the ramp."

****

Erin heard the engine rumble down Rafe's driveway. By the time she made it to the door, he and his partner were coming up the sidewalk. Her heart did a funny flutter. What the heck? She tried to turn away but failed. Nothing good could come from drooling or daydreaming about Rafe Sirilli. Her feet seemed to have taken root, rendering her brain's command to turn away useless. His long muscular legs covered the space between them in mere seconds. A smile lifted the corners of his mouth, but his face wore a troubled expression.

She opened the door and let him and Colton pass. "Something smells good."

The taut lines around Rafe's mouth relaxed. "We brought lunch."

Before she could speak, the sacks were whisked from Rafe's hand, and Colton was headed for the dining room. He glanced at her over his shoulder. "I hope you're not one of those health nuts who doesn't eat meat or fats."

"Ignore him," Rafe said with a laugh. "Colton loses his Southern charm if he gets too hungry." Rafe scooped a sack from the table, removed a burger and fries, then handed the rest to her. "Hide this, will you? I invited Linc to join us."

"Do we have to wait for him?" Colton helped himself to a french fry before backing away from the table. "I just wanted to make sure the fries were hot."

"He should be here any second." Erin bit back a smile when Rafe's forehead furrowed. He was curious as to how she knew that tidbit of information. "He was at home, so he called to see if I needed anything from my house. I asked him to grab my briefcase."

"How'd he get inside?" Rafe asked. "Don't tell me you still keep a spare key hidden under the flower pot by the door." The furrows between his eyes deepened.

"No, silly. I moved it after Jeff used it to let you inside. It's in a baggie and taped underneath the wheelbarrow in the backyard."

"You hide your house key under a wheelbarrow?" Colton grinned.

"I do now." They were teasing her, but she felt the need to defend herself. "I bought it at a yard sale and repurposed it into a flower bed."

"Flower pot." Rafe held out his hands, palms up, and pretended to be weighing something. "Wheelbarrow. They're the same thing to a thief."

"This isn't Dallas or Fort Worth. A lot of residents don't lock their doors at all."

"All I have to say is Linc had better hurry. I've had my share of cold burgers and soggy fries over the years. Not my favorite meal." Colton leaned over the dining table, nabbed another fry, and popped it into his mouth. The corners of his mouth turned downward. "Let's eat."

"I'll see what's keeping him." Erin picked up her cell and dialed Linc's number. The call went to voice mail. "He's not answering."

CHAPTER 16

Casanova's vision blurred. The trembling of his hands matched the volcano about to erupt inside his head.

Why was Erin doing this? Hadn't he proved himself? Passed test after test, demonstrating his love again and again? Still, she flaunted these men in front of him. Why had they picked up her mail?

And now Linc? Casanova had known the bastard was going to be trouble the minute they'd met. Linc had parked in front of her garage and was headed around behind her house. What was going on inside? Casanova dropped the binoculars and ran. Taking action in the daylight was dangerous, but exposing himself was a risk he had to take.

With no weapon, no plan, and only anger to fuel him, he boldly crossed the street and rushed to her backyard. The door was standing wide open, and Linc had picked up Erin's briefcase. Casanova ran inside, snatched a trophy off the bookcase and swung, hitting the bastard from behind. The top of the trophy broke off its base.

The neighbor staggered, lost his balance, and fell. His head made a soft thud on the carpet. He pushed himself up on his elbow. Panic rushed through Casanova. He couldn't be allowed to live. The heavy marble base of the broken trophy lay at his feet. He grabbed it and swung again. He continued until one side of the bastard's head and face looked like ground meat.

Linc lay still as death. A buzzing sound came from his pocket. Someone was calling, but there was no one to answer.

Where was Erin? Casanova raced through the house, searching. Empty. What did this mean? Where was she? Worse yet, who was she with?

Satisfied another bad influence had been permanently removed from Erin's life, Casanova planned his escape route. He'd taken a huge risk by walking across the street and had no intention of doing it again. He wet two kitchen towels and washed blood spatters off his face, neck, arms, and hands. The same towels were used to wrap up the pieces of the trophy. Careful not to touch anything, and thankful for the dark shirt he wore, he held the towels against his chest, left through the backyard, and took the long way back to his car.

There wasn't a twinge of regret in his heart. This death was not his fault. He'd killed the two girls and the reporter because they'd wronged Erin, but the neighbor's death rested solely on Erin's shoulders.

Now, he had to find Erin.

****

"I hate that we ate without Linc." Erin dropped her napkin in the empty burger sack.

"He wouldn't expect us to wait," Rafe said. "Agents and cops get used to eating cold food and leftovers."

"Amen to that." Colton slid his chair back from the table.

"Won't be the first meal he's missed." Rafe opened the refrigerator door. "Who wants another beer?"

"I do, but I'd better not." Colton's gaze caught hers. "He's right. It doesn't matter which brand of law enforcement you work for, you're going to miss a few meals. Spouses get used to eating alone."

"I'll take one. You're not telling me anything I didn't know," she said, using her most pleasant tone. "My adopted dad is a retired deputy sheriff."

"So I heard." Colton leaned forward and snagged a leftover fry.

Rafe set two beers on the table and leaned back in his chair.

"I'm left to assume I was the topic of conversation since you two stopped talking altogether when I joined you." His grin sent her heart tumbling.

"Not to burst your vanity bubble," Colton said, "but we were talking about different branches of law enforcement."

"That's right," she agreed. "I was just going to ask Colton what made him choose the law as a career."

"Not a topic for the dinner table." Colton's blue eyes deepened to almost navy.

Erin decided not to push the subject. "Then one of you can tell me what you learned from interviewing Grace and Melanie." A shield dropped across Rafe's face as he glanced at his partner. "I'm not asking you to reveal evidence. Just tell me if the girls are okay."

"Colton's going to keep an eye on them tonight." Rafe checked his watch.

"School's back in session tomorrow," she said. "You'll know where they are part of the time."

"Have you heard when you're going back to work?" Rafe's eyes softened, indicating his understanding of how important being reinstated was to her.

"Nothing yet." They sat in an awkward silence for a few minutes, but Erin sensed Rafe getting edgy. He'd checked his watch a couple of times in the span of five minutes. "Want me to call Linc again?"

"No." Rafe tilted the can and finished his beer. "Colton wanted to share surveillance duties with him."

"I spotted the perfect place to watch the entrance to the girls' neighborhood. If they leave, I'm on them." Colton stood and looked directly at Rafe. "You start feeling bad about me being there all night"—he flashed a brilliant smile—"bring me some coffee."

Rafe grunted or scoffed, she couldn't tell which, but it was some kind of communication between the two men, because they both laughed. He walked Colton to the edge of the sidewalk. Erin followed, stopping on the porch.

"You be caref—" Rafe said.

"Yes, Mom," Colton said, sliding behind the steering wheel of his pickup. "I'm thinking this could be fun. It's been awhile since I was on a stakeout without having to entertain you."

"As if," Rafe said, retreating to stand beside Erin.

****

Colton's gaze swept across the house and lawn before returning to meet Rafe's. "I can see you growing up here. Small town, close friends, neighborhood cookouts, and Friday night football."

He backed out of the driveway, leaving no time for Rafe to comment. Actually, Colton had sized up the place pretty well. How was a mystery. He hadn't been exposed to what Rafe would call normal family life. In fact, Colton had had a shitty childhood. Raised by his grandparents, he'd grown up in a particularly rough neighborhood in Houston. Football had bought him a ticket to college, and he'd made the most of his time at school. Not only was Colton street-smart, but he was intelligent as hell. He might dress and talk country, but it was a mistake to think him stupid.

Erin's hand slid up Rafe's back, spreading heat as she went. "Is everything okay?"

"Yeah." He caught her hand and pulled her closer to him. She molded herself against his body, fitting like a well-made glove. A combination of need and lust rushed through him, sending his blood south. That she drew such a quick reaction from him was scary as hell. "Better now that you're standing so close."

"I didn't mean to pressure Colton when I asked why he decided to go into law enforcement."

"You didn't."

"I made him uncomfortable. It was like a glacier formed behind his eyes."

Rafe wasn't sure about sharing too much of his partner's personal information with her, so he decided to keep things brief.

"Colton had a rough childhood. I don't know all of it, but his stepfather was abusive. Colton's mother had moved out and filed for divorce when his stepfather killed her and Colton's little sister and shot Colton."

"How horrible." Erin patted her chest. Sorrow filled her voice.

"Bastard committed suicide thinking he'd killed the entire family. Colton survived."

Erin buried her face in Rafe's neck. "I won't mention his past again."

"That's best. We'd worked together a long time before he told me."

"How long have you two been partners?"

"Forever." Rafe laughed. He pulled Erin under his arm and led her back to the house. "Three years in real time." He held the door open, allowing her to enter. He immediately missed the sensation of her body touching his. "I wouldn't want anyone else watching my back."

Erin walked to the stack of open boxes that he'd set to the side. She lifted the flaps and peered inside. "I worry that you talked to Grace and Melanie. Do you think they're in danger?"

"I wish I had a good answer for you. If whoever is selling the drugs learns they spoke with us, they might try to shut them up. Lucky for us, their neighborhood is gated. There's only one road in and out, which isn't uncommon for houses of that value. Colton will monitor the vehicles going in and out."

"Good." She pulled out a worn baseball glove and ran her fingers across the weathered leather. "Packing away all these memories must be hard."

"Not really." Her expression said she knew he lied. "I kept all that stuff for Luke. I left the cartons open so he could go through them. He'll want to keep some things even if they have to go into storage."

"When will he get home?"

"He's coming off his last assignment."

"And you're relieved."

"Hell, yeah. Those special ops guys pull some scary-as-shit missions."

"He won't be your baby brother any longer."

"He wasn't the last time I saw him. Jesus, the kid had almost caught up with me."

She replaced the glove, removed a school yearbook, and opened it. A few seconds later, her gaze lifted and met his. "This is yours."

Rafe put on his best puzzled look and challenged her. "Are you sure?" He knew the answer. Just didn't want to get into another conversation about the old days.

She raised an eyebrow. "The people who signed the book addressed their comments to you." She moved to the couch, sat, and kicked off her shoes. "Did you keep anything for yourself?"

"A couple of small things." Her counselor background was about to get her in trouble. She was asking too many personal questions. Maybe the truth would stop her before she got started advising him on regrets. "I don't have room in my life or apartment for a lot of extras."

Her head recoiled as if he'd slapped her.

Damn. That had sounded a lot harsher than he'd intended. But he'd spoken the truth, and he'd stand by what he said.

In the blink of an eye, she recovered. A knowing smile slid across her face. "Wow. I believe I found a raw nerve."

He smiled back at her. "Are you looking for a fight?"

"Me? I'm constantly looking for ways to avoid trouble. It's becoming a full-time job." The corners of her mouth lifted. "Sounds like a very lonely existence to me."

"I've made peace with how I live."

"It's your life." She dropped the yearbook into the box and

patted the spot next to her on the couch.

She didn't have to ask twice. He sat next to her. Her scent shot through him like floodwater over a dam. He fought the urge to nuzzle her neck and inhale the soft scent that was uniquely hers. Shifting his weight did little to relieve his growing erection. This case of lust was going to kill him.

"You should keep some of your dad's things. Rent a storage space if you have to, but someday, you'll have kids who will want to know about their family." She turned toward him, lifted her hand, and rubbed at the frown line between his eyes. "Oh, stop scowling. I'm not fishing, hinting, or trying to change your thoughts about marriage. I just don't want you to have any regrets."

He pulled her hand to his mouth and kissed her fingers. "I have plenty of them already."

"Are you talking about Nick? His death wasn't your fault. You must know that."

"I do." He pulled one of her fingers into his mouth and ran his tongue around the tip. Her pupils dilated, and her nostrils flared a fraction as she took in a deep breath. "We don't have time to list all my regrets, but you're right at the top."

"Really?" A small lift at the corners of her mouth sent his blood pressure through the roof. "How so?"

"Yep. You've always had this strange pull on my libido." He moved quickly, lifting her and pulling her across his legs, then turning her so she straddled his thighs. "I wish I had had a dollar for every hard-on you caused."

"Really?" Her eyes sparkled with mischief. "Why didn't you do something about it?"

He pushed a fallen strand of hair off her cheek. "Maybe because you hated me?" She relaxed, easing herself down onto his thighs.

"That's true enough."

"And I was leaving at the end of the year. You already

thought I was a dick. I guess I didn't want to prove you right by making a move on you then disappearing. Besides, I figured you'd kill me if I tried anything."

"There was that possibility."

Rafe swallowed the questions her answer had stirred up. Like, why had she been living under a bridge? What had happened to turn her into a runaway? He'd hold those questions for another time. Right now, his thoughts were on the rotation of her hips and the effect she was having on his erection.

"You know," he said, sliding his hand under her ponytail, tracing the bare skin on the back of her neck. "We can eliminate one of my regrets right here, right now." Her shiver was all the invitation he needed. One tug, and her lips met his.

Without breaking the kiss, he slipped an arm around her waist and pulled her closer. Now his erection not only strained against his zipper, it pressed into the softness at the juncture of her thighs.

A soft moan vibrated through her chest into his. Her hands cupped the back of his head as she took control, sweeping her tongue inside his mouth. Oh, yeah. Erin had grown up. She'd become bolder, more sure of herself, and Rafe liked her this way.

"Rafe?" She leaned her head back and whispered into his lips.

"Hmm?" He hoped her next question wasn't a tough one.

"I won't break." Her lips grazed his.

"And that's a good thing." He bunched the edge of her blouse, pulling it off in one motion, then ran his index finger over the tops of her creamy breasts. "Because I have unfinished business with you."

Before he could blink, she'd unhooked her bra and peeled it off her shoulders. His eyes feasted on her beauty before he lowered his head and took one delicious nipple in his mouth. Her back bowed, offering him better access to her delicate flesh. Her soft sighs swept him deeper and deeper into a world where only the two of them existed. He wanted her to call out his name. Wanted her to need his body as badly as he needed hers. Wanted this day to never end.

Erin's hand tugged at his shirt. She pressed her hands against his chest, forcing him to tear himself away from her rigid nipples.

"Sit back and be still for a minute." Her mouth was firm, but her eyes danced with mischief.

"Yes, ma'am." He liked this aggressive side of her. If she wanted control, he'd gladly give her the reins. This time anyway. Rafe leaned back against the couch and dropped his hands to his sides.

Half of his shirt was tucked in and half out. Her long slender fingers finished pulling the cloth from his jeans and then went to work on the buttons. The urge to help sent his blood boiling through his veins, but she appeared to be enjoying herself, so he watched the rapid rise and fall of her breasts as she worked.

"Lean forward." Her words had been barely audible. Mission accomplished, she tossed his shirt on top of her blouse. Her hands smoothed across his shoulders up to his neck, then glided down his chest. Her index finger drew a circle. "You didn't have this"—she gave the hair a slight tug—"back in school." Her gaze traveled over him, laying down a trail of napalm. "I like it."

"How do you know what I had or didn't have back then?" His skin sizzled under the warmth of her touch. Could she get any more sensuous? He didn't think so.

"You ran track. I watched you change shirts."

"You pervert." His hands had been empty too long. He remedied that by cupping her breasts in his palms and stroking her nipples with his thumbs.

"Hmm." Her eyelids fluttered closed, and her hips gyrated in that slow, insistent rotation again. "In fact, you were always the beautiful one," she said without opening her eyes.

"I'm calling bullshit on that." Rafe huffed out his denial.

She looked straight at him with one brow raised in defiance. "Go ahead. It doesn't make me wrong." The impish sparkle in her eyes shimmered.

"You want to see true beauty?"

He moved his hands to her backside, grabbed hold, and stood. Before he could tell her to hang on, her legs had wrapped around his hips, and she had his earlobe in her teeth. Shit, his knees weakened. He carried her to his bedroom, stopping in front of the dresser. He gently put her feet on the floor where she was facing the mirror. Standing behind her, he slowly peeled down her pants, kissing her from her waist to the backs of her thighs as he went.

"Rafe," she murmured.

"Shh." He turned her into his arms and covered her lips with his, sweeping his tongue in to sample her sweetness. Her hands tugged at his jeans, but he stopped her. "Not yet."

He faced her toward the mirror again, easing her lacy beige panties down and tossing them aside. "What you see in the mirror is beautiful." His hands held her breasts as if they were fine china, tenderly stroking her nipples until they were red and firm.

"You're embarrassing me."

"Your body is nothing to be embarrassed about. Surely, some man has told you how gorgeous you are."

"Not like this."

His hands skimmed lower, feeling her stomach muscles clench as he slipped even farther down past the soft curls. She spread her legs slightly, leaned her head back against his chest and closed her eyes.

"Keep your eyes open." Rafe slipped his finger inside her wet heat. She rocked against him, while her gaze seemed locked on his movements. When her knees relaxed, he wrapped his free hand around her waist to hold her steady, but didn't let up on the pressure on her core. "Your face is the most erotic thing I've ever seen. It's beauty defined."

Her breathing got faster and heavier. Her heated gaze met his. "You're going to make me come."

Rafe abandoned her sweet spot long enough to take her hand and place it between her legs, covering it with his. "Show me."

Together, they found a rhythm, circling her clit, his hand on hers, until she stiffened and gasped. Taking the cue, Rafe plunged their fingers deep inside her just as her inner muscles clenched and spasmed.

The corners of her mouth curved, and she arched her back like a cat. Sweat beads formed across Rafe's forehead. Her cry at release and her limp body against his just about sent him over the edge. He held her there, allowing her to tumble back to earth in her own time.

She lifted her gaze to his. "Inside me."

"Great idea." He swept her into his arms, walked to the bed, and carefully deposited her. When he started to join her, she stopped him by lifting her finger. Lying there with her legs slightly spread, her bare breasts begging to be kissed… Hell, he'd have moved a mountain if she asked.

"Not with all those clothes on. Lose the jeans and underwear."

God, he couldn't get out of his clothes fast enough. He fumbled a condom from his wallet and tossed it to her.

CHAPTER 17

Erin made no attempt to keep the smile from spreading across her face. She'd left her inhibitions on the floor in front of the mirror. Now, she felt no discomfort staring at Rafe's bare shoulders, muscular chest, or narrow waist.

But those features weren't what she found mesmerizing. His erection, jutting toward the ceiling, throbbing and beautiful, drew her attention. She couldn't pull her gaze away as he moved over her. She had to touch him. Reached for him, but he moved just out of reach.

"No fair."

"You touch me right now, and things will be over way too soon." His eyes gleamed with desire as he captured her hands, leaned forward, and kissed her.

Her bones melted into the mattress as his lips demanded and took everything she could give him. She buried her hands in his hair and held him to her, showing him how much she wanted him. Her heart pinched when he moved to her neck and nipped his way to her breasts, gently taking one and then the other into his mouth.

Way down deep, an ache blossomed. A need to hold him in her arms forever worked its way through her body as sure as blood flowed through her veins. She couldn't let the spark of affection she'd carried for Rafe all these years get out of hand. The last thing she needed was to fall in love with him.

He caught her hands and pulled them over her head and under the bottom bar of her brass headboard. "Don't move."

Tension balled between her thighs. The ache in her core turned to a throb, a need almost painful.

Rafe shouldered her thighs open wider and lowered his head. His fingers parted her outer lips, and he stroked her with his tongue.

Erin was lost in sensations. She lifted her hips, seeking more of the release his mouth offered, surrendering herself completely as he drove her higher and higher. The wave hit her rapidly, sending every fiber into convulsions. Her brain shut down, and nothing existed but the two of them. Tears filled her eyes, but she held them back, fearing he'd misunderstand.

His hand was splayed across her stomach as if to keep her from floating away, which she might have had he not been holding her in place. He placed small kisses in a trail up her body while she regained her senses.

"I could make love to you forever." His smile was that of a man who knew he'd pleased a woman. "You're so responsive."

She reached for him, pulling him in for a kiss and tasting herself as his tongue swept inside. "I respond to you," she uttered a confession. "I need you inside me."

Rafe retrieved the condom from the nightstand and laid back. Before he could open the package, she had to touch him. Had to feel his hardness in her hand. She wrapped her fingers around him, sliding her fingers up and down. His moan pulled her gaze up to meet his. Dark smoldering eyes were watching her every move. She squeezed. He groaned then leaned up and captured her mouth with his. Hot and needy. Deep and demanding. They matched each other's passion. Both were breathless when he broke away and ripped open the packet.

"You do it," he said, handing the condom to her.

"My pleasure." She spoke the truth, enjoying every second. When she'd covered him, he lifted her on top. She opened her thighs around his hips.

"You're in the driver's seat."

Erin placed the tip of his penis at her entrance. Sliding down slowly, she enveloped him inch by inch, pausing to allow her body to adjust to his size, until she'd taken all of him. She stilled for a moment, savoring the fullness their being joined gave her. Then she started a slow ride, leaning forward so her body was aligned perfectly.

He thrust hard, sinking even deeper, pushing farther into her body. Soon, they were in sync, moving together as if they'd been made for each other.

Her orgasm surprised her, rising more quickly than she'd expected. Nerve endings screamed for release, pushing her closer and closer. Rafe's hand slipped between them and found her most sensitive spot. As he rubbed in circles, his gaze locked with hers.

"Let go, baby. Let go," he said softly. "I'll come with you."

Her heart seemed to shatter in a million pieces as every part of her system rocketed to a place she'd never been. She wanted to laugh. Wanted to cry. Wanted not to be in love with Rafe Sirilli. She collapsed on his chest.

Sweaty and satisfied, her cheek resting on his shoulder, they lay in silence for a long time.

"God." She mustered the one word.

"You can still call me Rafe," he said with a chuckle, kissing the top of her head.

"Smartass. I was just about to give you a compliment, but now you get nothing." She laughed with him.

"You're wrong there. I got it all."

Every fiber of her being had turned to rubber. Satiated, content, and at peace with the world, she rolled off Rafe, waiting while he disposed of the condom, then cuddled up beside him. He snuggled her against his chest and smoothed her hair off her face before kissing her on the forehead.

She was on the edge of sleep when he spoke. "I'm glad you got to know Dad. I called when I could, but that wasn't a lot. Did you know he had heart problems?"

The tenderness and anguish in his voice were agony to hear, but that he'd opened up to her gave her hope. "No. Jeff had no idea either. Your dad's heart attack was a shock to everybody."

"Dad never wanted to appear weak or soft. Not even in front of family. He didn't tolerate it in his boys either. Nick felt like he was a constant disappointment to the old man."

"That was a lot of pressure—"

Rafe's cell buzzed from somewhere on the floor. His chest rose and fell with a big sigh. "I'd better get that."

Their moment of intimacy was over. Erin moved off his shoulder. Rafe pulled his jeans onto the bed and fished out his phone. She'd cling to the memory of today. It would be her lifeline, a piece of Rafe to hold in her heart after he returned to his first love. The FBI.

"I'll check it out." In one motion, he returned the cell to his pocket and slipped on his jeans.

"What's wrong?" Erin stood, sliding on her panties while he dressed.

Rafe zipped his jeans and reached for his shirt. "Maybe nothing. That was Jeff. He drove by your house and saw a car in the driveway."

"We forgot about Linc." She continued to dress. "But he shouldn't still be there."

****

A pinch of regret hit Rafe when she pulled her blouse across her breasts and started buttoning it. He walked around the foot of the bed to her, leaned down, looped his arms around her waist, and rested his forehead against hers. "Things ended a little too abruptly for my liking. I didn't get the chance to tell you how wonderful you are."

"We did okay for a first time." She moved away, flashed an impish grin, and finished dressing. "I'll call Linc."

Rafe grabbed his socks and shoes, then followed her to the living room. A glance at his watch sent a chill of concern up his back. In reality, Linc should have interrupted their lovemaking. That she had to leave a message sent off mental alarms.

"I'll head over. He might've forgotten something and ran next door to his house. I wouldn't have moved the car either."

"I'm coming with you," she said with conviction.

The set of her jaw made him think she used that face on the teenagers at school. "Save that I'm-the-boss look for your students. No way was I leaving you here alone."

"Let me brush my hair." She darted out of the room before he could respond.

"Good idea," he said to no one. Taking her cue, he went to the guest bath, splashed cold water on his face, then ran his hands through his hair. He glanced in the mirror. "Close enough."

Erin was ready to go and waiting for him. He clipped on his holster and badge then opened the door. She braided her fingers through his, standing close as he locked up. He tucked her in his car and wasted no time getting in and starting the engine. Rafe would have liked to enjoy the warmth of her body for a while longer, but his personal satisfaction took a backseat for now.

Linc Hawkins might've been sidetracked, but why wasn't he answering his phone?

"Want me to try Linc again?"

"Now who's reading whose mind?" Rafe joked, trying to keep her from worrying. "Go ahead."

He pressed the gas pedal harder, picking up speed to blend in with the highway traffic. She left a second message. This time imploring Linc to call as soon as he could.

"Something's happened to him. You think maybe the word slipped out he's a federal agent?" Her hand gripped Rafe's arm, icy fingers tightening. "I'm just talking to hear my head rattle. You can't know the answer to that."

"I haven't heard that phrase in many years. Dad used to tell us boys that after he'd gotten tired of listening to us argue."

"Jeff says that, too. Figures they'd use the same slang." Erin turned her head toward the window and fell silent.

Rafe broke the speed limit a few times, but within twenty

minutes, he drove into her neighborhood. Linc's car was parked in her driveway. Rafe called Colton and pulled him off surveillance. They wouldn't wait for him to arrive, but at least somebody knew where they were and what was happening.

"That's not a good sign, is it?" she said softly.

Rafe parked on the street and turned to face her. No way was he going to lie to her. "Hard to say. I don't want to take you with me, but I can't leave you alone in the car. I'll go in first but want your hand on my back at all times. Do not lose contact with me until I tell you it's okay. That way I won't wonder where you are."

She swallowed hard. "I understand."

"Did you bring the pistol Jeff gave you?"

"What? You know it's only legal if it's kept in the house."

One glance and he knew she'd lied. "I'll bet Dad took all of your money every time you played poker with the boys."

"Okay. Fine." She lifted a shoulder then reached for the leather satchel. "It's in my purse. If I get arrested it's your fault."

"I can bear the responsibility. Better a citation than a lifelong regret. And let me have your key to the front door."

She followed instructions. Then she removed the gun from her purse and jacked a shell into the chamber. Rafe was betting Jeff had taken her to the firing range more than once.

"Keep your pistol close."

"I will." She got out, holding the weapon nestled against her leg. "Linc should've heard the car doors close."

Rafe gritted his teeth. Erin was right, and he might be walking her straight into danger. She matched his stride, making it easy for him to maintain contact with her physically. They crossed the lawn, and Rafe quickly unlocked the door. He caught Erin and moved her behind himself before pushing inside. "Linc?" Rafe called out.

He'd hardly had time to say the name when he spotted the body on the floor. Erin cried out, but he caught her by the arm. "Not yet. Let me clear the house."

"Please, don't let him be dead." Her words were soft and low, as if she'd whispered in church.

"Call 911 and Beckett, but stick close to me for a minute." The quick glance Rafe had taken made him think it might be too late for Linc. Spatters of crimson were on the furniture, walls, and the briefcase that lay inches from his hand.

Rafe kept Erin close until he'd made sure they were alone with Linc. "We're clear," Rafe said. "Be careful where you step and don't touch anything."

Erin raced to the still form, stopping short of the pool of blood that spread across her carpet. Tears brimmed in her eyes. The color had drained from her face, but she leaned toward the body and pressed two fingers on his neck. She gasped. Hope flooded her face.

"He's alive. I feel a faint heartbeat."

"The scalp bleeds easily. Let's hope it looks worse than it is." Rafe had soft-pedaled his analysis of the situation for her benefit, and the steely glance she sent him said she wasn't buying. He liked that she expected the truth from people.

"Why would anyone attack him?"

"Lots of possibilities. Looks like rage to me." Rafe held out his hand, closing his fingers around her cool fingers as sirens screamed in the distance. "Let's get out of the way while I call Colton. Let the EMTs take over."

She slid her gun under her blouse and secured it behind her back. Rafe shoved his into his holster, snapping it in place, then led her to the porch. Police cars, a fire truck, and an unmarked roared in behind the ambulance. Wade Beckett emerged from the plain car and headed their way. He made quick introductions while the EMTs rushed inside the house.

"Tell me what happened." Wade removed a small notepad from his pocket. He lifted one shoulder. "I'm old school."

Rafe quickly explained Linc hadn't shown up as planned, so

he and Erin had come to check on him. "He'd stopped here to pick up her briefcase."

"Think he could've walked in on a burglar?"

Rafe shook his head. "No. You won't either after you see Linc. He wasn't just knocked out. The side of his head is bashed in."

Wade stuffed his notepad into his pocket. "You two hang out while I check inside." He didn't wait for an agreement, just turned and walked away.

Rafe appreciated the detective's direct, pull-no-punches approach. The truth might be harsh, but it remained the safest way to avoid misunderstandings.

"Can we go to the hospital with Linc?"

"Sure. We'll stick with him for a while. But I have to come back and get inside his house as soon as possible. If he has any information on the drug investigation that he hasn't shared with me or Colton, I need to know what it is."

A gust of wind caught her hair, sending loose strands swirling around an interesting scowl. Her brows dipped, and a look of confusion clouded her eyes. "Now?"

"That might sound cold to you, but there's a killer out there who's not going to stop. Linc would be the first to understand. These cases need attention."

Voices from inside the house grew louder as the ambulance crew brought Linc out on a stretcher. Erin fell in step with one of the EMTs.

"Linc," she said as the gurney was lifted into the ambulance, "stay with us. You hear? Hang on."

Rafe stepped up and slid his arm around her waist. She leaned into him as he led her to the detective. The three of them waited in silence as the ambulance backed out and sped away. The crime scene unit arrived and entered the house.

"We can't go back inside." Wade broke the silence. "Erin, I need a brief statement from you."

Erin's gaze held a sadness that ripped at Rafe's soul. Pain radiated from her. He got it. Seemed everywhere she turned, people were dying. She nodded and glanced briefly at the fleeing ambulance.

"Take it easy with her," Rafe said, leaving no doubt of his sincerity in his tone. "There's nothing she can tell you except Linc was down when we got here."

"I believe you," Wade said. "You've already explained why you were here. But it's her house and I need to hear what she saw."

With the crime scene unit in possession of the house, Rafe and Erin followed the detective to his car. Erin entered first, scooting to the far side of the backseat.

Rafe slid inside and listened while Erin gave her version of why Linc had been in her house and what she'd witnessed upon entering. Her cell buzzed, causing her to jump.

"It's Jeff."

"We're done here." Beckett stuffed his notepad into his pocket while Erin got out of the car and took the call. His gaze scanned the outside of the house, eventually stopping on her. "Everything keeps coming back to Erin. None of this shit makes sense."

Rafe didn't figure the comment required a response, so he moved farther away and called his office. His boss would know who to notify in Linc's division. Colton had already called it in and Linc's family were on their way.

Colton's truck stopped across the street. Rafe waited at the curb for him, then identified Colton to the cop keeping onlookers at bay.

"How bad?"

"Hard to say." Rafe kept Erin in his line of sight as he shifted positions to speak with Colton. "Linc was caught off guard. He had no defensive wounds. Did you see any activity at Melanie's or Grace's houses?"

"No, but I'm going right back. It's my job to keep your ass safe. I just came by to do a visual on you."

"We're both okay. Erin's shaken up pretty bad." Rafe glanced at her.

As if she knew they were talking about her, she ended the call and made her way to them.

"Colton." She smiled, but Rafe could tell it was forced.

"Ma'am." Colton tipped his hat.

"Did you tell Jeff it was a good thing that he noticed Linc's car in your driveway?" Rafe asked her. He stuffed his hands in his pockets to keep from fixing the strand of hair that had worked its way to freedom.

"I did." She pushed the stray hair off her face. "Since I'm going back to work, Wade said I could pick up a few more clothes. Anything I take has to be cleared and documented. My house is a crime scene, so I can't move back if I wanted to."

"You're going back to work?" Rafe asked.

"Yes." Her smile broadened. "The head of the school board called right after I hung up talking to Jeff. I've been reinstated. I can go back to work tomorrow."

"That's great news." Rafe understood she'd be glad to get back to school.

"That takes care of the daytime," Colton said.

"What does that mean?" She raised an eyebrow.

"Means we'll know where you are during the daytime. I'm going to check in with the narcotics boys. They'll want to know about Linc," Colton added.

"Let's get your stuff together, and then we'll go check on Linc."

CHAPTER 18

Hospitals had never been one of Erin's favorite places. She'd been in a couple of ERs back in her youth. Way back. Back in a time that she tried to keep blocked from her consciousness. But the smells and cool air washing over her sent a bolt of panic streaking through her.

Erin reached for Rafe when they neared the nurses' station at the emergency room. She found reassurance when his hand engulfed hers, folding her fingers inside his palm, holding her like a security blanket.

"You want to sit and let me ask about Linc?" Rafe's comforting tone gave her a smidgen of courage.

"No. Don't leave me alone. Okay?"

"I won't turn loose." His hand squeezed hers. "Not until you tell me to let go."

Two nurses lifted their heads to greet them. Both of them glanced at the badge on Rafe's belt. Erin figured he'd get more information than she would alone.

Rafe spoke first. "What can you tell us about Linc Hawkins?"

One nurse came out from behind the counter. "I was just in the trauma unit a minute ago. Mr. Hawkins is unconscious but stable. He'll have surgery as soon as his results come back from the lab."

"How bad is he?" Erin prayed Linc hadn't suffered a brain injury.

"The extent of Mr. Hawkins's injuries hasn't been determined, but I know his cheekbone is shattered."

"I was afraid his skull had been crushed," she said. Rafe's grip on her fingers tightened.

"You think that's not the case?" Rafe asked.

"I really can't say," the nurse responded. "One of the doctors will let you know as soon as possible. You're welcome to wait, but it could be awhile before one of them can talk."

"We'll be here." Erin couldn't imagine the pain Linc was going through or perhaps the long recovery he faced. Was he all alone? An FBI agent like Rafe, had he, too, shut out his family and friends?

The nurse stepped closer. "We have one of the best reconstructive surgeons in Texas on our staff. He'll do everything possible to reduce scarring."

"Thank you. When can we see him?" Erin asked.

"I really can't say. It won't be tonight for sure."

Rafe guided Erin to the waiting room and to a back corner where they could wait. Finding a comfortable spot was impossible. She'd been in a few waiting rooms. In fact, she'd been in a few of those small ER rooms where they pull the curtain closed and tend to your wounds.

"Hey." He nudged her knee with his. "We both hate that Linc was attacked, but there's more going on with you. Walking in this hospital triggered something." Rafe's eyes were dark with concern. "You can tell me anything, you know. It won't change the way I feel about you."

Erin's breath caught. An ache started in her chest. He'd been undercover, had worked drug cases. Her past probably wouldn't shock him. He draped his arm around the back of her chair and gently massaged the rigid tendons in her neck.

"I'm surprised your dad never told you. I'm sure Jeff confided in him." She took a deep breath. "I made more than one trip to the ER when I was a kid. I used to bring my mother in to get patched up. That changed when I got old enough for my stepfather to turn his attention on me."

"The bastard beat both of you." Rafe's body stiffened with his statement.

"They both would get drunk. They'd quarrel, and he'd take

his anger out on her. I tried to stop him once, and he broke my arm."

"I can see how visits to the hospital would bring all those memories back. Nobody ever got suspicious?"

"I lied just like I was told to do. My mother kept thinking things would get better. When I turned thirteen, his interest in me changed. He started out by sneaking up on me, standing too close. Then he began touching me, trying to force me to touch him." Tears surged, surprising and angering Erin. She willed them away. Rafe's hand moved to her shoulder, gripping her in a supportive gesture. "I begged my mother to make him leave me alone. She accused me of trying to take him away from her." The next words hung in her throat, sent her stomach churning, and started a pain in her heart. "For a while, I got really good at avoiding him. One day he came home early. I was alone in the kitchen, and he came up behind me. Grabbed my breasts and warned me that if I went to my mother again, he'd make me pay. He said my friends wouldn't recognize me when he got through."

Erin turned to face Rafe. What she saw in his eyes filled her chest with relief. His gaze held no condemnation, no disgust, only compassion and understanding. Would that change when she told the rest of her story?

"I lost it. Went crazy. Decided I'd rather fight than have him rape me, so I slashed out with the knife I had been using to cut potatoes. The blade sliced into his hand. He called me a bitch, and then he lunged at me. I still don't remember what happened next, but he was on the floor, and the knife was in his side. I ran."

"And lived under a bridge."

"Yeah. There's no telling where I'd be today if Jeff hadn't caught me stealing food."

"Did your stepfather die?"

"No. I hadn't hit one of his vital organs."

"For future reference, if you're going to stab somebody, go for the diaphragm. It's right below the lungs."

She rolled her eyes and finished her story. That Rafe wasn't passing judgment meant a lot. "I was a scared kid and didn't think anybody would believe me. Turns out, when I told Jeff my story, he believed every word."

"Where is this bastard stepfather today?"

"He died of cancer while in prison. Thanks to Jeff and Lotty, I found the strength to tell the police everything. I testified in court, and twelve people believed me."

"Your mother?"

"Who knows? The bastard swore he'd kicked her out after I knifed him. Said he had no idea where she went."

"She never came forward?" Rafe sensed the pain rolling off Erin. Her tone had shifted from calm to a bone-chilling icy.

"Never. I've always wondered if he killed her." Erin's chest rose and fell in a sigh. "So now you know the rest of the story. The snotty smartass you asked to the prom came from prime stock."

"I'm sorry we didn't go. You still owe me a dance."

"I'll try to be a little nicer to you next time you ask me to the prom."

"That's a deal."

****

Erin hadn't mentioned her father, and Rafe could tell she was through sharing. He felt honored she'd shared some of her past with him. After all she'd been through, she was a testament to what a person could overcome.

Even here in the harsh fluorescent light, he thought she was beautiful. Now she'd taken on a new glow. Damn, he was proud of her. He had to touch her, so he leaned over, cupped her face in his hands, and kissed her. Soft, warm lips met his. Enticing and welcoming. Reluctantly, he kept their contact brief.

"Everybody has a chapter in their lives they'd like to erase. Our history helps shape us, but our character makes us who we are. You're a smart, caring, amazing woman. I can't tell you how proud I am of the person you are today."

Her cheeks flushed at his compliment. "You turned out pretty good yourself." She glanced at her watch. "It's been hours since they took Linc to surgery. Maybe it's time I put my bad memories away and made peace with this hospital." She stood. "I'm going to see if the nurses have heard anything."

"Want me to go with you?"

"No. I can do this." She walked into the hallway and started in the direction of the nurses' station. "I'll be right back."

Rafe was on his feet and had her in his line of vision in seconds. Watching Erin walk, shoulders back, head held high, hips gently swaying, would never be a hardship. Her endlessly long legs gave her a graceful stride, the stride of a strong, beautiful woman.

He could watch her walk forever. The word *forever* brought his thoughts to a screeching halt, sending the hair on the back of his neck quivering. He refused to think in terms of *forever*. Planning on *forever* wasn't an option.

She struck up a conversation with one of the nurses. In minutes, the two women were chatting like old friends. As if she knew he was watching, she looked over her shoulder and smiled. She had managed to stir something inside him best left at peace.

The vibration from his cell got his attention. He pulled it from his pocket to find his boss on the line. Rafe moved to the end of the hallway to ensure privacy and still keep an eye on Erin. "Did you reach the Hawkins family?"

"I did. There's a shitload of them, too. Best I could tell, his mom, dad, and two of his brothers are on their way. I offered help with travel arrangements, but they're handling everything themselves. How is Agent Hawkins?"

"Don't know yet. We're still waiting to hear," Rafe said.

"I appreciate you getting involved in the case and helping a hometown friend. But I have to ask if you're okay. You haven't had time to grieve the loss of your father, much less get his things in order."

"I'm fine. This friend is important to me."

"Good. I'm glad to hear that."

Rafe caught movement from his right side. He turned, his hand instinctively reaching for the pistol riding at his right kidney. A small-framed woman wearing a loose-fitting, drab-green hospital jacket looked up at him. A surgical mask sagged just under her chin.

"Linc Hawkins family?"

"The doctor is here. Let me call you back." Rafe ended the call and directed his attention to the woman. Dark circles under her eyes gave her an alarmingly sad expression. The lady was either the bearer of bad news or she was extremely tired.

"Yes, ma'am. We're not blood related, but we're both federal agents. Linc's immediate family have been notified and are on their way."

"Doctor Winston." The diminutive woman shook Rafe's extended hand. Her fingers were icy cold, and for some odd reason, that surprised him. That and the fact her stoic expression hadn't wavered set his nerves on edge. "Mr. Hawkins is a lucky man."

Rafe quirked an eyebrow at such a preposterous statement. The good doctor chuckled, changing her sad expression to that of a pretty but tired woman. "Lucky because his skull remains intact. His cheek was a different matter. That procedure took a little longer than usual as I had to piece him back together. We'll watch him closely for the next twenty-four hours. Once he continues to gain strength, we'll turn our attention to additional reconstructive surgery. You should go home. It will be hours before you can see Mr. Hawkins."

Erin! Rafe whirled in the direction of the nurses' station, expecting her to be hurrying toward him and the doctor. She was nowhere in sight. Furious at himself for turning away from her, he felt his heart pounding against his rib cage. Dr. Winston was still talking when he sprinted down the hall.

"Where is the young woman who was asking about Linc

Hawkins?"

"She went to the restroom." The nurse pointed. "It's just around that corner."

Rafe ran to the door with the word WOMEN on it. He put his hand over the word and pushed. "Erin," he called loudly. Giving no thought to whether or not the place might be occupied, he hurried to the first stall. Empty. As was the next one. He was alone. "Damn it."

He rushed into the hall, unsure of which way to look. Panic boiled through his veins.

Erin was missing.

My fault! The two words reverberated through his mind. He hadn't been there when Nick needed him. He hadn't been there when their dad died. And now, he'd let Erin down.

"Rafe?"

He whirled to find her walking straight toward him, a cup of coffee in each hand. His knees almost buckled. And his heart rate? That didn't slow down one bit. "Damn it. You disappeared. I was seconds from declaring an emergency, placing hospital guards at every exit, and calling the cops."

She held her arms forward as if to make sure he saw the cups in her hands. Fire flashed from her eyes. She fucking had the nerve to be mad at *him*.

"I can do without you overreacting."

"Overreacting?" Rafe stormed toward her, ready to raise hell with her for scaring the shit out of him. But when he reached her, stood face-to-face with her, looking into her beautiful eyes, he pulled her into his arms instead. He held her tightly, hoping she couldn't feel his heart beating a rhythm against his chest wall.

Erin's spine went rigid, stiff as a board. He hadn't given any thought to the two coffees in her hands. He released her, took his cup, taking a long drink of the lukewarm sludge.

"A simple thank-you will suffice." Her words were chilling, but the tone in her voice suggested humor.

"Don't do that again. I can't take it." He wrapped his free hand around her elbow, smiled apologetically at the frowning nurse who'd heard his tirade and come running, then led Erin back to the waiting room. "I turned my back on you for less than a minute, and you disappeared. What was I supposed to think?"

"I didn't realize the coffee machine was that far down the hall. I was already there and figured we could both use a shot of caffeine. Maybe I was wrong."

"After all this is over, we're going to sit down and figure out why I panicked. Losing control goes against my nature, my training, everything I've learned. Staying calm can be the difference in living or dying sometimes." Rafe struggled with his reaction to her being out of his sight for a few minutes. He dragged his hand through his hair.

"Maybe you care more about me than if you'd been protecting a stranger." Erin set her cup on a table and brushed her fingers across his forehead, patting his hair back into place.

Her words had defined the situation perfectly. She'd cut right through his bullshit and looked into his heart. He couldn't let her know she was right nor could he let his emotions get out of hand.

"Linc's doctor and I had a brief chat."

"How is he?"

"I'll explain on the way home." Rafe tossed back the cold coffee and stood. "He's going to live, but he's apparently got some reconstructive surgery ahead of him. We can't see him, so let's stop by the nurses' station, leave our phone numbers for them and his family, and then we'll get out of here. You're bound to have a to-do list."

She looked up at him. Her head tilted to the side. "A to-do list?"

"You're going back to work tomorrow, remember?"

Her lips spread into a smile. "I'd forgotten. You're right. I've got things to do."

****

Leaving the hospital was no hardship for Erin. Even with the renovations and updating that had been done, she'd hated being inside. Outside, she breathed in the night air and tried to concentrate on tomorrow.

Rafe's hand resting on the small of her back as he guided her to the car made concentrating on anything except the heat he generated very difficult. Erin should have felt guilty for scaring him, but she couldn't. Instead, it gave her hope that he actually felt something stronger than friendship for her.

"My going to work in the morning relieves you of your babysitting responsibilities, at least during the day."

He opened the car door, waited until she settled in the seat, then leaned inside. "You're not out of the doghouse. I haven't decided if I can trust you enough to drop you off and pick you up."

He was too close. So she leaned forward and kissed him. The intention was to plant a sweet, innocent peck on his lips. Instead, his hand clasped the back of her head and held her tightly while he ravaged her mouth. Erin was almost panting when he released her.

"Never scare me like that again." Before she could gather her thoughts, he'd closed the door, walked around and seated himself.

When his phone rang, Rafe fished out his cell. "What's up?"

Erin was amazed that in a blink of an eye, he was chatting with Colton as if the earth hadn't just rotated off its axis. The romantic air previously filling the interior of his car vanished, replaced by the cool, calm voice of the law.

The one-sided conversation was easy to follow. Grace had left her neighborhood, and Colton had followed. Not only was it a little late for the teenager to be out, but she hadn't turned on her headlights until she was well away from her home. He'd also notified his contact with the narcotics division, and the decision to stay back and not interact in any way had been made. Colton was on a fact-finding mission.

Chills raced up Erin's arms. Could Grace be involved in drug trafficking?

CHAPTER 19

Erin didn't try to engage Rafe in conversation during the drive. He was deep in thought after his call from Colton. Once Rafe had parked in the driveway of the Sirilli home, he'd unloaded the suitcase of work clothes that she'd packed while at her house, then carried the bag to her room. For the next few minutes, she'd concentrated her efforts on unpacking even more of her belongings. She now had more than enough clothes to last a few days.

She'd opened up her heart and shared information with Rafe, facts she'd never felt comfortable talking about. His smoky gray eyes had been full of understanding. His nonjudgmental attitude had added to her growing respect for him.

"You up for a cup of coffee before bed?" His deep baritone drifted from the doorway across the room and caressed her skin.

She turned and grabbed the headboard for support. Warm-up pants rode low on his hips as he ran a towel over his damp hair. His bare chest still had water droplets riding above his collarbone. In a couple of long strides, he stood in front of her, bringing with him the musky scent of soap and a woodsy shampoo.

His eyebrows dipped. "You okay?"

She swallowed, following with a weird-sounding cross between a giggle and a laugh. "That's the dumbest question I've ever heard."

"How so?"

"Are you for real? How many times do I have to tell you? You're hot and sexy and half-dressed. You're really good to look at." She pulled the towel from his hands and finished drying him.

"You see something I don't. When I stand in the mirror, nothing 'good' looks back at me." His gaze raked down and back up her body. "Unless you're standing in front of me naked."

Heat rushed up her cheeks at the mention of the mirror. "Stop it. I think I'll get my shower."

"Need your back washed?" He moved to block her path.

"You just got out." Every nerve ending sizzled. His nearness had a needy ache building low in her belly. No one had ever fired her libido so fast.

"I'm sorry. I should've waited for you." He moved a step closer.

"About that coffee." The desire to touch him was too much. She stroked her fingers across his nipples, trailing down to the loose waistband. "I'd rather have hot chocolate."

"Keep that up and I'll buy you a chocolate factory." He unbuttoned her blouse while he talked.

"Hmm. A challenge if I've ever heard one." She pushed her hand past the elastic, wrapped her fingers around silken steel and stroked the already hardened length. A smile crept up her cheeks as he expanded with her touch. "I love to feel you grow in my hand."

The next few seconds passed quickly as her clothes were removed and tossed to the floor. Erin tugged, and his warm-ups hit the floor. She dropped to her knees and took his erection in her mouth. The low, guttural moan coming from Rafe spurred her on. She pumped his erection a couple of times with her hand before releasing him and pulling him deep inside with her tongue. His hands sank into her hair, and strong fingers guided her movements. His taste was salty, warm, and for her alone.

"Stop," he commanded, backing away quickly. "We have all night. I'm not blowing it in the first five minutes."

He shoved her empty suitcase to the floor and sat Erin on the bed. "Lie back."

Just as her head hit the mattress, his strong hands caught her hips and pulled her closer to the edge. He knelt, pushed her thighs wide, and draped her legs over his shoulders. In this position, she was unable to see Rafe, but she trusted him completely, so she closed her eyes and relaxed.

Her folds were gently parted, and a cool stream of air caressed her moist skin. Slowly, he kissed, probed, and laved until Erin lifted her hips, begging for more. Rafe intensified his efforts, picking up speed, delving deeper inside her core with his tongue, then withdrawing to suckle her clit. Back and forth, until she pleaded for release.

"Please. Please."

His thumb found the perfect spot as his tongue drove her closer to the edge. Her orgasm exploded hard and fast. Large quakes stormed through her body. They slowly subsided only to be followed by smaller aftershocks.

He kissed her inner thighs and worked his way up to her breasts. As he cupped each one, his thumb circled a nipple.

"You're beautiful all the time. But immediately after you've come, you're breathtaking." He kissed her tenderly, stood, and offered his hand.

Were they done? Didn't look like it to Erin. His erection looked larger and harder than before. "You said we had all night."

"We do. Let's get you that shower. Then we'll talk about hot chocolate."

She took his hand, leaning into him for strength while they made their way to the bathroom. Erin grabbed two towels while Rafe adjusted the water temperature. She stepped in behind him and ran her hands across his abs, kneading and teasing. "Don't make me wait any longer. I need you inside me."

He turned, pulling her into his arms for a blistering kiss. His hand lifted her leg and placed her foot on the bench seat. Today her height proved to be a real advantage, because with very little maneuvering he was at her entrance. "Inside me. Now."

Rafe lifted her slightly and slid deep with one powerful thrust. "Like that?"

"Yes, just like that." She captured his mouth, taking her turn at sweeping her tongue inside and tasting the warm interior.

His thrusts were hard and fast, and Erin matched his movements. Her leg raised put her at the perfect angle, and with each stroke he pushed her closer. The warm water sluiced across their bodies as sensation piled on top of pleasure to the point of pain. The release exploded from deep inside, rolling and pitching her as if she'd been caught in a powerful wave. He continued the hard and deep thrusts until she stilled. Then he drove deep inside her, tilted his head back and groaned, pulsing again and again.

Rafe wrapped his arms around her, sat on the bench seat, and pulled her onto his lap. His head rested on her breasts while water washed over them. She smoothed his wet hair off his face and dropped her cheek to the top of his head.

Erin didn't know how long they stayed like that, clinging to each other after such an intimate round of lovemaking.

The rest of the shower was taken in silence, with Rafe washing her tenderly and dropping an occasional kiss to the freshly rinsed part of her anatomy. He turned off the water, stepped out, and offered her a towel. What was running through his mind? Had he figured out she was falling in love with him? Had she scared him away?

Combing her hair, she caught him staring at her in the mirror. "What is it, Rafe? We've come too far to have secrets."

"I didn't use a condom."

"Not to worry. My periods were so erratic the doctor put me on the pill years ago."

"I wasn't worried. I keep envisioning a little girl who looks just like you, and it scares the shit out of me."

"Why would that scare you?"

"My mother killed herself because she couldn't handle the pressure of being married to a member of law enforcement. It was more than Nick could bear."

"Your mother suffered from depression. She'd been treated for it for years. Don't you remember times she couldn't get out of bed? Refused to dress, cook or clean?"

"How do you know all that?"

"Jeff saw it firsthand. He never could understand why your dad kept it a secret. Maybe he wanted you boys to blame him instead of her."

Rafe's gaze held hers in the mirror for a few minutes. "I'll fix that hot chocolate now."

****

Rafe left the bathroom, grabbed his warm-up bottoms and a T-shirt off the floor. He tugged them on before heading to the kitchen. A sound sent him back after his pistol. It shouldn't be Colton, since he was committed to the drug case. Rafe silently moved down the hall toward the light burning in the kitchen. The fridge door was wide open, and all he could see was a butt wearing fatigues.

"Listen, kid. I could have shot you. Why didn't you make some noise?"

Luke straightened and turned around. The smile was that of his younger brother, but the body belonged to a well-trained Army Ranger. "Who are you calling a kid?"

Rafe pulled Luke in for a bear hug. "You've grown up."

"I've put on a few pounds. As for making noise, there was enough of that coming from the shower. I didn't figure you'd want to be interrupted."

Rafe glanced toward the back bedroom then back at Luke. "You keep what you heard to yourself."

"Not a word. You should do a better job of securing the premises next time."

"How did you get in?"

"I picked the lock." He returned to his position, studying the almost empty fridge.

"You'll have to settle for a sandwich."

"Works for me. So who's in the bathroom?"

Rafe walked to the hallway entrance and listened. The hair dryer was running. "Erin Brady. She's staying here." Rafe gave Luke a down-and-dirty overview of the situation with her and the drug investigation.

Luke finished building his sandwich and followed Rafe to the dining room table. "I can help."

"Thanks. I may need you. How long will you be home?"

"As long as you need me. This was my last tour. With the military ramping down, I figured now was a good time to cut ties. I'm available for full-time work."

"If you're staying in town, the house is yours. I've been packing things, thinking we wouldn't need the place or the stuff in it. I set aside some things I thought you might want."

"You did the right thing. I haven't decided where I'll settle down. But I've got enough money saved up not to get in any rush."

Rafe stood, retrieved their father's will, and rejoined Luke. "I hate this, but it's something we should discuss."

"What is it?"

"Dad's will. Along with the house and property, Dad had a couple of sizable life insurance policies. There's more than enough for you to travel, open your own business, or just take your time deciding what you want to do." Rafe handed the envelope to Luke, who put down his supper and read.

Luke folded the papers and tucked them under his plate. "I hate that neither of us was here for him."

"Me, too. He was gone by the time I found out. I was hard to reach, and you were impossible. Don't let it feed on you."

"He was very proud of you both." Erin swept into the room, bringing with her a positive tone and a wide smile. She extended her hand to Luke. "Hello, Luke."

"I remember you, ma'am." Luke stood at attention. He held on to her hand a little too long.

"I'm not surprised. By the time you made it to high school, my story was all over the newspaper. Welcome home." She extracted her hand from his big paw. "I'm sorry you're here under such sad circumstances."

Luke frowned and dragged a hand over his buzz-cut hair. After a second, he nodded. "I do remember. You did the right thing, putting that bastard in prison. But that wasn't why I remember you. I always thought you looked like a movie star."

Rafe ran his finger inside the neck of his T-shirt. It seemed to get tighter with Luke's flirting. "Erin has to go to work in the morning. After I drop her off, I'm catching up with my partner. You take your time getting settled. We've got plenty of time to decide what to do with the house."

"I just got here," Luke protested. "We need to talk."

"Rafe's going to stay up and visit with you. I've got to be up early. See you tomorrow."

He watched her walk away. She'd dried her long hair, leaving it loose and hanging in swirls around her shoulders. A knot formed in his throat. After he left, would she fall in love with some other guy? Settle down and have kids? The little girl he'd imagined earlier flashed through his mind again. That knot moved from his throat to his heart just thinking about the possibility. A band formed around his chest and tightened when she walked out of sight. He jumped when Luke's hand clamped down on the back of his neck.

"You got it bad, big brother. What are you going to do about it?"

Rafe shook his head. "Nothing, kid. Nothing at all."

CHAPTER 20

Erin hadn't slept well, and the circles under her eyes reflected that fact. She finished applying makeup then pulled her hair back into a low ponytail. Her nerves were jumping all over the place. Would she be welcomed back? The hurt she'd felt when people had stared and wondered if she were truly innocent had been embedded in her mind. She took several deep breaths and pushed those negative thoughts from her mind. She had good friends at work. Friends who'd stood up for her from the very beginning. She straightened her shoulders and walked to the kitchen toward the male voices.

"Good morning," she said.

"Morning," Rafe and Luke said in unison. Rafe had dressed in jeans and a pullover, apparently ready to drive her to school.

Erin felt a twinge of leftover disappointment from last night. She'd half-expected Rafe to join her in bed. Even after she'd reminded herself that this affair was temporary, sleep had been elusive.

Rafe stood, walked to the coffeepot, poured her a cup, and brought it to her. Leaning down, he kissed her forehead. "You look beautiful."

"Thanks." She fumbled the handoff, almost dropping the hot liquid down her legs.

Luke cleared his throat. "That's an understatement. None of my teachers looked like you. I might have broken the rules more if they had."

Rafe steadied her hand, ensuring her grip was secure on the handle, then turned his gaze on Luke. "Don't you have something you need to do? Anything?"

Luke stood, chuckling to himself. "You still don't play well with others."

Rafe laughed at his brother. "I wasn't playing."

"I'm going to shower. Do you want to go with me to talk to Dad's attorney? He can guide us through probate or walk us through the legal system." Luke held his hand up, sipping his coffee. "I know that sounds callous, but Dad would want us to honor any of his outstanding debts."

"You're right," Rafe said. "I went through some of his bills. His credit card doesn't have but a couple of hundred dollars due. We should check with the funeral home, ask if he has an outstanding balance."

Luke turned toward Erin. The resemblance between the brothers was amazing. Luke's gray eyes, lush mouth, and quick wit reminded her of a younger version of Rafe. "Sorry," he said. "I don't mean to throw water on your first day back to school."

"Not at all. If there's anything I can do, please don't hesitate to ask."

"I will." Luke slapped Rafe on the shoulder on his way out. "Later, bro."

Erin put her cup in the sink. "I need to get to school a little early. There's a lot to catch up on before the day starts."

Rafe pulled her into his arms, leaned his head back, and pinned her with his gaze. "Promise me that you will stay inside the school building until you see me waiting out front."

Erin reached up and pushed a wayward lock of hair off his forehead. "I promise."

****

Erin opened the door to the administrative offices and stepped inside. The smile on Mrs. Henley's face eased any residual tension left in Erin's shoulders.

"There you are." Mrs. Henley bustled from behind the counter and surprised Erin with a hug.

"I'm so glad to see you," Erin said. "I truly appreciate you for the constant support and for believing in my innocence."

"There was never a doubt. I have your office key right here." Mrs. Henley stuffed her hand into her blazer pocket and pulled out a key. "We've all been waiting for your return."

"That's good to hear." She nodded her head in the direction of the principal's office. "Is he in?"

"He had an appointment downtown. But he wants to see you today."

"I'll check back in a couple of hours." Erin opened the door and stepped into the hall. She felt as if she'd just returned home from a long journey. The shining tile floor, the metal lockers, and the banners promoting extracurricular activities seemed to welcome her as she made her way to her office.

She placed her hand on the doorframe of her office, feeling the cool wood against her skin, and unlocked the door. Inside, she resumed her routine of turning on the lights, opening the blinds so the sun flooded her work area with light, and then she sat in her desk chair. Everything about being back felt right. Firing up her computer, she dug right into her emails and messages.

"Hey, stranger." Carla stood in the door. Her smile was just the distraction Erin needed.

Erin stood and hugged her friend tightly. "Gosh, it's good to see you."

"I hear there are a few covered dishes in the teachers' lounge. Maybe even a cake. Come on."

"Now I know why my stomach was growling." Erin fell in step with her friend and chatted away as they went to lunch.

The teachers had set up a stop-and-go luncheon. For forty-five minutes, Erin was welcomed with open arms. By the time she returned to her office, she was on the verge of tears because of the wonderful reception she'd received. She settled at her desk and went back to scheduling appointments.

A knock on her door drew her attention. She motioned for

Principal Mueller to enter.

"Welcome back." A smile crept up his cheeks. "Do you have a minute?"

Erin glanced at the clock. "I'm sorry you had to come to me. Time got away from me. Please, come in." She waved to the same chair Penny had been sitting in when the entire scandal started. "I appreciate your support with the board."

He waved off her compliment. "Walk with me. The coach is concerned for a student, and I'd like you to speak with the boy."

Erin was on her feet before he finished the sentence. "Certainly." She grabbed her notepad and a pen before joining him. "What's going on?"

"It's Sean Porter. Coach is going to bench him if he doesn't get his grades up."

Erin easily matched the principal's stride step for step. "Why didn't he send Sean to my office?"

"Coach thinks the boy is also having problems at home. We thought he'd speak more freely if you both spoke to him."

Principal Mueller stopped at the exit to a stairwell and opened and held the door for her. "Sean's waiting in the coach's office. You go ahead. I don't want him to feel like we ganged up on him."

"I'll let you know how it goes." Erin jogged down the stairs. She stopped at the second-floor landing when she heard a scuffling sound coming from behind. Swallowing, she turned quickly. No one was there. Shaking off her jumpy nerves, she hurried down the final steps, pushed the metal bar on the door, and stepped outside.

The prick in her neck happened quickly. She opened her mouth to scream, and a cloth was stuffed into her mouth. Someone held her from behind. She struggled to free herself, but her legs and arms grew heavy. Fighting against sleep proved futile.

****

Casanova's heart pounded painfully against his rib cage. Absolutely everything rode on the next few minutes. The minute he'd heard she was returning to work, he'd known this was a sign. He'd parked his car at the side exit, out of sight and safe because the practice field was empty this time of day. Scooping his soon-to-be bride into his arms, he placed her in the backseat. As a precautionary measure, he covered her with an old blanket.

Casanova drove carefully, minding the speed limit and using care not to draw attention. It wasn't unusual for him to go home for lunch, so he pulled into his garage, got out, and lowered the door. Once inside safely, he almost wept with joy. He'd done it. He and Erin would be together forever.

Erin would write a letter announcing that she needed some time alone and would be out of touch for a while. By the time she rejoined society, they'd be an old happily married couple. People would see how happy they were, and no one would ask questions.

Time was critical, so he carried Erin inside and down the stairs to the storm shelter. The ladder's narrow steps presented a problem, and he slipped once, banging his elbow and her head against the wall. Her moan sent his heart racing again. Once he had her on the bed, he removed the cloth from her mouth then ensured she was breathing easily.

She was beautiful, eyes closed, resting peacefully. How stunning she would look in the wedding dress. He lifted it gently and laid it across her body. He leaned down and placed a chaste kiss on her lips. "I'll be home soon, my love."

Casanova hurried up the stairs, closed and secured the heavy metal door, then placed the carpet in its proper place. A flutter of irritation washed over him. He'd worked so hard for this moment, and yet, he couldn't stop and enjoy it. He shook off the self-pity.

Later, when Erin understood everything he'd done so they could be together, she would demonstrate her appreciation, making all his hard work and patience worth it.

****

Erin tried to ignore the headache while she fought her way to consciousness. She opened her eyes to total darkness. A scream hit the back of her throat, but she swallowed it back. Remaining calm would be difficult, but nothing good would come from her losing control.

"Hello? Is anybody there?" Silence answered her. "If somebody is here, please say something."

Erin pushed herself up. Something soft slid off her chest and onto her lap. A quick check told her it hadn't been a piece of her clothing. Whatever it was, it didn't belong to her, so she shoved it to the floor. Questions jammed her mind, flooding in like a high-speed train. Panic bubbled up again.

Stop. Get a hold of yourself.

There had to be a way out, and she had to find it. Cautiously, she stood and scooted one foot along the floor. Then she repeated the process, shuffling her feet and holding her arms out in front of her. Terrified of what she might find, but more afraid of what would happen if she didn't try, she moved at a snail's pace. The question "why?" kept coming to mind.

She'd taken only five steps when her hands found a wall. The surface was cool to the touch. If she could only see her surroundings, she could figure out what to do. One hand over the other, she shuffled sideways before finding a corner and second wall. Wherever she was, the room didn't seem to be very large. Best she could tell the room was the size of a jail cell. Something flicked across the top of her head. Startled beyond words, she stumbled backward. Her arms flailed through the air as she tried to maintain her balance. Unable to steady herself, she fell, landing on the cold, hard floor. Pain shot from her tailbone up her spine to her head.

Erin screamed her frustration and anguish. Her voice reverberated, bouncing back at her, sounding as if she was in a tunnel. She brushed a hand across her cheek to find tears running down her cheeks. When had she started crying? Angrily, she wiped her face dry. Now wasn't the time for fear or self-pity. But the dark was maddening.

She stood and resumed her hand-to-wall shuffle. Determined to locate a window or door, she clenched her jaw and forced herself to move.

Hope flooded her heart when her fingers wrapped around the bar of what might be a ladder. Yes. She ran her hand up the cool metal and grasped another rung. Searching, she located a secure place for her foot and started an ascent. Her footing was bad, and her sense of balance a disaster. The top of her head crashed into some barrier. Tears rushed to the surface with the impact, but she ignored them, running her hand over the surface until she found a handle or lever. Clinging to a rung with one hand and trying to move the metal bar used every muscle and ounce of strength she could muster.

"Help," she cried out. "I'm here." Refusing to give up, she pulled, pushed, and tugged until her voice grew weak and her limbs began to tremble and cramp.

Exhausted, she slipped and slid back to the hard floor. Sweat had soaked through her blouse, and a shiver raced across her shoulders. Erin gathered her strength and felt her way to what might be a small bed. Her hand felt something soft. Was that what she shoved to the floor? She pulled it next to her, tried to figure out what the yards of material were, using that to occupy her mind. Anything to blot out the word *trapped*, which circled in an unending loop through her thoughts.

To stave off the rising panic, she had to do something, anything. She stood, put her hands on the wall, and resumed her search. Her knee bumped into something, pulling a yelp of pain and surprise from her clenched teeth. She knelt and opened a small door. The interior light of an apartment-size fridge shone brightly. The bulb was small in size and wattage, but the faint illumination it provided was very welcome. Relief washed over her as her tense nerves relaxed a little.

Erin opened the door all the way and looked around. A chill shook her body. She'd been placed in a dull-gray metal bunker. One small cot, the fridge, and a camp potty left little room to move around. Hanging from the ceiling was a pull string attached to a bare light bulb. That's what had brushed across her head earlier.

She stood, reached up, and then tugged on the string. It took a second for her eyes to adjust to the glare. Erin picked up the pile of white material on top of the cot. Bile charged the back of her throat. In her hands, she held a wedding dress. She was to be somebody's bride. Expected to wear yards and yards of lace for some madman.

She charged the ladder, quickly reaching the top. She pounded with her fist until she couldn't raise her arm any longer. Despair wrapped around her like a damp gray blanket on a cold winter day.

What if nobody ever found her?

What kind of monster had done this?

Principal Mueller had left her at the top of the stairs, hadn't he? Had he helped set her up? He didn't seem capable of attacking Linc or murdering two young women and the photographer. He was a politician, an executive, and a bit of an awkward flirt. But she'd seen through his façade, known he was insecure, full of self-doubt, and that his handshaking and backslapping were a cover-up.

Had he quietly followed her down the stairs? If not him, who? Had Coach Evans tricked the principal into sending her out the side door?

She had no memory of how she got to wherever she was. Where the hell was *here*? And how long had she been here? She didn't wear a watch, choosing to check the time on her cell. But without either one, she had no way of measuring what day today was or if it was day or night. She shut the fridge door, crawled onto the cot, and pulled her knees to her chest. Tremors racked her body.

Rafe. He'd probably gone in the school looking for her and by now was searching for her. Had he exploded in anger or kept his cool? He'd use all of his resources to find her. Of that, she had no doubt. The question most pressing was would she be alive when he found her? And who would tell Jeff and Lotty?

The silence seeped into her soul. The sound of her heart racing roared in her ears. Her imagination pulled at her sanity like a runaway horse.

How strong was her mind? Could she endure living in captivity? Damn right, she could.

Erin replaced fear with anger. Many years ago, she'd become an expert at being a survivor.

CHAPTER 21

Parked in a visitor's spot right in front of the school, Rafe lifted his sunglasses off and put them on the dash of his car. Nothing would hinder him from spotting Erin when she came outside.

Today had been productive. Colton had provided his information from last night's surveillance to the narcotics squad, and bright and early this morning, the local PD had picked up Grace and hauled the sleepy young woman downtown. She'd recently turned eighteen, which meant she could be questioned without the department having to wait for her parents to fly home. Rafe would've liked to know what was going down, but this was Colton's case. Erin was his responsibility.

Funny how badly he'd missed having her around today. Even while he and Luke worked through family issues concerning their dad, she'd popped into Rafe's thoughts entirely too often.

His gaze shifted to the car's clock. Erin was five minutes late. The hair on his arms rose. The hell with waiting. He got out, jogged up the sidewalk, and walked in the school.

"Mr. Sirilli." Mrs. Henley met him just inside the building. "What brings you here so late in the day?"

"I'm giving Ms. Brady a ride home." He moved to go around her.

Shaking her head, she said, "She's already left."

An icy hand gripped his heart and squeezed. "Impossible. She promised to wait for me. I've been outside for over thirty minutes. She'd have seen me waiting."

"I don't know what to tell you." Mrs. Henley lifted a shoulder. "I just walked down to her office to remind her that Principal Mueller wanted to see her today, but she wasn't there. I assure you, her office is empty."

Rafe ran full speed, sliding to a stop at the closed door. Erin's office was dark. He tried the door handle. Locked. His stomach dropped to his shoe tops.

Erin was gone.

"I told you," Mrs. Henley said, arriving a few seconds after Rafe. She huffed out each word.

"Do you have keys for this office?"

"Not with me. Aside from there being confidential information inside, Ms. Brady is a stickler for everything being kept tidy."

"I need that door unlocked." Rafe felt the nerves in his jaw bunch. Her eyes widened. He was scaring her, but it couldn't be helped. She glanced back toward the front of the school as if looking for help.

"Is the principal still here?" He paused until she nodded. "Get him and the keys, while I call the cops." Rafe took out his cell.

She turned and hurried away.

Rafe's first call was to Wade Beckett, who after being apprised of the situation took over the necessary notifications. Next, he called Colton and repeated what he'd just shared with the police.

"I'm on my way."

Rafe decided against alerting Erin's adoptive parents until he had more to tell them. Shoe heels hitting the tile floor sent hope rushing through his system. He spun, hoping to find Erin hurrying to him, full of explanations and apologies. His neck muscles tightened. The footsteps belonged to the principal and Mrs. Henley.

"What's this about Ms. Brady missing?" Principal Mueller's superior tone slid up Rafe's spine like a knife.

"I believe Erin has been kidnapped."

"And what are you basing that on?"

"I don't have time to explain it. You'll have to take my word. I need to look around her office."

"Shouldn't you wait for the police?" Mrs. Henley protested.

"Mr. Sirilli is FBI. Of course, he can go inside." The principal's tone had changed. He unlocked the door and moved out of the way. "Mrs. Henley, you go on home. I'll stay just in case I can help."

The conversation between the principal and his assistant barely registered with Rafe. His attention was keyed on Erin's workspace. He stood very still while his gaze traveled across every inch. Faint and soft, her perfume filled his senses. Just like her home, books, pictures, and student memorabilia lined the shelves. The computer was off, her chair pushed away from her desk, and the light had been off. Had somebody wanted it to appear as if she'd left for the day? Mrs. Henley's previous comment about Erin's love for organization told a different story.

A folder lay open on the desk with papers scattered around it as if she had been in the middle of something. The blazer she'd worn to work this morning remained draped over the back of her chair. A ceramic mug sitting on a coaster was half-full. The Erin he'd come to love—scratch that, care for—would never have left stale coffee to sit overnight. She was much too fastidious for that. But the deciding factor for him was her promise. No way would she have left with anyone other than him.

"I want every inch searched." Wade's voice boomed through the empty hall. "Call in more uniforms if you need them. Remind them to treat the school grounds as a crime scene."

Wade's voice, issuing instructions to his team, did little to ease the panic Rafe fought to keep under control. Nor did telling himself that nothing could be gained by him losing it calm his churning stomach.

Rafe introduced Wade to Principal Mueller.

"Norman. Please call me Norman," the principal said as the two men shook hands. "You, too," he said to Rafe.

Wade handed Norman a business card. "Norman, we're going

to need you to stick around. There may be areas of the school we'll need you to unlock."

Norman seemed not to have heard. His gaze was on Wade's card. "You're with homicide? You think Erin is dead?"

"We hope not." Wade gave the principal a humorless smile. A patrol officer approached, and Wade spoke with him, turning back to say, "There's a reporter out front. We're not letting him or anyone else inside. It would be best if you didn't speak with the press."

Norman shook his head. "I won't."

"If you'd like to wait in your office until we've completed our investigation, that's fine."

The principal's lips thinned. "I'll have to notify the president of the school board and district police as to what's going on. They'll expect me to have answers."

"Of course, you have protocol to follow. Suggest they not speak to the media." Wade nodded his agreement. "The crime scene unit will take over shortly. My men are searching the premises. If we can complete our work before morning, the school can open on time. And you'll be notified when you can access Ms. Brady's office in case there are files you need in there."

Rafe waited until he and Wade were alone. "Erin didn't willingly walk out of here. We agreed I'd be waiting out front for her. Her blazer is still here, and there is a half-full coffee cup on her desk. Ask one of your men to start opening drawers. I'm betting you'll find her…"

A uniformed female held up a purse. Rafe's chest constricted even more. He rubbed his chest bone to ease the pressure. "That's Erin's."

"You look like you're on the edge, clinging by your fingertips. I can't have you around if you're going to fall apart. FBI or not, technically this isn't your case. It's mine."

"I'm fine," Rafe snapped, tamping down the fire in his belly.

"You can stay or go, just don't interfere with my people."

Wade's radio squawked and a voice said, "Are you expecting the feds?"

The detective's eyebrows rose in question. "Are you expecting your partner?"

"Yeah."

"Send him back," Wade said into his radio.

"Will do," came the reply.

"I'll go escort him back," Rafe said, but he couldn't walk away without speaking his mind. Erin's disappearance might not be his case, but he intended to find her and the bastard responsible. "You're wasting your time here, Wade. Whoever has her was too smart to leave a calling card. Somebody tricked her into leaving or took her by force."

"We'll see if we can get a timeline on who saw her last. Get an idea of when she left."

"In the meantime, the men on that list she gave you need to be interviewed."

Wade stuffed his hands into his pants pockets. Rafe stood his ground, allowing the detective to consider Rafe's opinion. His impatience ate away at him.

"Okay, I'm issuing the FBI an invitation. I'll clear it on my end. Do you have a copy of the list?"

"Not with me. I can have it in twenty minutes."

"No need to go that far. I'll call my office. One will be waiting for you at the front desk. Go do some interviews."

Rafe released the pressure in his chest with a big breath. "Thanks."

"And stay in touch," Wade said to the back of Rafe's head.

****

Rafe scanned the list they'd just collected. Glad to have the addresses in hand, he got in Colton's pickup and buckled his seat belt.

Colton turned the key, and the engine roared to life. "Where to?"

Rafe read the address out loud. "I want the coach first. Terry Evans is just arrogant enough to think he could get away with kidnapping."

Colton entered the information into his GPS, slipped the gearshift into reverse, then backed out. "How are you holding up?"

"I'm fine." The imaginary strap around his chest tightened. "Why wouldn't I be?"

"Don't bullshit a bullshitter. You finally found a woman who got to you. Your brother and I think it's cool."

"You met Luke? I forgot to tell him that you were staying at the house."

"Yes, you did. He was in the kitchen when I unlocked the front door and strolled in."

"Sorry. I take it you two had a nice visit."

"We made it just fine. Shared a cup of coffee. Seems like an okay guy."

"He is. I'm glad he's home. Keeps me from having to guess what to do with Dad's belongings. Besides, now that he's out of the military, I don't have to worry about him."

"Have you asked him what he wants to do?"

"No. I figure he'll find something he likes. Why?"

"He's looking at the Texas Rangers or US Marshals Service."

"He needs to choose something safer."

"He's been sleeping with danger. It's in his blood." Colton chuckled. "He's not walking away from the military to run a tire shop."

"Fuck you. He could be a landscaper or banker."

"I'll let you tell him that."

The droning voice of the GPS announced their final turn and that their destination was two-tenths of a mile on the right. Colton pulled down the driveway and killed the engine. The coach's home sat back off the street behind large trees and a green lawn. It had pale brick trimmed out in gray and a slate-colored roof. Rafe thought the place looked like a small prison.

"Neighbors are pretty damn close." Colton pulled his sunglasses down the bridge of his nose and stared over the top of the frames. "But, then, so were the neighbors where the girl in Ohio was kept for eighteen years."

Rafe checked his watch. Had it been only a few hours since he'd gone inside the school to see what was keeping Erin? The clock was ticking and the pressure was building in his chest.

Before they reached the porch, Coach Evans opened the door. First impressions for Rafe meant a lot, and the coach looked surprised and curious.

"Coach, this is my partner, Colton Weir. We'd like to speak with you for a minute. May we come in?"

He shook Colton's hand and stepped back, waving them inside. Neither Rafe nor Colton sat, but the coach plopped down in a chair and propped his feet up.

"What's this about?"

Rafe went straight to the point. "Erin Brady is missing. We believe she's been kidnapped by someone she knows."

"Terry?" An attractive woman walked into the living room, drying her hands on a kitchen towel. "Hello. I thought I heard voices."

"My wife, Lauren." The coach made introductions. "The counselor at school is missing."

"Gentlemen, please sit down." Mrs. Evans waved toward the couch. "How can we help?"

"We're speaking with all Erin's coworkers." Rafe turned his attention to the coach. "Did you see her today?"

"Yeah. I stuck my head in her office to welcome her back."

"Did she have anybody with her?"

The coach's wife sat on the edge of her husband's footstool.

"Don't burn my supper," Evans snapped.

Pink rushed up her cheeks, but she stood. "You're right, of

course. I'd better check on it."

Colton, who'd remained standing, cleared his throat. "Mrs. Evans, may I trouble you for a glass of water?"

"Bring the man a fresh bottle out of the fridge," the coach commanded.

Evans might be smart, but Rafe knew Colton wanted to speak with Mrs. Evans alone. "No, thanks. I prefer tap." He fell in step behind Mrs. Evans. "You hand me a glass, and I'll do the rest."

It was up to Rafe to keep Evans busy for a few minutes. If Colton could get Mrs. Evans to open up, they might actually learn something useful.

"He'll keep her busy with small talk, give us some privacy." Rafe leaned back in his chair and crossed his legs. "You were telling me about how you stopped by to welcome Ms. Brady back to work."

"Right. Nobody was in her office. I have a couple of players who are damn close to becoming ineligible. I wanted her to speak with them about their grades." Evans glanced toward the kitchen.

"You have a nice place. Mind if I take a look around?"

The coach dropped his feet to the floor and leaned forward. "What's that supposed to mean?"

"It means I don't have time to waste. Either you have something to hide or you don't. With your reputation as a bully, guess who I thought of first? We can end this one of two ways. Colton can keep your wife busy while I look around, or I'll get a warrant and tear this place apart in front of her."

"You don't have grounds for a warrant," the coach fired back.

"Try me." Rafe glanced at his watch. It seemed to mock him, reminding him that time wasn't on his side.

"Fine." The coach propped his feet back on the stool. "Look all you want."

Colton joined Rafe after he'd thoroughly searched the house. A shed out in the backyard certainly looked like a good hiding place.

"You'll need this to get inside." Colton passed Rafe a key.

"You get this from the wife?"

"Yeah. Nice lady."

"You learn anything from her?"

"Nothing of value. She made small talk, but she kept looking over her shoulder as if she feared the coach would burst through the door any second." Colton glanced back toward the house. "I kind of wish he had."

Rafe swung the shed's double doors wide. A riding lawn mower took up half of the space. Yard tools hung in perfect order on a wall rack. The workbench had been laid out the same way. Every tool was straight and easy to find. "Too tidy," Rafe said.

Colton removed a garden spade and walked around, stabbing the sharp point into the dirt floor. Rafe shifted items and sorted through a bag of rags, looking for anything that might belong to a woman. "If this bastard has Erin, he's stashed her someplace else."

"We should see if Evans or his wife owns additional property." Colton hung up the spade.

"Good idea. Let me return the key." Rafe walked to the back door and knocked.

"I'll do it."

Rafe stepped back a few feet and let his partner take over. Seconds later, Mrs. Evans opened the door.

"He really doesn't like to be disturbed while he's having his evening meal."

"Did your husband kidnap Ms. Brady?"

Her head moved left then right slightly.

Colton took out his card and handed it to her. "Call me if you need help."

She stuffed the card in her pocket and stepped closer. "Thank you."

"There are places you can go for help. Places where you'll be safe."

She nodded and closed the door.

"She won't call," Colton said, shaking his head.

They walked away in silence. Both were worried about the coach's wife and what went on behind closed doors. Rafe joined Colton in his truck and read over the names on the list

"Who's next?" Colton asked.

"We wasted a lot of time on Coach Evans. I'd have put money on him." Rafe's nerves were stretched thin. His shoulders ached, and his fear for Erin worsened with each passing minute. "Charles Parker is the history teacher. The list says he's single. I'll call Beckett and ask for real estate information on the coach."

The GPS voice irritated the shit out of Rafe. Odd, the flat monotone had never bothered him before. It wasn't like Erin's upbeat and confident voice.

Was she hurting? Cold? Hungry? He refused to believe her life was in jeopardy. If the stalker believed himself to be in love with Erin, he'd keep her alive. But Erin would never give in. The more she protested and argued, the more dangerous her stalker would become.

"Stay with me." Colton's slow drawl interrupted the fear building in Rafe's mind.

"I'm fine."

"You're not fine." He held up one finger. "But that's okay. Just don't go bat-shit crazy on me. I fucking don't need to fight you and this bastard who has your woman."

"She was my responsibility. Mine."

"We'll find her."

"And the son of a bitch who took her." Rafe ground out the words. "I've never wanted to kill another human being, but this guy..." He clamped his teeth together for a second. "If he's hurt her in any way, you'll think bat-shit crazy."

"We'll find her. And justice will take its course."

"I'm not looking for the court's justice. I'll exact my own justice."

"You know I've got your back. Just hold it together."

Rafe leaned back in the seat. The Glock pressed against his kidney, reminding him of its presence. They headed for the history teacher's house. Rafe silently begged the fates to protect Erin. Colton, no doubt, was measuring Rafe's sanity, which was a good idea, because he was doing the same.

CHAPTER 22

Erin woke with a start. How could she have fallen asleep in this hellhole? The initial burst of adrenaline had worn off, and the resulting crash had left her weak and exhausted. Still, drifting off had been dangerous. Staying alert and strong were the way out. Out of what? Out of where?

Away from whom?

Her muscles ached as she stood and stretched. Her right hand throbbed. She'd pounded on the hatch door until her hand was bruised and swollen. Her bladder was about to explode, but just the thought of being caught on that toilet ended those basic urges.

How long had she slept? An hour or twelve? It felt as if she'd been down here for days. She had no idea whether it was day or night. A shudder racked her body.

God, she was thirsty. The refrigerator had been empty, but for some stupid reason, she felt compelled to open the door and look. It was still running and still bare.

The wedding dress, which she'd wadded up and thrown aside, seemed to mock her. This whole thing was a little too *Phantom of the Opera* for her. She'd never listen to that music again. Erin reached to rip the dress to shreds.

The seed of an idea stopped her. Did the crazy bastard expect her to marry him? That would never happen, but to stay alive, she might have to pretend. Could she pull it off? What would she do if he wanted to have sex?

A sound from above sent her heart racing. The door lever moved. Erin grabbed the dress off the floor and spread it across the foot of the cot. Her heart raced, and the sound of rushing blood filled her ears.

Was she being rescued? Or was she about to meet the monster?

She stood, backed as far into the corner as possible, and waited. Faking bravery used to be one of her specialties, but she'd been a kid back then. She'd draw on those skills and maybe brazen her way out of this trap. Could she pull it off?

The hatch opened, and a foot appeared on the top rung. Whose shoe was she looking at?

"You found the light pull." Principal Mueller made his way down the ladder and into the small space. His tone wasn't that of a predator. His face wasn't snarled with evil. He was joyful, which made his words even more chilling. "I'm sorry I didn't leave it on. I'd planned on coming home sooner, but in my position, I had to stay until the police left."

"Why did you do this?" Her anger, coupled with a large dose of terror, threatened to boil over. His behavior was beyond insane.

He tilted his head and smiled. "My silly sweetheart. This was the only way. Now no one will disturb us or interfere with us being together. When we're ready, we'll rejoin society."

"There is no *we*."

"Of course there is, and I see no reason for you to deny it. Why else would I have killed those people for you? Remodeled my home? Installed this safe room for your use? Only a person in love would do that. I'll never allow anybody to hurt you."

All the blood drained from her head. The extent of his break from reality made Erin lightheaded. How had he kept this side of his personality a secret? At school, he'd displayed such a proper demeanor that she'd never once thought him unstable.

She crept to the edge of the cot, pushed the wedding dress aside, and sat down.

His smile broadened, and he clapped his hands like an excited child. "Don't you love the dress? I hope it fits. I had to guess at the size, but I knew right away that it was perfect for you."

That he'd ordered the dress with her in mind sent her stomach into a downhill slide. She wrapped her arms around her middle. "Principal Mueller." Erin tried to sound calm as she stood. She smoothed the front of her blouse, trying to look calm. She walked the few steps it took to stand in front of him. "I want you to step out of the way, so I can leave."

"Sweetheart, you never have to address me as Principal Mueller again." He lifted his hand and tried to touch her cheek, but she backed away. "In fact, I much prefer you call me Casanova."

"And why would I do that?"

"It's the nickname you gave me. I've grown quite fond of it."

Her hand went to her face where he'd almost touched her. Had she heard him correctly? She'd never referred to him by any nickname. How could he stand there and spew that babble with a straight face?

"You must be mistaken. I haven't called you anything except Principal Mueller."

"Of course you have," he said. "I'm not deaf. I heard you." His tone had shifted to impatient.

An argument formed on the tip of her tongue, but Erin pulled her frustration and anger into check. Determined to keep her voice steady, she concentrated on enunciating her words. "I want to go home. People will be looking for me."

"I was afraid of this." He spoke as if talking to a child. "I had hoped leaving you down here for any length of time wouldn't be necessary. I can see you've denied your feelings for me so long you've lost your way."

He moved toward the ladder. She had to stop him. "Please. Don't do this."

"It's for the best. You need some time to collect your thoughts. I blame all of those outside influences. The men. They've successfully come between us." He shook his head as if disgusted. "Can't you see they don't love you? No one will ever love you like I do." His eyes darkened as he spoke. "And those horrible girls telling lies about you. Everything that's happened over the past few weeks has messed up your thinking. Now that all of the outside influences have been eliminated, you'll realize we're meant to be together. You're safe now. I'll always protect you."

The principal was insane. Completely out of his mind. "Kidnapping me is not protecting me." She lashed the words out at him.

He advanced, closing the distance between them. Flat, emotionless eyes stared down at her. "I killed for you. Sent a message to the world that lying about you wouldn't be tolerated."

"You killed Penny and Sara." The world collapsed from under her with his smile. Tears flooded Erin's eyes.

"Of course I did. Do you think any of those men who've been sniffing around you would kill to protect you? Not likely."

The realization that she might spend the rest of her life in captivity hit her hard. "You need to let me go. Please," she said, softening her tone. "Let me walk out of here."

"No." He whirled and started up the ladder.

Erin grabbed his leg. "Don't lock me in. I hate being down here."

"I'm very disappointed in your lack of gratitude for everything I've done. In fact, I planned to bring you your purse, but that wasn't possible. Some alone time is exactly what you need. Think about writing a letter to the media. You need to explain how you want to be left alone. Later, you can put pen to paper, and then I'll mail it for you."

"I won't do it. Rafe Sirilli will never stop looking for me." She grabbed again for his leg.

"Then he can die, too." The principal's foot lashed out, kicking her in the stomach.

She stumbled backward and landed on the cot. Her shoes slipped off of her feet and fell to the floor, landing with hollow thuds. The skirt of the wedding dress, with its yards and yards of lace, fluttered up around her thighs. Erin shoved the dress away.

"Where am I?"

Mueller stopped at the top of the ladder and turned to look at her. "You're at home. I had the house remodeled, installing this storm shelter. After we're married and life returns to normal, we'll come down here during bad weather."

"This is not my home." Normal? Normal wasn't a word she'd use to describe him.

"You'll come around," he said. "I'll bring you food and water later."

The door slammed shut, the sound echoing like an explosion. What kind of storm shelter had the lock on the outside? To Erin, it felt like he'd closed the lid on her coffin.

She'd handled their first contact poorly. Gaining his confidence should have been her goal, not pissing him off. Instead, she'd reminded him that he was holding her against her will, making him suspicious of her every action. Before he returned, she had to gain control of her fears and formulate a plan to escape.

Erin took down her ponytail and dragged her fingers through the knots in her hair. Oddly enough, straightening her clothes and putting her shoes on made her feel more in control.

Time passed slowly. Not knowing how long she'd been down here was maddening. When she felt as if the room was getting smaller, Erin paced the few steps from wall to wall. The waiting was torture. Not to mention that she was growing thirstier with each minute.

Dozens of news stories about women held as sex slaves for years ran through her mind. He seemed to believe that by holding her captive she'd surrender. Could she make him think she'd had a change of heart? Play up to him so he'd believe he'd won her over?

The dress could be the key to her escape. But would it backfire if she wore it too soon?

Erin heard a noise. Was she hearing people talking or was that a TV? She jumped up, rushed up the ladder, and tried to listen. Her imagination was running away with her.

The silence. The hunger. Her thirst. She returned to the cot, hugging her knees to her chest. Nerves frazzled, she dozed off and on. But she refused to turn off the light. That and hope were all she had, and she clung to them both, using them as a lifeline.

Rafe was hunting for her. He'd turn over every rock, unearth every possible clue until he found her.

What if the principal grew tired of her? Realized he couldn't force her to love him? He'd kill her. Waiting for Rafe to save her wasn't an option. She had to do this herself.

****

Rafe ended the call by apologizing again. As expected, Jeff had chewed Rafe a new one for not contacting him and Lotty sooner. He'd put off upsetting the Paulenskis, hoping to have better news.

A hand clamped down on Rafe's shoulder. He grasped the wrist and whirled. "Goddamn it, Luke. I could've hurt you."

"Sorry." His brother pointed to the plate he'd placed on the table. The bologna sandwich and a bottle of water didn't appeal to Rafe. "Eat. Drink."

"I'm not hungry." Rafe studied his brother. Luke's gray eyes seemed darker tonight.

"You know the speech about keeping your strength up better than I do, so suffice to say, eat it or wear it."

"Thanks." Rafe took a bite without noticing the taste. "It's late. What are you doing up?"

"I feel odd. Being home, not having a purpose, all this luxury, it makes me edgy."

"You'll adjust. Give yourself some time to get used to civilian life. You've been through some rough shit."

"You ever have nightmares?"

"Not anymore. But you were in deeper than I was, and

longer, too. If you need to talk, I'm here." Rafe's time in the military as a sniper hadn't been a picnic, but he knew that the Rangers were called on for some of the toughest assignments ever.

Luke reached over and picked up Erin's list. He studied the pages. "The check marks mean you talked to them?"

Rafe nodded, understanding the change of subject. Luke would open up about his experience overseas at his own pace.

"Nobody stood out?"

"Everybody has their skeletons. My money says the coach either physically or mentally abuses his wife. The history teacher is clean. Nice guy and very gay. I promised to keep that confidential. Erin worked closely with the head of the special-ed department. His wife and two kids met us at the door. Another nice guy. The principal is single. We stopped back by the school and questioned him."

"What did you think about him?"

"He was more worried about the board and whether or not the students would be allowed in the classrooms tomorrow than what had happened to Erin."

"What now?"

"Tomorrow we work the list. We're digging into info about everybody's property. She could be anywhere."

"I'm available for grunt work. Use me. I can take care of myself."

"I'll bet." Rafe studied his brother. Aside from his formidable physical appearance, Luke had plenty of hard-core military training to back up his claim. Luke had always been intelligent as hell.

Their mother would have been proud of her baby boy. Luke probably didn't remember much about her. Being four years younger than Rafe and Nick, his memories of her might have faded. After the first few years of her suicide, he'd stopped talking about her altogether. But so had the rest of the family.

"Colton said the local police made a couple of arrests on the drug case."

"So I heard. Our original hunch on Grace and her brother paid off. He hadn't been at college this year. Too busy running the drugs to Westbrook Hills from Laredo."

"What about the girl?" Luke asked.

"Don't know. She's old enough to try as an adult. She'd been covering for him since he started pushing that poison." Rafe looked down and surprised himself. He'd not only polished off the sandwich, he'd eaten every chip on his plate.

Luke returned the list and picked up the empty plate. "I don't suppose you could be convinced to get some rest."

"I'll sleep after I find Erin and kill..." Rafe bit off his sentence.

"Don't do anything to end your career." Luke carried Rafe's trash to the kitchen.

Water running, followed by the scent of coffee being scooped into the pot, indicated Luke planned to stay up. No way was Rafe turning down the offer to help. Somebody took Erin out of the school, and Luke could use his expertise to locate the most logical point of entrance and exit. Maybe the cops missed something.

"Can't a guy get some rest around here?" Colton stood at the end of the hall, fully dressed and wide awake. "Do I smell coffee brewing?" Without waiting for an answer, he walked through the dining room into the kitchen, where a muffled conversation started.

Colton's claim that he couldn't get any sleep was a load of crap. His partner had disappeared long enough to grab a shower and change clothes. Rafe couldn't continue sitting around doing nothing. He called Beckett who agreed to squeeze out a workspace for him and Colton at the precinct.

"Colton," he called out. "Beckett's getting a dedicated space for us. We'll have access to their systems and ours."

"I'm in." Luke set a travel mug full of coffee on the table. "I want to help."

CHAPTER 23

The waiting was making Erin crazy. The principal had left to get her something to eat, but he hadn't returned. What if he never returned? Had a heart attack and died? No one would know she was down here.

She'd sat cross-legged on the floor and tried to meditate. Failing that project miserably, she'd stretched out on the cot and tried to envision green fields of corn, children playing, but again, she'd failed. She'd slept in fits. Battled her panic and lost. She'd succumbed to bouts of depression and tears of despair, followed by fits of anger, where she screamed and cursed the principal.

How long had it been since she'd had water? The one essential thing for life, and she couldn't remember her last sip.

The door opened, and Erin sprang to her feet. Blood rushed from her head, and the world turned blurry for a second.

The principal carried a plastic bag over his arm as he descended. "I'm sorry you had to wait." He removed a bottle of water and handed it to her.

She opened it and took a long drink. Nothing had ever tasted so good. The cool liquid slid down her throat. "Thank you."

Mueller's appearance had changed. No suit and tie now. He wore jeans, boots, and a pullover shirt. On his belt, he wore a scabbard holding a big hunting knife. "I had to get some rest. This morning the school board met, and I had to bring them up-to-date."

He paused. His eyebrows pulled together. Should she have said something? All she could concentrate on was the aroma coming from the sack he held.

"What?" she asked

"You have no sympathy for my problems, do you?"

"I'm sorry. It's just that I'm very hungry."

"I figured." He removed a small box from a local fried chicken restaurant and handed it to her. "I picked up a couple of packages at the post office today. Would you like to come upstairs and see them?"

Erin savored her first bite of chicken for a second before answering. "Yes, please."

"How do I know I can trust you?"

"I won't try to get away. I'd really like to have a shower."

Principal Mueller studied her face. Erin smiled and continued eating.

"Finish your meal. I'll be right back."

Panic closed her throat, and she coughed. "You won't forget?"

"Never." He left, but closed the door behind him.

Erin cleaned up every bite of the food he'd brought, polished off the water and was wiping her fingers with the single napkin when the door reopened.

A coiled nylon cord landed hard on the floor. He followed. "Give me your foot."

"What are you going to do?"

"Do you want a shower?" He stood in front of her, holding a white plastic tie.

"Yes." She had no intentions of refusing him, but she didn't want to make him suspicious by sounding too eager. "But how will I take off my clothes to shower with a rope around my ankle?"

He didn't respond as he wrapped the plastic tie around her ankle then slid one end through the loop. He made sure the tether was tight enough so she couldn't slip her foot out. "Stay put," he commanded. He held the other end of the cord in his hand and tossed the wedding dress over his shoulder. Once he'd climbed the ladder, he called to her. "Come up here."

Erin didn't have to be told twice. Careful not to get her feet tangled, she climbed to the top. Her heart dropped. He was securing the other end of the cord to his wrist. He'd tethered her to him. She quickly scanned her surroundings, looking for an escape route.

"When I remodeled the house, I had extra insulation installed. We have neighbors, but no one will hear us if we argue." His gaze raked over her and a smirk lifted his lips. "If you're one of those women who are vocal during sex, no worries."

Her mouth went bone dry. There would be no sex between them. He'd have to force her, and the fight preceding the rape would be epic. He was a couple of inches taller than she was and had a good forty pounds on her, but that wouldn't stop her from fighting.

He laughed a low, throaty sound. "You're blushing. I like that." He rolled the excess cord around his arm until he stood by her side. "Shower is this way."

Erin walked in front of him down the hall. How did he expect her to undress? Could she convince him that if he left her alone long enough to shower, she wouldn't try to escape? It was a bluff she'd have to try.

His hand on her shoulder stopped her. He opened a door and stepped back, waving her to go in first. "I hope you like it."

Erin's knees buckled, forcing her to grab the doorjamb for support. The room was white. Sterile. Cold. Not just the walls. Everything in the room was white. The headboard on the king-size bed, the dresser, and the matching end tables were all a light-colored wood. The lamps, drapes, and the large throw rug? All white. The only relief in the room was a floral arrangement of red roses on the nightstand. "My God," she muttered.

"It's beautiful, isn't it? Helps me sleep."

"It does?" She worked at keeping her tone calm.

"White reminds me of you. Pure, whole, and angelic. The red makes me think of the passion we'll share. Each night I crawl between the sheets and pretend you are in bed with me." His free hand slid around her waist. "I can't wait to see your naked body lying in our tangled sheets."

Erin's skin turned clammy and cold, yet sweat beaded her forehead.

"Tonight"—his lips were next to her ear, almost touching—"there will be nothing to stop us from demonstrating our love. We don't have to hide our desire anymore."

Her flesh recoiled at the idea of him touching her intimately. He was so deluded that he expected her to sleep with him. No, not deluded. Insane.

He turned her to face him. His fingers dug into her flesh.

"I'm insane?"

She'd said that out loud? If she denied it, he'd see right through her. "You kidnapped me."

"I saved you!" His grip tightened painfully. "Here I'd hoped your alone time had helped you get your priorities straight."

"My priorities?"

"Oh, I accept some of the blame. You made your affection for me known, but I waited too long to let you know that I felt the same way. My mistake was allowing you to hang out with those FBI men. They corrupted your mind." His voice had gotten louder and shriller with each word. "I should've killed them all."

"You bashed in Linc's head, didn't you?" The fried chicken churned in her stomach.

"If your neighbor dies, his death will be on you. He had no business going in and out of your house as if he belonged there. All of them were interfering with us being together. Just like that photographer, who paid for hiding and taking your picture and scaring you.

Erin opened her mouth. She had to force words out. "You killed the guy who hid in my tree?"

"Damn right I did. I'll kill anybody who hurts you or interferes with us being together."

The principal's lips had thinned, and the nerves in his jaw

muscles twitched. She had to calm him down. The principal's hold on reality was slipping fast. Escaping had to be soon.

"Is the bath through there?"

"Yes." He released her waist, walked her over, and opened a door.

The one ray of hope vanished. A skylight flooded the room with bright sunshine. But it was the only window in the room. She pulled a smile from somewhere and ran her hand over her blouse. "I can't take this off with the rope on my ankle. I understand that you don't trust me, but there's nowhere for me to go."

His gaze narrowed. Silence hung between them. "Fine." He tightened his grip on her waist. "Don't test my love. Not again. I can and will put you back in the storm shelter."

"I understand."

The hunting knife made quick work of the plastic tie. Erin bent and rubbed her ankle. Her mind raced. So the bathroom wasn't her way out. She'd have to find another way.

"Thank you," she said in the sweetest tone she could muster. She turned her back, reaching to close the door. *Please God*, she prayed. *Don't let him watch me undress.*

"I will be right outside. I think you'll find everything you need. This is our bathroom, and I've been slowly stocking it with everything you might need."

The snick the door made when it closed sent relief rushing through Erin. She turned the hot-water faucet to full blast then looked around. Maybe she could find a weapon, something she could hide in the waistband of her slacks. The small storage closet had everything but a sharp object. On the shelves, she found shampoo, conditioner, a hair dryer, and deodorant. Nothing of any value when it came to self-defense.

How much time would he allow? How much restraint was he willing to show? Unwilling to risk it, she quickly stripped and stepped into the steamy shower to adjust the water. Cleaning her body and hair in record speed, she used that time to think, to plan. Her head was tilted back as she rinsed the shampoo from her hair when the door opened then quickly closed.

Naked and wet, she'd never felt so vulnerable. Was he in the room? Planning to join her? She peered through the frosted-glass shower door. Unable to see, she turned off the water and wrapped an oversized white towel around her body. Then she stepped out onto the tile floor.

She was alone, but her clothes were gone. In their place was the wedding dress. The bastard had tricked her, planned this all along.

That monstrosity could hang on the door until the end of time. No way was she putting it on. She tightened the towel, located the dryer, and went to work on her hair. Maybe she was wrong. Maybe he'd taken her things to launder them for her.

Behind her, from almost every position she stood in, the snowy white wedding dress taunted her in the mirror. Her clothes weren't going to be returned. This was his way of forcing her into the dress. She had the overwhelming urge to turn the dryer on the lace and see how he liked a melted sham of a dress.

The rubber band broke when she tried to anchor her hair off her face. She rummaged through the drawers, finding nothing to use as a replacement tie. The bastard had thought of everything, including a brush, comb, and even a toothbrush, but there were no clips or rubber bands.

Now was the time she needed Rafe to burst through the front door and rescue her. She shook her head to stop that kind of thinking. She'd spent many years learning to depend on no one but herself. She paid her own bills and made her own decisions. But looking in the mirror at the frightened woman staring back at her, she admitted she'd welcome a hero rushing in to stop the bad guy.

A knock startled her. Damn Casanova, or whatever the hell he called himself. She wanted to throw open the door and rush him, but she remembered his knife. A weapon like that belonged with a hunter, not the timid principal of a school. A conversation with Rafe flashed through her memory. Something about stabbing a person in the diaphragm.

The knock came again. "Come out here. I want to see you in the dress."

His demanding tone sent her blood boiling. Putting on that wedding dress meant surrender. She clutched the towel tightly and opened the door.

"I have no underwear. Do you expect me to walk around in that dress with no bra and panties? What would your mother say about that kind of perversion?"

The back of his hand landed squarely on her cheekbone. Erin fell backward, landing hard on her tailbone. The tile floor sent rockets of pain up her spine. The towel fell off, exposing her body to his eyes.

Time seemed to stop as his gaze raked across her skin. She felt as if she needed a scalding-hot shower. She quickly covered herself with the damp terry cloth, ignoring the pain in her cheek.

"My mother tried using that tone of voice on my father. She learned quickly he wouldn't tolerate her disrespect. What would she think? Who knows? Dad dumped her out at the bus station many years ago. Told the whore to never come back."

He grabbed Erin's ankle and affixed a new plastic tie on her along with the rope. She held the towel tighter as he pulled her to her feet.

"Put on the dress or go downstairs. Your choice."

Tears rushed to the surface. Erin blinked repeatedly, trying to stem the flow. As if recognizing the sheer hopelessness of her situation and against her will, tears marched down her face in steady streams.

She bent over, picked up the cord, and then handed him the slack. Shoulders back and head high, she walked into the hall and to the door to the shelter. Without another word, she descended the ladder.

"Have it your way." His end of the nylon cord landed at her feet. Moments later, the wedding dress fluttered to the floor. Then the door slammed shut.

Erin screamed. Grabbed the dress and ripped at the lacy overskirt. Her tears came from rage and frustration, and this time she allowed them to flow freely. Not since her stepfather had she wanted to physically hurt another human being. But given the chance, the principal would know her anger.

Eventually, her fit of temper subsided. And once again, she was alone in the silence. Chills raced up and down her body. Wrapped in a bath towel and with no way out, she'd allowed her defiance to seal her fate. Had she made the right choice? How long would he wait before returning?

Escape from this hellhole was impossible. But could she do whatever was necessary to stay above ground? To live, to survive, she had to come to terms with her situation.

CHAPTER 24

Rafe drained the cup of coffee, tossed the paper cup into the trash, and refocused on the surveillance video from the school. Wade had set up the conference room so Rafe could watch and study all the different angles from the different cameras. Damn that he'd found nothing suspicious. Caffeine, anger, and frustration were keeping him going.

Erin knew he cared for her, right? How big a deal would it have been to confess she'd always hold a special place in his heart? Someday, she would've understood that his lifestyle had put them on different paths.

He'd tell her face-to-face when he found her. And he would find her.

She was the focus of a massive manhunt. The patrol units were on alert to Erin's disappearance. The television station had already run a story on their hourly newsbreak. A few crank calls had come in, but for the most part concerned citizens had reached out and offered their services. Erin had a lot of people in her corner.

Rafe had spent hours going over backgrounds and real estate information. With no clues to work with, finding Erin was as likely as catching a handful of smoke. Still, somewhere there was a hint, something that would grow into a clue.

"Good morning."

Rafe looked up to find Luke standing in the doorway. He wore jeans and a white shirt and had obviously found his old Stetson. "Morning. You find anything?"

"Not yet." Rafe motioned to an empty chair. "What'd you learn from your time with Colton?"

"The narcotics squad is an interesting group." Luke turned

the chair backward and sat down. "That college dude is spilling his guts. Colton says none of the names he's provided are on Erin's list."

"So no help there."

"What if Erin's kidnapper's name isn't on her list?" Luke asked.

"That's a real possibility. Still, this isn't a random kidnapping or a stranger abduction. The bastard sent her a message. 'You test my love.' It was too familiar, too intimate to be from a stranger. He issued a warning."

"So he didn't approve of what? You?"

"Yeah." Rafe dragged a hand through his hair. "I think so." He stood, poured another cup of stale coffee, and offered it to Luke.

"No, thanks. Colton went for food. I asked him to bring you a carton of milk."

"Milk?" Rafe turned his attention back to the surveillance video. "If you're going into law enforcement, you'd better forget milk."

"Just drink it when he gets here. Your stomach will thank you for it." Luke slid his chair next to Rafe's. "What do we do next? Colton is still officially assigned to the drug case. He's going to the school with a couple of detectives this morning. Now that they've arrested the college boy, he's talking, and a few more students' names have surfaced."

"Good. The more they learn from Grace and her brother, the closer they'll get to the supplier in Laredo."

"We should go to the school, too." Luke pointed to the monitor. "Looking at the layout, the south exit is the logical extraction point. Even if the cops searched. area, we might see something."

"We are going to the school." Rafe kept his thoughts to himself. "I want to look for myself. I also believe the administrative assistant, Mrs. Henley, knows more than she thinks."

"I can hear you now. I'm not hungry." Colton entered the

conference room in a hurry. "I was so damn hungry I ordered extra of everything, so eat up." He emptied three bags of food, one orange juice, and two milks. "Little brother must be worried about your digestive system."

"We don't have time for this. And Luke doesn't know I can operate for days on nothing but coffee."

"I've gone days with less." Luke opened his container. "There's nutrition in milk. I've had days I would have killed for a glass. So fuck off."

"Touché." Colton chuckled, pushing the carton in front of Rafe. "Drink your milk."

Rafe wolfed down a breakfast sandwich and polished off his drink. One of these days, he'd tell Luke that Colton knew plenty about war and going hungry. Nobody knew for sure exactly what he'd done or where he'd served as a SEAL. It was a topic he didn't discuss, and Rafe didn't bring up.

"You ready?" Rafe stuffed his trash in one of the sacks. "Thanks for breakfast." He clapped Colton on the shoulder. "We're going back to the school."

"I'll be finished with the drug case today or tomorrow," Colton said. "I'm not leaving. I'll ask for vacation time. If I don't, I'll be called back to work."

"Thanks." Rafe was grateful. He didn't try to talk Colton out of taking time off. It would've been a waste of breath. "I'll text Beckett. Let him know where we're going."

When Beckett returned the message, Rafe said, "Says he's going to the YMCA to interview the manager."

Rafe and Luke left the building and hurried to the parking lot. A dull ache had formed at the base of Rafe's skull. Normally, he thrived on pressure situations, loved solving the puzzle and bringing some lowlife to justice. This was different. He struggled to keep the panic below the surface. His imagination as to what Erin might be enduring sent his mind into turmoil.

Luke extended his hand. "I'll drive."

"You think I can't?"

"You tell me. You're standing next to the wrong car." Luke tapped the roof of somebody else's vehicle.

"Fuck." Rafe handed over the keys. "I'm a little distracted."

"And that's okay." He walked two rows over and opened the passenger door for Rafe.

****

Luke drove and Rafe tried to pull his thoughts together. He got that bad things happened to good people. He'd come to grips with that fact a long time ago. But this was Erin. She'd survived hell as a kid. Made a great life for herself. He had to make things right for her.

Luke drove into the school's parking lot and turned off the engine. Rafe got out and waited at the curb.

Luke held out the keys. "Want these back?"

"Keep them." They entered the building just as the bell rang and the hall emptied.

"Good memories, huh?" Luke stopped and looked around.

"Not so much." The high school was where Erin went missing.

"I'm sorry." Luke's voice trailed off. "That was stupid of me. You were thinking about Erin."

"Won't stop until I find her. There's something I'm missing. Something that will lead me to her." Rafe led the way to the office area. Mrs. Henley was at her desk, speaking with a student. Her gaze swung from Rafe to Luke and back.

"Good morning, gentlemen," Mrs. Henley said. "Give me just a moment?"

Rafe nodded, moving to the row of chairs that lined the wall. He sat and Luke joined him. "You remember Mrs. Henley?"

"Sure." Luke lowered his voice. "She was the librarian when I graduated. Always called me Lucas."

Rafe chuckled. "She still does."

The student left, and Mrs. Henley motioned for Rafe and Luke to join her. She stood and extended her hand to Luke. Her smile was sincere.

"Lucas," she said. "It's good to see you. I'm pleased Rafael brought you by today."

"We'd like to speak with you," Rafe said. "Is there somewhere we can have some privacy?"

She glanced around the office. "Is this about Ms. Brady?"

"Yes, ma'am," he said.

She asked one of the other women in the office to cover for her. "Let's use Principal Mueller's office. He had to run an errand." She led the way. "Please take a seat and tell me how I can help."

Luke sat but Rafe was impatient. Sitting wasn't an option. He handed her a copy of Erin's list of names. "I value your personal opinion. I assure you that nothing you say will find its way back to your door. I'd like your honest take on each of the men who interacted with Erin."

With a slight nod, she took the piece of paper from him and studied it. Time dragged on as she read, looked to the ceiling for a moment then went back to the list. He wanted to rush her, but he didn't push, knowing it could backfire and she'd miss something.

The principal's office hadn't changed much in the years since Rafe had been inside. The bookcases were still filled with dusty tomes on state and government policies and procedures. The desk was still cluttered and the chair overstuffed. He noted there were no family pictures, but then, the principal was single.

"My least favorite is Coach Evans. Just about anybody you ask will say the same thing. Well, except the football boosters. They love a winning season. I've met Coach's wife. Timid little thing. No doubt, scared to death of him. Did you speak with him?"

"Yes. He gave us permission to search his property. I don't like him either, but we found nothing that would point to him. That's why I thought you might be able to help. Maybe one of these men said something or did something that made you uncomfortable?"

She nodded again and went back to the list.

"Principal Mueller has been here for a couple of years, but I know very little about him. He's a decent-looking man, but he never brings a guest to any function."

"So he's a loner?" Rafe asked.

"Hard to say. I've heard whispers that he's gay, but I don't buy it. I've seen him try to flirt. He just doesn't know how."

"Odd that he doesn't have one picture."

"That is odd. He's had a picture of our school picnic on his desk for a long time." Mrs. Henley scanned the room. "I don't see it now."

Rafe moved around the room while Mrs. Henley went through the list, noting any small idiosyncrasy she had noticed. Luke made notes as she spoke. When she reached the end of the list, she shook her head.

"I haven't helped you one bit. I'm sorry."

"But you have. You've helped more than you know." He walked to the door and stopped. She and Luke joined him.

"It's good to have you boys home. I'm sorry for the loss of your father."

"Thank you," Luke said. "It was good to see you, too."

Mrs. Henley walked with Rafe and Luke to the outside steps. "If I think of anything, I'll call you."

"Word will get back to the principal we were here. You won't get into trouble for talking to us?" Rafe asked.

"With Casanova?" She glanced over her shoulder. "I doubt it. He's hardly here anymore. Always off on errands. Makes me wonder if he's interviewing for another job. Besides, what's he going to do? I'm retiring at the end of this year."

"Casanova," Luke repeated. "You just said he didn't know how to flirt. How'd he get that nickname?"

She grinned up at Luke. "He stumbles around women like a

drunken sailor. It's a tongue-in-cheek name. I hung it on him after witnessing him trying to make a joke."

Rafe wasn't smiling. "Do you remember who the object of his interest happened to be?"

"I could've showed you if the picture had been on his desk. In it, he's staring kind of moon-eyed at Ms. Brady."

Rafe pulled his business card out and handed it to Mrs. Henley. "I need his home address."

She blinked a couple of times. "You don't think...I'll run inside and get it."

Rafe dug out his cell and called Wade. "We need to get over to Mueller's. It's looking like he could be our guy. I'm on my way."

"Wait a minute. You can't go cowboy and kick in his door."

Rafe disconnected and ran to meet Mrs. Henley.

CHAPTER 25

Erin shivered. How long had she been down here? Dozing off and on made it even more difficult to keep up with time. Why she tried was a mystery. Some things were impossible.

The towel had dried a long time ago, but it didn't offer the warmth she needed to stave off the chill. The wedding dress had yards of material, but she'd preferred the cold to wrapping that thing around her body. She'd curled into a tight ball, using the thick terry cloth as a blanket.

Her legs had cramped, and she'd been forced to get up and walk around. With the nylon cord still attached to her ankle, she'd carried the loose end to keep her feet from getting tangled. The muscles had finally relaxed, but the pain in her calves reminded her to keep moving.

She'd been careful not to drink too much, rationing herself to small sips. Eventually, she'd finished the lone bottle of water he'd tossed down to her the night of her shower. Why did her thirst worsen the minute the damned thing was empty?

It was all about mind control, which was exactly what Mueller was trying to do to her. She'd read stories where the captured party had been completely brainwashed. Could she convince a madman that she'd gone just as crazy as he was?

She stared at that hideous dress. How would he react when he saw the damage to the lace? So he had an abusive father and his mother had abandoned him. She didn't accept that as an excuse for his actions. Her fingers trailed across her swollen cheek and eye.

Her anger and frustration disappeared. In its place, she felt a calm resolve wash over her. The towel silently slid to the floor. She picked up the dress, wound the cord around her leg, stepped into the dress, and pulled it on.

Erin paused to just breathe as she held the strapless bodice to her chest. Her heart pounded, and her hands shook, but her mind was made up. Reaching around, she tugged the zipper up as far as she could. He'd underestimated her size but not by much. A couple of more days with minimal food and water and the dress would fit perfectly.

She ran her hands over the lace, smoothing the material. Then she backed up to the edge of the cot, sat down, and waited.

Was he upstairs asleep? At work? On his way home? Her stomach growled. She hadn't eaten since the fried chicken. How long ago had that been? Last night? The night before? Surely, he'd feed her soon.

****

Casanova had sported a hard-on most of the day. He couldn't count how many times today that he'd flashed on her sprawled naked on the floor.

He'd driven to Fort Worth to pick up a package. If Erin didn't respond positively to this surprise, he'd be forced to resort to corporal punishment. It would be entirely up to her as to how she was treated. If she failed to come around, he'd be forced to leave her downstairs until she became more compliant.

The local hamburger joint drive-through provided one meal. Call him too careful, but he wasn't ordering anything that could be construed as dinner for two.

Casanova couldn't wait to check on Erin. She'd been alone, wearing nothing but a towel and with only a bottle of water for almost twenty-four hours How could she not admit that she loved him? Was she deliberately trying to hurt him? He quickly changed into his jeans and T-shirt, sliding the leather scabbard holding the hunting knife onto his belt. He hoped to use the knife to cut off the plastic tie, but only Erin could make that happen.

He carefully removed the floor molding and folded back the

carpet. The door opened easily, but Erin didn't come into view. He'd bent over backward to please her with nothing in return. Tonight would be different.

****

The door to freedom opened. Erin's moment had come. Her ability to play along with a maniac would soon be tested. She stood and smoothed the front of the dress, folding under a few torn edges of lace.

The principal descended the ladder holding a small sack that smelled of food. The second he saw her, his expression shifted from serious to surprise. His gaze roamed from her bare shoulders to her feet and up again, leaving a slimy trail behind. She resisted the urge to wipe off her arms.

"You look beautiful."

"Thank you." She tried a timid smile and a little-girl curtsy.

He walked over to her, studying her for a minute. "Why did you put on the dress?"

She'd expected him to distrust her motive. "Because you asked me to." She quickly responded to his arched eyebrow. "And I was cold."

"Both good reasons." His gaze narrowed while he studied her swollen eye. "I hope you learned not to make me angry."

So him striking her was her fault. She'd expected that, too. "I won't do it again." She carefully touched the bruise.

"See to it you don't. If I take you upstairs to eat, will you behave?"

"Yes. Going upstairs would be nice." Stay calm and convince him she was trustworthy.

He studied her for a second before picking up the loose end of the nylon cord and securing it to his wrist. He climbed the ladder first.

Erin considered what would happen if she jerked hard on the cord. Would he fall to the hard floor? Would it knock him out? If she could at least stun him, she might be able to get the knife. It was too risky. If she failed, she might not ever get another chance. Her opportunity would come upstairs.

"I'm waiting." She felt a tug on her ankle.

"Coming." Climbing in that horrible dress wasn't easy. She stepped on the hem a couple of times, tearing the dress even more. Once upstairs, she followed him to the dining room.

His home was nicely furnished. Nothing elaborate, but it was neat and clean. That every window had been covered with heavy drapes troubled her. How long had he been planning to kidnap her?

"The dress doesn't fit." He caught the back of the dress, and the bodice slid down a little. If he'd noticed the torn lace, he didn't mention it.

"It's fine."

He pulled out a chair, and she obediently sat. The tops of her breasts were exposed. The bastard had lowered the zipper. Erin tugged the bodice up higher.

"No need to be modest. Soon, we'll intimately know every inch of each other's body." He leaned over and kissed her cheek, causing her to jump.

"Eat." He pulled a chair close to hers.

Their thighs touched, and Erin forced herself to pretend she wasn't repulsed. The soggy burger had lost its appeal, but her body needed the nutrition, so she took a big bite.

"I thought about you all day." His voice was low.

"You did?" Erin kept her attention focused on the meal in front of her.

"How could I not? You naked, wrapped in a towel, with all those delights barely covered. It drove me crazy. Knowing you're wearing nothing under that dress already has my dick hard."

"I appreciate you bringing me this food." She chose to ignore his statement. "It's delicious."

"Don't pretend there's not a sexual pull between us. Here, in our home, we can act out any fantasy. Tell me how you like it, and I'll do it."

He grabbed her hand and tried to force it to his lap. She jerked her arm away. Dear God, no way was she touching the sick bastard's erection. He caught her wrist and squeezed. The pain was better than touching him.

"I'm not a patient man, Erin. I won't tolerate you pulling away from me. As my wife, you will spread your legs for me whenever I say. Whether or not you enjoy it is strictly up to you."

She couldn't speak. Could not find her words. His personality changed so quickly she didn't know what was safe to say.

"No argument? Good. You're learning. Now finish your supper."

"I'm not hungry anymore."

"Eat it now or tomorrow night. My daddy taught me to never waste food."

Erin battled back tears. Her hands trembled as she picked up the cold burger and forced herself to take another bite. Where was her bravery now? Her plan to escape? Hope was fleeing. The longer she chewed the more difficult it became to swallow. Finally, she forced down the last morsel.

He stood, walked toward the bedroom, jerking the cord and forcing her to follow. He pointed to the bed. Lying across the bedspread was a white bridal veil and a small box.

"Open it."

Erin hands trembled as she lifted the lid. Inside were matching gold bands. "You can't make me marry you."

"You will put on the veil." He grabbed the comb and stabbed it into her hair. "Tonight we'll have a private ring ceremony. Later, perhaps we can have a legal ceremony."

"No," she blurted.

He buried his hand in the veil and her hair, wrapping it around his fingers. He jerked her head back. His lips crushed hers as he tried to kiss her. Erin thrashed her head from side to side. He shoved her onto the bed. The face of evil loomed over her as he straddled her body and wrapped his hands around her throat.

As his grip tightened, cutting off her breath, a calm came over her. She cupped his cheek with one hand and ran the other up and down his back.

He released her neck. "I knew you'd come around."

Erin gasped for breath. "Do what you want," she croaked out the words.

He lifted up and began pulling all the lace up around her waist.

She kept stroking his back until she felt the handle of the blade. She shifted under him to distract him while she freed the knife. Following Rafe's instructions, she lifted it high and jammed it into his diaphragm.

He screamed and collapsed on top of her. She shoved him hard, pushing him to the side. Her feet found the floor, and she started to run but then remembered. The cord.

The principal wasn't moving. Was he dead? No, his breath was labored, but he was very much alive and dangerous. She had no choice but to climb onto the bed, put both hands on the handle and remove the knife. She closed her hand around the handle and pulled. The blade moved but didn't break free. She gritted her teeth and twisted the handle, trying to free the blade. The slurping sound the blade made as it exited his body would forever be etched in her memory.

He grabbed for her. His hand disappeared into the lace skirt, and he pulled her toward the bed. She grabbed the material and jerked. It ripped, freeing her again.

Erin moved as far away as the cord would allow and furiously sawed at the sturdy nylon. The principal shoved himself up, writhing in pain and anger. He was coming for her.

The sharp blade finally sliced the cord. Free, she ran toward the front door.

"You're dead," he said through gurgles.

"You first," she said, opening deadbolts. The night breeze blew across her sweaty face. Freedom was only a few steps away.

Erin gathered what was left of her skirt and ran. She didn't look behind her. Didn't listen for footsteps. She ran. The outside lights were on at the second house down the street. Two teenagers were shooting hoops in the driveway. She'd never been happier to see other human beings.

Both boys froze at seeing her. No doubt, wearing a bloody dress and holding a knife in her hand, she looked like a zombie from a television show.

"Ms. Brady?" one of the boys asked.

She smiled with relief. "Yeah. Call 911."

Both of them ran into the house.

At last, she looked behind her into the night. All she saw was the light from an open door. Was the principal dead? The tears finally came. Poured from her. She dropped the knife to the lawn and sat down on the curb. Once again, she'd faced pure evil and survived.

CHAPTER 26

Rafe was out of the car and running toward the ambulance before Luke killed the engine. "I'm here, baby. I'm a few steps away," he said into his cell. That she'd called him from somebody's phone meant her injuries weren't life threatening. Nevertheless, he had to see for himself. She'd managed to say she'd stabbed that bastard Mueller, but most of their conversation had consisted of her softly sobbing.

He hurried across the street but was stopped by a couple of patrol officers. He slowed long enough to show his ID.

"Let him through," the officer called out.

The small crowd parted, and Rafe's heart catapulted into his throat. Sitting on the stretcher in the ambulance, Erin looked like a homeless waif. Only this waif was wearing a bloody wedding gown. One side of her face was bruised and swollen, and the dress was a rag.

"Rafe." She handed off the phone and opened her arms to him.

In three strides, he was inside the ambulance and on his knees beside her. He folded her body against his chest, rocking her as her whole body quaked. It ripped his guts open to imagine what she had been through.

"Take me home," she whispered.

He glanced at the EMT, whose eyebrows pulled into a frown.

Rafe smoothed the hair off Erin's forehead. "I'd like nothing better. First, you have to be checked out by a doctor."

She shook her head.

"You're hurt and probably in shock. Please let a doctor take a look at you."

"You'll stay with me?"

"Just try and get rid of me." Rafe nodded to the EMT, signaled to Luke, then moved to the small extra seat. "Put your head right here, so I can talk to you."

She lay down on the stretcher and breathed a big sigh. Rafe stroked her tangled hair. He noticed the bruises on her neck. That bastard Mueller had choked her.

"How is she?" Rafe asked the EMTs.

"Looks to be superficial bruising. Her vital signs are good."

"Rafe?"

"Hmm?" he said, swallowing the lump in his throat. He leaned over so she could see his face.

"Where's the principal?"

"I don't know." Rafe glanced at the EMT.

"Second ambulance was dispatched to take the dead guy to the morgue," the EMT answered.

"Right where he should be." Rafe kissed her forehead again.

"I'm sleepy," Erin whispered. Her eyelashes fluttered.

"Adrenaline crash," the EMT said. "Sleep all you want. You're safe."

The doors slammed closed, and the ambulance sped off. They were on the freeway before Rafe relaxed. He leaned closer to Erin, resting his hand on her shoulder. She jerked, frowning in her sleep.

"I'm here. Nobody's going to hurt you." He whispered those words again and again, hoping that the sound of his voice would ease her fear.

Once they arrived in the emergency bay, things happened fast. The nurses asked questions he couldn't answer, prompting him to call Jeff.

Luke, who'd followed the ambulance, led Rafe to the waiting room. Less than thirty minutes later, Jeff and Lotty had joined the wait. Rafe found no peace in sitting, so he paced.

Colton's voice pulled his attention to the doorway. "Any word?"

"Nothing. The nurse said somebody would come tell us when the doctor was through with the examination."

"What about Mueller?"

"All I know is the bastard's dead."

"Erin took him out?" Colton asked.

"Yeah. I didn't ask her what went down. She'll have to talk about the entire episode soon enough."

A young doctor joined them. Tall and thin, he wore navy slacks and tennis shoes. The dark circles under his eyes said the good doctor hadn't slept in a while. His appearance was quite a contrast to his crisp white coat. Jeff took the lead, introducing himself as Erin's father.

"The news is good," the doctor said. "Other than a few bruises and dehydration, Ms. Brady is fine. She's dehydrated, so we're keeping her overnight to get some fluids into her. She's being moved to a room soon. It's late, and it would be better if you let her rest. I gave her a sedative." His gaze swept the small group. "She asked for Rafe."

"That's me." He stepped forward. "I'm staying the night. If she wakes up, she won't be alone."

The doctor smiled. "Come with me."

"Call us," Lotty said.

"I will." Rafe followed the doctor down the corridor.

He stopped at the nurses' station. "This gentleman is staying with Ms. Brady tonight."

A nurse stood and walked around the counter. "She's in four-fourteen."

"Thanks." After he'd entered the elevator on his way to the fourth floor, he leaned against the handrail, allowing the band around his chest to relax a little. His cell vibrated. A smile inched its way up his cheeks as he read the text. Beckett had decided tomorrow would be soon enough to take Erin's statement.

He stopped in the doorway to Erin's room. Clothed in a faded blue hospital gown and covered by white sheets, she looked so fragile. A wounded bird who had fought her way to freedom. Her room was dark except for a small overhead light, but he could see her bruises even as he eased into a chair next to the bed. He wanted to touch her, hold her in his arms, and kiss her until she laughed with joy. Instead, he sat silently, grateful she was alive.

Her body jerked in her sleep. He stroked her arm, hoping this wasn't a nightmare disturbing the first peaceful rest she'd had in days.

Even if it was the right thing to do, leaving her was going to be hard. All he could offer her was a life full of loneliness and fear. Fear that every time he went undercover, he'd return to her in a body bag. That kind of anxiety was the last thing she needed. Erin was the bravest and strongest person he'd ever met. She'd been through enough for one lifetime and deserved somebody stable. A man whose job and lifestyle weren't full of danger.

He moved the chair closer, leaned his head back, and just watched her breathe. It was a beautiful thing.

****

Erin opened her eyes, staying very still while her surroundings came into focus. Was it really over? Now what? Was she supposed to feel guilty? Experience remorse for taking another human being's life? Lying between the cool clean hospital sheets, she couldn't make herself feel bad.

"Hello, sleepy head."

It was the one voice she wanted to hear. One she'd like to wake up to every morning. "Morning." She turned to face him. Unshaven and disheveled, he looked tired but beautiful. She couldn't imagine waking up to a nicer face. "You spent the night."

"I did." He stood and straightened his shirt, tucking it back into his jeans and making her mouth water. "How do you feel?"

"Safe. Stiff. Will you hand me the control to the bed?"

"I'll do it." Rafe picked up the remote. "Say when."

"That's perfect. Thank you."

"Are you too stiff for a hug? Because I'd very much like to hold you."

Erin opened her arms. "I thought you'd never ask."

"I see our patient is awake." A nurse entered the room. "Time to take care of the necessities and take a look at your bruises." She glanced at Rafe.

"I'll go check on Linc."

"Are you Rafe Sirilli?" the nurse asked, and Rafe nodded. "There's a detective in the waiting room. He asked me to ask you to stop by."

"Will you call Jeff and Lotty?" Erin asked. "She'll know what to throw into a bag and bring to me."

"No problem. I'll let them know you're awake."

The nurse closed the door behind him and turned to Erin. "Feel like you can walk to the restroom?"

"Absolutely." Erin swung her feet to the floor. A hand on her back startled her. She stiffened and pulled away.

"It's okay. You're safe now. After what you've been through, you may be jumpy for a while."

Erin had washed up and finished breakfast when Rafe stuck his head in the door. "All clear?"

"Yes. Come in," she said.

Rafe and Beckett filed into the room. Each took a chair, one on her left and the other on her right. Wade looked as worn-out as Rafe.

"Did you see Linc?" she asked Rafe.

"No. His family had him transferred to Dallas. They left early this morning. They wanted him closer to home while he recovers."

"I wish him the best. The principal said he should've killed all of you, that Linc's injuries were my fault."

"None of this is your fault. I wish the crazy bastard had come after me." Rafe rested his hand on top of hers.

The detective cleared his throat. "I worried you'd figured out who had her and kill him."

"There was a good chance that would've happened."

Erin's heart squeezed. Rafe cared for her a lot more than he wanted to admit.

"Beckett has promised not to tire you out."

"I'm fine." She turned to face the detective. "I expected you earlier," she said. "You have lots of questions, right?"

"I have a few answers, too. The crime scene unit uncovered a lot of surprising facts about the principal. For one, he wasn't who he claimed to be. Turns out he was a convicted sex predator. He moved here using a stolen identity. We don't know, yet, if he killed the guy or just stole his information."

"So Norman wasn't Norman." Erin's mind filled with questions. "So the fake identity allowed him to get past the school board's background check."

"Also probably why he was here in a smaller school district. We'll keep digging until we learn more."

Something stirred in Erin's memory. "He wanted me to call him Casanova. Said I'd given him that nickname."

"Mrs. Henley referred to him as Casanova," Rafe said. "He must have overheard her and thought it was you."

Erin listened and answered questions. Reliving the few days as a captive was hard, but it had to be done. When they were finished, she had nothing to worry about except getting on with her life. Somewhere in the conversation, Rafe had slipped into FBI mode. His formal tone sent a strong message when he suggested she find somebody to help her work through the trauma. Before they'd finished talking, Erin knew what she had to do.

Beckett stood. "I'll see you around." He placed his hand on her foot and patted her. "Be well."

Rafe got to his feet and shook Beckett's hand. "I'll touch base with you before I leave town."

"You go, too," Erin said. "Get some rest. Jeff and Lotty will be here soon. I'll ask them to stop by your place and get my car and things."

"There's no hurry."

"You and Luke will have an easier time closing out the estate without my stuff there."

Erin searched his face for any sign of disappointment or pain. If he minded being dismissed, he was hiding it well.

"Okay. I'll talk with you soon." He leaned over and kissed her forehead.

The pain in her heart was sharp, cutting a corner piece off and sending it out the door with him.

Alone, she stared at the empty doorway. So the horror was over. She was no longer in trouble with the law, meaning Rafe had completed his favor to Jeff. Rafe could return to work, go undercover, and disappear for weeks at a time.

She'd learned something from this experience. Life was too short to sit back and watch from the curb. If Rafe wanted her, he'd have to take the first step.

****

Sweat poured off Rafe. The weather had turned unseasonably hot and humid on the very day he and Luke had picked to load furniture onto a rented trailer. The church he'd attended as a kid still had its small store where people in need could pick up items for free.

"Are you sure you don't want to keep the house?" He and Luke hoisted a chest of drawers onto the bed of the trailer.

"I'm sure."

"You decide what you want to do next?"

"I've given the future a lot of thought. I had no idea Dad had amassed such large investments. According to the attorney, Dad had been investing for years. I'll have more than enough money to pay for any additional schooling I need. I'm not sure what it will take, but someday I'll pin a Texas Ranger badge on my shirt."

Rafe's chest filled with pride. "Figures you'd pick an organization where you could keep the white hat."

"Easy about my hat," Luke joked.

"You've picked an elite group. That's a hard organization to get into. But they'll be damn lucky to have you."

Luke went inside and returned with two cold beers. He passed one over to Rafe. "You still have to take that box of Erin's things to her." He chugged down a big swallow. "You think Jeff left it here on purpose?"

"Hell, yes. He and Dad always thought they knew what was best for us kids."

"Want to know what I think?" Luke dropped his empty can into a large metal trash can.

"Now, why did you ask? You're going to tell me anyway."

"I think you're afraid."

"And what would I be afraid of, little brother?"

"Getting killed."

"If that worried me, I'd already be dead." Rafe set his beer can down and hopped up on the trailer bed. He carried the chest of drawers forward, making room for what was left in the house.

"Not for yourself. For Erin. You finally realize that you're not ten feet tall, bulletproof, and invincible. If you got married, she might wind up a widow. You don't want that on your conscience."

"Okay. Let's say you're right. So what? It is what it is."

Luke stopped dead still and laughed. "Dad used to say that all the time."

"I know."

"Just remember, if you're dead, you won't have to worry about your conscience." Luke laughed again, this time at himself.

"Who are you? Some high school valley-girl?" Rafe couldn't help but join his brother in laughing at his nonsensical wording.

Luke flipped imaginary long hair over his sweaty shoulder and went back in the house for another load.

With Colton back in Dallas, it had given Rafe and Luke a few more days to get reacquainted. Sending their mother's china cabinet to a new home had been tough, but it had reminded Rafe just how fragile a family was. How easily it could fall apart. He and Luke had drifted apart over the past few years. Rafe wouldn't let that happen again.

They made a good team, and soon, only a few pieces of their dad's belongings were left to deal with. The Realtor would get rid of the beds for them.

Luke slid behind the wheel and drove away, headed for the delegation of church members and friends of their father who waited to unload the furniture.

Rafe showered, dressed, all the while pretending to ignore the box of Erin's clothes that Luke must've set in the middle of the living room floor.

Two days ago, she'd dismissed Rafe as if he'd been a pesky student. That in itself had confused and pissed him off. He'd made love with her. Recognized the passion and emotion in her eyes. Heard the soft sigh of relief in the back of that ambulance when he'd held her in his arms. Damn her, she cared for him. She cared a lot. And she was strong. Just how strong was the question.

He scooped up the box and headed for his car. There were things he needed to say before he left for Dallas. If he could keep his own emotions in check and do what was right, maybe this time they'd part as friends.

CHAPTER 27

Erin checked the peephole. Her heart vaulted to the back of her throat. Rafe was on the other side of her door. She'd vacillated between hoping he'd come and dreading having to put on a charade if he did. Her heart felt physical pain when she thought of him driving away, never to return. But she couldn't make his decisions for him.

She swallowed hard, opened the door, and waved him inside. "Thank you for bringing the box by. Just put it by the coffee table."

He did as instructed then turned to face her. "It's amazing what a couple of days' rest will do. The bruising has already started to fade." He reached over as if to stroke her cheek.

Erin stepped back, stumbling over her own feet. He couldn't touch her. If he did, she'd cave. Confess her feelings. Then where would she be? Alone and right back where she started.

Damn him, he kept coming. She kept backing away. The breakfast bar stopped her.

"Why are you running from me?" His gray eyes bore deep into hers.

"It's better this way."

"What way? Why did my touch just suddenly become repulsive?" His eyes flashed wide. "Oh shit. Of course, you don't want anybody to touch you. I'm an insensitive dick." He moved to the other side of her dining room table.

"It has nothing to do with Mueller or whatever his name was." This wasn't going as well as she wanted. "You know what's going to happen if you touch me." It was her turn to advance on him. "We'll wind up in bed. Afterward, you'll drive away feeling guilty, and I'll regret my moment of weakness."

"I make you weak?" One corner of his mouth lifted into his sexy grin.

"You came to say good-bye." If he'd just be honest, she'd make it through this without making a fool of herself.

He dragged his hand through his hair. Shuffled his feet like a little boy in trouble. He was waging war with himself. Just how much did he care? And could he come to terms with it? "You could ask me to stay."

"No." She begged her heart to stop racing. "I can't."

"Damn it, Erin." He moved two steps toward her. "You moved home to get out of the craziness of the bigger schools, but there are tons of needy kids in Dallas. Lots of smaller districts would jump at the chance to have you on their staff."

"I said that to keep Jeff and Lotty from feeling guilty." Still no declaration. Her heart folded in her chest. "Sorry, but I need more than a job offer."

At his silence, she turned toward the door. She straightened her shoulders and put her hand on the knob.

"I thought I'd lost you," he said. "I've never felt that kind of fear. The paralyzing kind of fear where nothing on the planet makes sense any longer. Is it fair to ask you to live through that?"

"You lived through it. What makes you think I can't?" She swung the door open and waited for him to leave.

His hands landed on her shoulders. He lashed out with his foot and kicked the door shut. "Then marry me, tough guy. Make me the happiest man on earth."

An unexpected laugh burst from her. "That's your idea of a proposal?"

"Tell me what you want. Want me to get down on one knee? Take you on that date we never had?"

"Yes," she whispered as her throat tightened with emotion.

"Yes to which one?"

"The first one." She waited until he'd sorted through all the options. "I love you. And I'll make a great FBI agent's wife."

His lips crashed down on hers. Demanding, needy, pleasing. Finally, Erin was home.

"I love you more," he whispered against her lips.

"So, from now on, if I dial 666—"

"I'll come running."

ABOUT THE AUTHOR
& OTHER TITLES...

Author of <u>Hell or High Water</u>, <u>Cold Day in Hell</u>, and <u>No Chance in Hell</u> from the Lost and Found, Inc. series, I live in Texas with my husband and our rescue dog, Buddy. I write alpha males and kick-ass women who weave their way through death and fear to emerge stronger because of, and on occasion in spite of, their love for each other.

The <u>Green-Eyed Doll</u>, <u>The Last Execution</u>, and <u>Someone to Watch Over Me</u> are available single titles. <u>No Greater Hell</u>, book four of the Lost and Found, Inc. series, is scheduled for a 2015 release.

Get up-to-date information on new releases. Sign up for my newsletter at <u>http://www.JerrieAlexander.com</u> and connect with me on <u>Facebook</u> and <u>Twitter</u>.

If you enjoyed this book, please help me spread the word. Facebook and tweet your approval. A review on Amazon and/or GoodReads would be greatly appreciated. Send me an email if you post a review—I'd love to thank you personally.

PRAISE FOR *HELL OR HIGH WATER*

"I adored this story. Jerrie Alexander has done it yet again. Her weaving of suspense and romance is masterful. Her characters both main and ancillary are well-written. For those who like romance you will be satisfied and for those suspense lovers you won't be able to put this book down either."

~ *The Book Maven*

PRAISE FOR *COLD DAY IN HELL*

"The sexual tension and sizzling chemistry between Ty and Ana has the temperature rising even higher than the sweltering heat of the jungle, as they escape from the relentless pursuit of the cartel henchmen, who threaten their existence. Cold Day in Hell is an entertaining story filled with action, suspense, and romance, which will keep the reader enthralled until the very end!"

~ *InD'tale Magazine*

PRAISE FOR *NO CHANCE IN HELL*

"The cast in the Lost and Found Inc series warm my heart with the love, trust, and confidence they have for each other. Marcus is a true alpha, protective and overpowering, but at the same time pure sweetness, loving, caring, attentive, and affectionate. The way he cares for Diablo, just made me melt. The romance, attraction, between Marcus and Chris is fresh and potent, palpable. All these factors mixed into this tale, makes it fascinating, one to be remembered."

~ *Books and Spoons*

4480298R00146

Printed in Germany
by Amazon Distribution
GmbH, Leipzig